August 2014

Dear Friends,

One of my most frequently asked questions is, "Where do you get your story ideas?" The answer is different with every book. Most of the plots I develop are a direct result of something that has come about in my own life. *Love Letters* is no exception.

Shortly after my mother died, I found the diary she'd written during World War II. It was one of the older versions—a five-year diary—with only a few lines for each day. Every page of Mom's diary was a love letter to my father. Her heart was in each entry. I read through the journal with tears in my eyes. At one point my father arranged, through his sister, for Mom to get roses on her birthday. Her entry that day said: *Roses from Ted. Oh my heart.* Later, when my father was captured and held inside Germany as a POW, it was months before Mom received word he was alive. Day after day, the only words she wrote were: *No letter from Ted. No letter from Ted.* And then there was one heart-wrenching entry that spoke of all her fears and angst that read, *Oh God . . . please.* Once she received the notification that Dad was alive, Mom didn't write in her diary again.

After reading through Mom's diary, my mind started spinning with the idea of writing a book that involved love letters. My heroine, Jo Marie, knows what it's like to lose her husband on a battlefield. Paul wrote her a letter just in case he didn't return home. And a young couple, Roy and Maggie Porter, whom you're about to meet, broke up in college only to be reconciled by a love letter. And then there's Ellie . . . I do this, you know. I get so excited about a plot that I tend to give the entire story away in a reader letter. I'll resist as best I can and let you make the discovery for yourself.

So, my friends, settle back, get involved in the story, and my hope is that when you finish the book you'll heave a breathless sigh and feel strongly enough to write a love letter to the one who holds your heart.

One of my greatest joys as an author is hearing from my readers. You can connect with me on my website at DebbieMacomber.com or on Facebook. In fact, if you feel so inclined, you can write me a love letter and mail it to P.O. Box 1458, Port Orchard, WA 98366.

Enjoy.

Warmest regards,

Debbie Macomber

BALLANTINE BOOKS BY DEBBIE MACOMBER

ROSE HARBOR INN

Love Letters
Rose Harbor in Bloom
The Inn at Rose Harbor

BLOSSOM STREET

Blossom Street Brides
Starting Now

CHRISTMAS BOOKS

Starry Night
Angels at the Table

For a complete list of books by Debbie Macomber,
visit her website, www.debbiemacomber.com.

Love Letters

DEBBIE MACOMBER

Love Letters

A Rose Harbor Novel

BALLANTINE BOOKS

NEW YORK

Published in the United States by Ballantine Books, an imprint of Random House, a division of Random House LLC, a Penguin Random House Company, New York.

BALLANTINE and the HOUSE colophon are registered trademarks of Random House LLC.

LIBRARY OF CONGRESS CATALOGING-IN-PUBLICATION DATA
Macomber, Debbie.
Love Letters : a Rose Harbor novel / Debbie Macomber.
pages cm — (Rose harbor)
ISBN 978-0-553-39113-8 (hardback : acid-free paper)
ISBN 978-0-553-39114-5 (ebook)
1. Love stories. I. Title.
PS3563.A2364L678 2014
813'.54—dc23
2014023995

Printed in the United States of America on acid-free paper

www.ballantinebooks.com

2 4 6 8 9 7 5 3 1

FIRST EDITION

Book design by Dana Leigh Blanchette

To Steve and Robin Black,

for their friendship, UPTick wines, and for gifting

Wayne and me with our very own row of grapevines.

May they produce an endless flow of wine!

Love Letters

Chapter 1

~

If someone had told me, as little as two years ago, that I'd own and operate a bed-and-breakfast in this tiny berg of a town called Cedar Cove, I would have laughed my head off. But then I never expected to be a widow at the age of thirty-six, either. If I've learned anything—and, trust me, life has been filled with several painful lessons—it's that the future doesn't come with a printed guarantee.

So here I am in ninety-five-degree heat, stripping beds, scrubbing toilets, and baking cookies. An even greater surprise is that I'm loving it. Well, maybe not the toilet-scrubbing part, but just about every other aspect of this new life I have carved out for myself.

It's been two full years now since I got the news that my husband is dead. And while I never thought it would be possible, there are times when I can smile again, feel again, even laugh. All three are surprises. When I got word that Paul had been killed in a helicopter crash on some unpronounceable mountainside in Afghanistan, it felt as if my entire world had imploded. I needed to hold on to something to keep from spiraling out of control, and that something turned out to be Rose Harbor Inn.

Nearly everyone advised against me buying the inn: my family, my friends, my employer. Again and again I heard that this was a drastic change, and I should wait a year. Give it twelve months, I was lectured. That's the proverbial wisdom, and while I politely listened, I silently went about making my own plans. It was either do something different—all right, drastic—or slowly go insane.

Has it been easy? Hardly. Eking out a living by renting rooms, doing a good majority of the work myself, hasn't helped build up my investment portfolio. I have yet to see a penny in profit, but I'm not going under, either. For the most part I've invested every cent back into the inn.

After I purchased the inn, I changed the name and had a new sign constructed and installed. I'd decided to call my new home Rose Harbor Inn. Rose is my surname, Paul's name, and Harbor because I needed to find a protected environment in order to heal. And my sign hung proudly in front of the inn with my name, Jo Marie Rose, etched below.

In addition to the new sign, there were certain necessary repairs, some cosmetic and others unavoidable. Thankfully, friends introduced me to Mark Taylor, the local handyman.

Mark.

What an enigma he was. I've seen him nearly every day for the past year, sometimes two and three times a day, and I still know hardly anything about him other than his name and address. Okay, so he's a great carpenter and he craves my peanut-butter cookies. Not knowing more felt like a pesky bug bite with a constant itch. My imagination ran wild. I wanted to uncover Mark's secrets, conjuring up a dozen reasons he refused to talk about himself. Some of those scenarios were outrageous, and there were a few scary ones lurking in the back of my mind as well.

I've been on a mission to pry some small bit of personal information out of him. So far I've had little to no success. I might as well try chiseling marble with a marshmallow. The man is as tight-lipped as they come.

The washing machine beeped, indicating that the cycle had ended.

The Hendersons, who'd recently checked out, had been in town visiting their son, who was stationed at the Bremerton Navy base. He'd recently become engaged to a local woman, and the couple had flown in from Texas to meet their future daughter-in-law. Lois and Michael were a delightful couple and I'd enjoyed hosting them.

I had two names on the books for the upcoming weekend. Both would arrive sometime Friday afternoon. After a while, names become a blur in my memory. People come and go, but for whatever reason, I specifically remembered both parties who had booked this weekend.

The first was Eleanor Reynolds, and she'd sounded quite proper when we'd first spoken. I'd guesstimated that she was either an accountant or a middle-aged librarian. Since that time I'd changed my mind. I'd spoken to Ellie twice—she asked that I call her that—since our original phone call. Once when she canceled and then a third time when she rebooked. The woman couldn't seem to make up her mind. Seeing that I hadn't heard from her in the last few weeks, I had to assume she would keep the reservation and arrive sometime this afternoon.

By contrast, Maggie Porter had been a breath of fresh air, chatting and happy. This was a getaway weekend she was planning with her husband, Roy. Right before the Fourth of July, Maggie's in-laws, who had apparently heard what Maggie was planning, had called and paid for the weekend as an anniversary gift for the young couple. I looked forward to meeting Maggie and her husband.

Rover barked, which told me someone was coming up the front walkway. I glanced at my watch, fearing I'd let time get away from me. This happened more frequently than I cared to admit. Rover, my rescue dog and constant companion, raced to the door. I recognized Rover's bark, which told me I had nothing to be anxious about. It wasn't a guest arriving early; it was Mark Taylor.

Great. I'd been hoping it was him. I fully intended to drill him and this time I wasn't going to let him sidetrack me or sidestep my questions.

I held the door open for Mark. He'd broken his leg last May and it'd healed nicely. I couldn't detect even a trace of a limp. I'd been upset with him for how long it'd taken him to plant my rose garden. What should have taken only a matter of a few days had stretched into weeks and weeks.

As you might have guessed, patience isn't my strong suit. To be fair, his injured leg didn't exactly speed up the process. When the rose garden was in and blooming I was less irritated. Next on my agenda was the gazebo, which I wanted Mark to build. I'd given him a photo of exactly what I envisioned, but that had been weeks ago.

I longed for that gazebo. In my mind, I pictured Rover sitting with me while I sipped coffee or tea at sunset, watching the sun casting a net of pink and orange shadows across the sky as it slowly went down behind the Olympic Mountain Range. I could get the same view from the deck in the back of the house, but I liked to reserve that spot for my guests. It was a picture of the sunset that graced my brochure. Mark took that photo. Actually, he's quite good at photography, although he brushes away my praise as if receiving a compliment embarrasses him.

Mark came into the inn and paused long enough to look down at Rover. He muttered something about the dog being nothing but a worthless mutt.

I bit down on my tongue to keep from defending Rover. Mark was like that. He'd make a comment just to get a rise out of me, but I was onto his game and I wasn't falling for it.

"You got a minute?" he asked.

"Sure. What's up?"

He didn't answer me directly. Instead, he went into the breakfast room where I served my guests and placed a rolled-up piece of drafting paper on the tabletop. "I've finished the plans for the gazebo."

This was a surprise. I'd expected it would take another five or six months for him to get around to that. From the first, he'd let it be known that he had other jobs that took priority over mine. This was something else he did, I suspected, hoping to irritate me. To my way of thinking, my money was just as good as anyone else's, or so one would think. Despite my best efforts, I had yet to figure out how Mark established his priority system. Not that it mattered. However he calculated it, my projects were generally placed near the bottom.

"That's great," I said, and hoped to sound encouraging, but not overly so. I didn't want to be disappointed when it took far longer than I wanted for him to start the project.

He unrolled the sheet of paper and anchored it with the salt and pepper shakers on opposite corners. The free corners curled up slightly.

I glanced down and immediately liked what I saw. "When did you draw this up?" I asked.

"A few weeks ago."

And he was only showing it to me now?

"Do you like it or not?"

I wasn't the only one who struggled with patience.

"I do," I assured him, "but I have a few questions."

"Like what?"

"What's it going to cost me?"

He rolled his eyes as if I'd made an unreasonable request. "You want an estimate?"

"That's generally how it works," I reminded him.

He sighed as if insulted. "I would have thought by now that you'd trust me to be fair."

"I do trust you, but building a gazebo can't be cheap, and I may need to budget for it. I don't suppose you take payments?"

He shrugged. "Nope."

"That's what I thought." As it was, he preferred to be paid in cash.

"Okay, fine, I'll get you an estimate but if you complain about delays, then you have no one to blame but yourself."

"Can you give me a general idea?" I pressed. To this point, the cost of everything Mark had built for me had been more than reasonable.

In response, he took out a small spiral pad he kept in his shirt pocket and riffled through several pages. He studied the sheet, then frowned and closed his eyes as if mentally tallying up the final estimation. When he opened his eyes, he named a figure I could live with.

"Sounds good," I said, trying to disguise how pleased I was.

"It's a go?"

I studied the design once more. It was basically a carbon copy of the picture I'd cut out of a magazine and handed him months ago. As far as I could see, it was perfect and would add a great deal of curb appeal to the inn.

"It's a go." I rubbed my palms together. I was excited now, and I didn't care if Mark knew it. Rover wagged his tail as if he, too, was pleased.

"Good." He replaced the salt and pepper shakers to the middle of the table, collected the paper, rolled it back up, and secured it with a rubber band.

Mark wrinkled his nose. "You baked cookies this morning?" he asked, and then frowned. "In this heat?"

"It was early."

I tend to be an early riser, always have been. My friends, before they married and had children, often slept until ten or eleven on weekends. Try as I might, I rarely made it past seven. Eight at the very latest.

"How early?"

"Four."

Mark shook his head and grimaced as if he'd unexpectedly tasted something sour. "Too early for me."

"Is it too early for a taste test?" It went without saying that he was looking for me to make the offer.

"I could be persuaded."

I've never known Mark Taylor to turn down a cookie. Not that anyone could tell he had an addiction to sweets. Mark was lanky, at least six-three, possibly six-four, and thin as a pencil. He seemed perpetually in need of a haircut. He was an attractive man, or he could be if he were inclined to care about his appearance, but clearly he wasn't. Appearances didn't seem to matter much to him. By contrast, I was what Paul had referred to as "round in all the right places." I was one of those women whose weight constantly went up and down and then up again. To combat this, I routinely exercised, mostly by taking Rover on long walks. I enjoyed gardening, too. This summer I'd taken to growing out my hair, which was dark and bounced against the top of my shoulders. Almost always I secured it at the base of my neck with a hair tie.

Mark followed me into the kitchen. Rover led the way. The peanut-butter cookies were on the cooling racks. I handed Mark a plate and said, "Help yourself," while I poured us each a cup of coffee.

We sat down at the table across from each other. I rested my elbows on the tabletop and studied the handyman.

He'd downed three cookies before he noticed that I was intently watching him. "What?" he asked, frowning at me.

Cookie crumbs had collected at the corners of his mouth. He had a nice mouth, I mused. "Pardon?" I asked.

"You're staring at me."

I shrugged. "I was thinking this morning."

"Did it try your brain?" he asked.

His meager attempt at humor fell decidedly flat. "Very funny."

"Okay, fine, I'll ask the obvious question. What were you thinking about?"

"You."

"Me." He reached for his coffee and took a sip. "Not the most interesting subject, I can assure you."

"Quite the contrary. It came to me that we've been friends almost from the time I bought the inn and I know next to nothing about you."

"Nothing to know."

"Have you ever been married?"

His frown darkened. "Seems to me you've got better things to occupy your mind."

"Not really. My guess is you've never had a wife. Remember, I've been inside your house."

"Big deal, and as I remember it, you came without an invitation."

I was quick to defend myself. "I brought you dinner after you broke your leg."

"I wasn't interested in eating," he argued.

"Don't change the subject." I refused to let him sidetrack me by starting an argument. "There isn't a single personal item on display in your entire house. No pictures, no photographs, nothing."

He shook his head as if he didn't know what I was talking about. "So I don't have a knack for interior design. Are you suggesting I watch that network you like so much where a woman can take a Coke bottle and a fishing pole and make a dinette set out of it?"

"No," I clarified. "I'm thinking you might be part of the Witness Protection Program."

Mark had taken a drink of his coffee and started to laugh, spitting a mouthful of liquid back into the mug.

"I'm serious," I told him.

"Then you've got a creative imagination."

"Fine, you're not under the government's protection. You didn't answer my question."

He sighed as if bored with the subject. "Which question?" He reached for another cookie and stood.

"Have you ever been married?" I asked a bit louder this time. I wanted him to know I was serious and determined to unearth his secrets.

"Can't imagine why you'd want to know something like that. Doesn't really seem like any of your business."

I guess that was meant to put me in my place. "Just curious," I said.

He set the mug in the sink. "Don't be. I'm not that interesting. See you later."

And with that, he walked out the front door.

"Well, well, isn't he the prickly one," I said to Rover, who cocked his head to one side as if he agreed. Unwilling to let the matter rest, I reached for the phone. Fine, if he wanted to be that way, I would go to plan B. I punched in the number for my friend Peggy Beldon.

Peggy and her husband, Bob, owned the Thyme and Tide, another local bed-and-breakfast. It was Peggy who'd recommended Mark as a handyman. She'd become a friend and was always helpful and informative. Never once had I gotten the impression that she viewed me as competition. In fact, she'd often sent her overflow customers in my direction. I was grateful to Peggy for the advice and guidance she'd so generously shared with me.

"Jo Marie," she greeted, and sounded pleased to hear from me. "What can I do for you?"

"I have a question," I said, a little embarrassed to be so openly curious about Mark.

"Sure, anything."

"I was wondering what you know about Mark Taylor."

"O-k-a-y." She dragged out the word as if my asking had taken her by surprise.

I wanted to make something clear first, though. "It's not because I have any romantic interest in him."

"I didn't think so," Peggy said. "The reason I hesitated is because there isn't much I can tell you. I don't know that much about him."

"Does anyone?" I pried. Mark was the most secretive man I'd

ever met. I was certain there was a story there, possibly a dark and sinister one.

"I can ask Bob if you like. He's gone at the moment but is due back anytime now. I was heading to the bakery in an hour or so. We could meet there and I'll fill you in on what Bob tells me."

"Perfect. I'll meet you in an hour." One way or another, I was going to unearth Mark Taylor's deep, dark secrets.

Chapter 2

Ellie Reynolds's stomach was in knots, twisting and churning as she rode the shuttle bus from Sea-Tac Airport into Cedar Cove. She prayed she was doing the right thing by meeting Tom Lynch. Her mother's warnings rang in her ears like cacophonous church bells drowning out her thoughts, until Ellie felt she was about to go deaf.

She clenched her hands together as she looked out the bus window. The middle-aged woman sitting in the seat across the aisle from her held her knitting in her hands. As if guessing at Ellie's unrest, the other woman offered her a reassuring smile. Ellie smiled back and turned her head away to study the landscape. In many ways, the terrain resembled Bend, her home in Oregon.

Over the years, Ellie had visited the Seattle area twice before. Once as a Girl Scout in fifth grade, and then again in high school when she was part of a choral group that performed at a Christmas function in the city. Both Ellie and her mother had stuck pretty close to home for the majority of her life. Seattle was the "big city." Visiting it had been a grand adventure when she was sixteen. Now, at age twenty-three, she felt like a disobedient child who'd defied her mother's wishes.

Ellie decided she couldn't think about her mother. Instead, she would think about Tom. Right away a warm, happy feeling stole over her. They'd been communicating for months via Facebook, text messages, phone calls, and emails. She'd never felt this strongly about any man, especially someone she hadn't met in person. They had a great deal in common and had really connected. They both liked fish tacos and stargazing, long walks, and classic novels. In fact, they met through an online book club.

Tom was a former submariner who worked in the Navy shipyard in Bremerton. The minute her mother heard that small bit of information, it'd thrown her into a tizzy. Sailors were notorious for having a girl in every port; they were men with loose morals, or so her mother claimed. But Ellie refused to believe it about Tom. He was like her, a bit shy and reserved, unless she was nervous. Silly as it seemed, when overly anxious, like now, she could blurt out the most nonsensical information to a stranger that she wouldn't consider sharing with her closest friend.

Despite her mother's warnings, Ellie wasn't worried that Tom was using her. Everything she knew about him told her he was kind and thoughtful, intelligent and studious, and not the stereotypical sailor who played on others' emotions. She couldn't make herself believe he would do anything to hurt her. She trusted him, and if his photo was anything to go by, he was as open and honest as she believed. She was willing to go by faith and trust her gut feelings. What counted was his heart.

They would meet face-to-face for the first time this weekend. Tom was the one who'd suggested she stay at Rose Harbor Inn. Ellie prayed once more that she was doing the right thing. She made the reservation at the inn in May, almost three months ago, and twice since then she'd changed her mind. They'd set the date for August, and Tom had been pleased and excited that they would meet at last. She was, too.

Her mistake, she realized, was telling her mother about Tom. The instant Virginia Reynolds heard that Ellie planned to meet this man she'd met through Facebook, she had become rattled and unglued, certain Ellie was about to make the worst mistake of her life. After constant badgering from her mother, Ellie had given in and canceled the trip. When she'd told Tom she'd changed her mind, he'd offered to contact her mother and reassure her that his intentions were honorable. Ellie was touched, but thought it ridiculous that at her age she had to justify to her mother what she did and who she met. Eager to prove she was capable of making her own decisions, Ellie rebooked the inn a short while later. Tom stood by his offer. He'd be happy to chat with her mother, answer her questions, and give character references if needed.

Ellie's cell phone dinged, indicating she had a text message. Hoping it was from Tom, she dug her phone out of her purse and sighed with frustration when she saw it was from her mother.

Please let me know you're OK, Virginia Reynolds had written.

Landed. Am safe. Ellie quickly typed back.

Thank God. You don't know how worried I am.

I'm fine, Mom. Ellie sighed and returned her cell to her purse, ignoring the next ping, certain it was her mother yet again.

The root problem, Ellie realized, was her parents' failed marriage. A thousand times through her childhood, Ellie had heard her mother claim that men weren't to be trusted. Men would stomp on your heart and then walk away as if it meant nothing. That had been Virginia's experience, and she was willing to do whatever was necessary to protect her only child from the same fate.

Following her parents' divorce, Ellie had become the entire focus of her mother's world. Virginia had dedicated everything to Ellie: Her time, her resources, and her love were all directed toward Ellie. At times she felt her mother was suffocating her. Ellie craved to forge her own path and then instantly felt guilty, knowing she was everything to her mother.

Her phone rang, and again, hoping it was Tom, Ellie grabbed it out of her purse.

Her mother.

Ellie let the call go to voice mail. The woman across the aisle sent her a curious glance, which Ellie ignored. The problem was, Ellie fully understood her mother's concerns. Taking off to meet a man she knew only through phone calls and emails and text messages was risky on any number of levels. The bottom line was her mother was right. Ellie really didn't know Tom Lynch. He could be a serial rapist or a criminal or even a mass murderer. And as her mother said, Ellie could be walking into a nightmare that would haunt her for the rest of her life. She'd begged Ellie to let her travel with her for this initial meeting. For a time, Ellie had actually considered the offer. It didn't take long for her to decide otherwise. This was something she wanted—no, needed—to do on her own. She was cautious and would meet Tom in a public place.

If, after they met, they decided there was something to this relationship, then they would continue getting to know each other. He would come to Oregon next, and introduce himself to her mother. It made sense to Ellie, and while she was somewhat introverted, she wasn't stupid. She had her own apprehensions about this. Even she had to admit her relationship with Tom was unconventional. She'd be the first to concede this wasn't the way a woman generally met a man for the first time. And while she didn't have a lot of dating experience, she trusted her gut and her heart, and both told her that Tom Lynch could be trusted.

With her phone still in her hand, Ellie checked her email and saw that Tom had sent her a message, asking her to let him know when she arrived. Her fingers fairly flew across the tiny keyboard as she responded. Although reluctant, she did have to admit that Tom had seemed a tad bit secretive, something her mother had taken delight in pointing out at every opportunity. Ellie hadn't tried to argue; all she told her mother was that she trusted her instincts. Which, in retrospect, probably wasn't the wisest of responses. That declaration had instantly sent her mother into a long tirade against Ellie's father. At one time, Virginia, too, had trusted her heart, and look what it had gotten her. Ellie could almost mouth the words along with her mother.

Going against her own parents' wishes, Virginia had fallen in love with a young man she met while in college. They'd been crazy about each other. From the first, her mother's parents had had questions about Scott Reynolds. They hadn't liked or trusted him. After only one meeting, her father declared that Scott was too slick, too cocky, and, perhaps worst of all . . . superficial. Both her parents had warned Virginia against falling in love with a man who was overly confident of himself. They had someone else in mind for their only daughter, someone far more suitable. From the start, they were convinced Scott would break Virginia's heart. And they were right.

Because she was in love and ruled by hormones, Virginia hadn't listened to her parents. Scott and Virginia had defied her family, and against their advice had continued to date. Love had blinded Virginia from the truth. To complicate matters, Virginia and Scott had eloped.

For a short while, Virginia admitted, she'd been blissfully happy, especially when she learned she was pregnant with Ellie. Scott dropped out of school and took a job driving a taxi. He'd been thrilled with his baby girl, whom they named Eleanor after Virginia's mother, in the hope that her parents would look past Virginia's defiance and make Scott a part of the family. Right away Scott had called her Ellie, and the name had stuck. As first-time grandparents, Virginia's family threw their loving arms around Virginia and Eleanor. They made an effort with Scott, Virginia claimed, but his dislike of her mother and father drove a wedge between them.

It wasn't long before Scott's fascination with being a husband and father wore thin. They struggled financially, living on what Scott made driving a cab. Her parents offered them a loan, but Scott wouldn't hear of it. That was when their problems started. Virginia couldn't understand why he insisted they had to make it on their own. They argued often, especially when Virginia started spending a lot of time with her mother at the family home. Scott was often late coming home after work, and when Virginia questioned where he spent all his time, he claimed it shouldn't matter, seeing that she was rarely at the apartment anyway. She seemed to prefer her parents' company over his.

Then one horrible day Virginia's father swore he saw Scott with another woman. When she'd confronted him, Scott had insisted this so-called other woman was a coworker and a friend, in addition to being thirty years his senior. Virginia refused to believe it. As far as she was concerned, Scott could no longer be trusted. With suspicions running rampant, it wasn't long before the marriage was over.

Once Virginia filed for divorce, her parents took her back into the family home, willing to forgive their daughter for being a fool for love. Ellie came with her and had only fleeting memories of her father.

And now it seemed history was repeating itself. Ellie had defied her mother over a man, too, a man she had yet to meet.

The bus stopped and a middle-aged couple that was sitting in the back got out at a community known as Gig Harbor. While the driver unloaded their suitcases, Ellie studied the quaint buildings that butted up against the picturesque waterfront. She didn't know a lot about Cedar Cove, but she hoped it was as charming as this small town.

Once the driver was back on the bus, Ellie asked, "How much longer until we reach Cedar Cove?"

"We aren't far now," he said, twisting around to get a good look at her. "I should have you there in less than forty minutes."

Ellie offered him a feeble smile. Her stomach knotted again, tighter this time. Even now she had a hard time believing she was actually defying her mother.

"Just a couple more stops first," the driver added, and, turning around, started the bus once again. "A short stop in Purdy and Olalla, and then Cedar Cove."

"Okay."

"Do you have someone meeting you at the bus stop?" the driver asked, looking at her in his rearview mirror. "A family member or a friend?"

"Yes." Well, sort of. As soon as she'd told Tom her plans, he'd offered to take time off work to pick her up. Ellie had declined. For their first meeting, she wanted to look her best, and she preferred not to do it following a flight and wearing traveling clothes. Surely there was a taxi in town that could deliver her to the inn. When she'd asked Jo Marie about catching a cab, the innkeeper had surprised her and offered to meet her at the stop just off the freeway where the bus would leave her.

"Looks like we're in for lovely weather," the older woman sitting across the aisle casually mentioned. Ellie had noticed her a couple times earlier. Every time Ellie's phone beeped, she caught the woman glancing in her direction.

"This is the best time of year to visit. You are visiting, aren't you?"

"Yes," Ellie said.

The other woman was busily knitting without so much as looking at her hands as she wove the yarn around the needles. "I come every year to visit my children and grandchildren. My daughter and son-in-law both work, and I didn't want them to take time off to come collect me from the airport. My grandson is meeting me at Park and Ride in Olalla."

"I'm meeting someone for the first time. He works in the Navy shipyard," Ellie said. She braced herself, anticipating some form of censure from the older woman. If this knitter was anything like her mother, a warning or comment would soon be forthcoming. When the other woman didn't say anything, Ellie realized how ridiculous she was being. Her mother had brainwashed her into expecting negativity.

"We met over the Internet in an online book club," Ellie added, testing the waters yet again. "Well, actually, he asked to be my friend on Facebook. His online book club had a link with mine . . . it's a long story." She suspected the older woman didn't know that much about social media.

"I understand that's the way a lot of young people meet these days."

"Like I said, this is our first face-to-face meeting," Ellie continued. "I admit I'm nervous." And talkative, which wasn't a good combination, but she couldn't help herself.

"It's rather romantic, isn't it?"

Ellie smiled. It was romantic and risky and silly all in one. "I think I'm half in love with him already. Funny, isn't it, when our entire relationship to this point has consisted of phone calls, emails, and text messages?"

"It's my opinion that love rarely makes sense," the other woman commented. "I'm Martha, by the way."

"Ellie."

"Pleased to meet you, Ellie."

"My mother doesn't approve of me doing this," Ellie said, keeping her voice low and guarded.

"It's hard for us to let go of our children." Martha's look was thoughtful, as if she was remembering something from her own past. "When Marilyn married Jack, I hated the thought of her moving to Washington State. It's all the way across the country from New Jersey. I was sure she'd made a mistake, but she loves living in the Pacific Northwest. The truth is, I enjoy coming out each summer for a visit. Marilyn owns a hair salon on Harbor Street; that's the main street in Cedar Cove. Where are you staying, dear?"

"Rose Harbor Inn."

"I know it; the inn is right up the hill from Marilyn's shop. The view of the cove is magnificent from there."

Tom had mentioned the same thing. The view was one of the reasons he'd recommended Rose Harbor Inn. From the deck, not only was the lighthouse within sight, but she'd be able to see the Bremerton Shipyard as well.

Ellie's cell pinged, and a quick look told her it was her mother yet again. She didn't know why she bothered to look.

Another text. Another warning. Ellie sighed and saw Martha glance her way. "Mom again," she said, replacing her phone. "She's convinced I'm making a fool of myself."

"And if you are?"

"Then I'll never live it down."

"Are you being foolish?" Martha asked, in a friendly tone.

"Perhaps I am," Ellie admitted, stiffening her back, "but frankly I don't care."

Martha's smile was warm and gentle. "As a mother, I can understand her fears. For my own children I would have loved to pass on the treasure that cost me tears and struggles and prayers, but I can't. My mother's heart wanted to spare them disappointment and pain, but life doesn't work that way. We each have to experience hurts in order to grow. We each must forge our own path. I'm sure your mother means well."

Ellie wished her mother viewed life that way.

Martha left the bus in Olalla. "My grandson recently got his driver's license. He's excited about picking me up." She placed her knitting inside a quilted bag. "Good luck to you and your young man."

"Thank you," Ellie said, "for everything."

The driver helped Martha out of the bus and then retrieved her suitcase. A young man wearing a Seattle Seahawks T-shirt arrived in a minivan a couple minutes later, and Martha waved as he parked the vehicle in the Park and Ride lot.

Ellie was the last one on the bus.

"It won't take long now," the driver assured her. "We're only a few miles to the Cedar Cove exit. You can phone your ride, if you want."

"Okay." Ellie reached for her phone and the sheet of paper where she'd written down Jo Marie's name and contact information. The innkeeper answered right away, almost as if she'd been sitting by the phone, anticipating her call.

"Rose Harbor Inn." Jo Marie sounded cheerful and upbeat, and instantly Ellie felt welcomed.

"It's Eleanor Reynolds," Ellie said, and then clarified, "Ellie."

"Oh yes, I was expecting your call. I'll grab my keys and head out the door right now. You don't mind if I bring Rover with me, do you?"

"I don't mind at all." Ellie was fond of animals. Tom was, too. One of his most lengthy emails was about the dog he'd had while in grade school and how he'd taught Ranger to catch a Frisbee in midair. It'd broken his heart when Ranger had died when he was in the seventh grade. Ellie had always had cats, but she hoped one day to have a dog, too.

"I'll see you in a few minutes," Jo Marie promised.

"Thank you." Ellie disconnected the line and exhaled a slow breath. She felt better than she had since she'd boarded the plane for the short ride between Bend and Seattle. No matter what her mother said, she had a good feeling about this adventure. A very good feeling.

Chapter 3

~

Once I got the call from Eleanor Reynolds, I loaded Rover into my car and made a quick run to the Texaco service station off the first Cedar Cove exit on Highway 16. I saw her right away, standing alone with her one piece of luggage, looking a bit lost and nervous.

Rover leaped from the backseat into the front as soon as I turned into the parking lot. We'd made this trip before, picking up guests who rode the shuttle bus from the airport into town.

I pulled into the parking space in front of the mini-mart and turned off the engine. Although we'd spoken three times over the phone, I had yet to get a good picture of what to expect from Eleanor Reynolds. She was younger than what I'd assumed, especially after our initial conversation.

"Eleanor?" I questioned, and quickly revised it to "Ellie? Ellie Reynolds?"

The woman looked up and nodded. "Yes, that's me. You must be Jo Marie?"

Rover barked from the front seat of the car. "And Rover," I added.

"You're young," Ellie said, as if surprised. "I guess I was expecting someone closer to my mother's age." She reached for her suitcase and headed toward the car.

"I was just thinking the same thing about you."

"People say I sound much older on the phone. Elocution was important to my grandmother." And then, as if she felt the need to explain further, she added, "We lived with my grandparents while I was growing up."

I opened the car trunk. "I hope you enjoy your stay in Cedar Cove."

"I know I will," she said, smiling broadly. She effortlessly set her suitcase inside and then came around to the passenger side.

As soon as he realized Ellie was getting in the car, Rover returned to the backseat. Ellie climbed inside and then turned around to pet Rover. He basked in her attention and then immediately settled down, circling on the seat several times before finding a comfortable position.

Ellie clipped her seat belt into place. "I hope this isn't too much of an inconvenience," she said. "I would have been happy to catch a cab."

"It's no problem. I do it all the time; it's part of the service the inn provides."

"I got the schedule for my return trip, too . . . in case I need it," she added.

I was about to question her but changed my mind. She seemed a bit anxious and reached for her phone twice, checking emails, during the short drive back to the inn. "It's my mother," she mumbled. Then, as if she'd made a momentous decision, she added, "I'm going to ignore her; otherwise she'll ruin everything."

Apparently, a comment from me wasn't necessary, and frankly, I was just as glad, because I wasn't sure what to say. "I'll leave you to get settled in your room while I run an errand, if that's all right."

"Oh sure," she was quick to assure me. "Contrary to what my mother believes, I don't need a babysitter."

"No, you don't." The poor girl clearly had mother issues. She hadn't said anything about her mother during our short phone conversations previously. What little I was able to read between the lines told me Ellie's mother was convinced this trip was a huge mistake.

"I met a wonderful grandmotherly woman on the bus," Ellie continued, chatting away as if she was eager to tell me about the experience. "She was so wise and reassuring. I could be making a big mistake coming to Cedar Cove, but if so, then it will be a learning experience."

Her meaning was lost on me, but I nodded as if I understood. We pulled up to the inn and Rover obediently followed us inside. I hadn't taken him for our morning walk yet, and he instantly trotted over to where I stored his leash, letting me know he was eager and ready to follow routine.

"In a bit, Rover," I told him. To his credit, he'd been patient, and I appreciated it. I glanced at my wrist; it was nearly time to meet Peggy.

Ellie signed in and I handed her the key to her room and showed her around the communal areas of the inn before leading her up the stairs to her room.

"Are there other guests this weekend?" she asked.

"A married couple and a local resident."

"Local resident?" she repeated, as if she found it difficult to understand why someone from town would opt to spend the weekend at a bed-and-breakfast.

"Yes, Peter McConnell called this morning. Apparently, he's having some plumbing work done on his house and the water's being turned off. He'd normally go out of town, but he's working a half-shift on Saturday and needed to be in the area."

"Oh."

"He won't check in until late this afternoon. I don't know how much we'll see of him."

"I plan to be busy myself," Ellie told me. "I'm meeting a . . . friend. A male friend . . ."

Ah, so that was it. No wonder her mother was concerned. Well, good for Ellie. It was long past time that this bird left the nest.

Once Ellie was comfortably settled in her room, I left with Rover to meet Peggy Beldon at the downtown bakery. Eager to exercise, Rover all but dragged me down the hill toward the waterfront. The day couldn't have been any more beautiful. The sky was cloudless and a luscious shade of blue that made it difficult to look anywhere else. The waters of the cove were flat and clear, with an occasional eagle circling overhead, seeking out a meal. It wasn't unusual to see one swoop down and grab hold of an unfortunate salmon, swimming too close to the surface.

I saw Peggy even before I reached Harbor Street. She sat at a table outside, luxuriating in the warmth of the summer sun.

"Hi," I said, joining her. "I hope I'm not late."

"Not at all," Peggy said, reassuring me. She'd dressed comfortably in capri pants with a red checkered shirt over a matching red sleeveless top. Her hair was shorter, which told me she'd had a recent haircut.

"You look all summery," I said, as I pulled out the chair across from her and sat down. Rover settled by my feet, pressing his chin over the top of my foot. Peggy had ordered me a cup of coffee. "Thanks." I lifted the cup and took a sip. "It's my turn to buy next."

"No worries."

Now that I was comfortable, I got to the subject that was prominent on my mind. "Were you able to talk to Bob about Mark?"

"I was." She leaned slightly closer.

"And?" I was unable to hide the eagerness in my voice.

Peggy shrugged. "I wish there was more to tell. Bob met Mark for the first time at the local hardware store."

"How long ago?"

"I asked him that, too, and he seems to think it must have been five or six years now, but I don't think it was near that long. My guess is about four years, but I could be off. It seems like he's always been around."

"So Bob met Mark at the hardware store and the two struck up a conversation?"

"Yes."

"Did Mark mention where he'd moved from?"

"Not that Bob remembered. All Bob remembered was Mark telling him that he was new in town and looking for odd jobs. Said he was retired, which Bob found humorous, seeing that Mark couldn't have been more than thirty-five at the time."

"Did Bob happen to ask Mark why he moved to Cedar Cove?"

"You'll have to ask Mark that yourself. But why not?" Peggy asked, motioning toward the view. "It's beautiful here, and a good place to raise a family."

"But as far as I can tell Mark doesn't have a family."

"True."

I wished Bob had known more. The fact was, I already knew just about everything he'd mentioned to Peggy. Well, not the part about Bob and Mark meeting, but everything else.

"Did you notice that he likes to be paid in cash?" I asked. Frankly, I couldn't help wondering if this was his way to avoid having to pay taxes. It seemed underhanded and not in line with what I knew about him.

"I didn't know that," Peggy said, frowning slightly. "Bob is the one who deals with the finances. He never mentioned that. You should ask Mark."

"I did." Many times, but I had yet to get a satisfactory reply. I guess I'd put too much emphasis on the small idiosyncrasies I'd noticed about him that made me suspicious. This habit led me to believe he didn't want a money trail going back to him and that he wanted to keep his identity hidden from the outside world.

"Bob liked him right away," Peggy added, breaking into my thoughts.

This surprised me. Mark wasn't a likeable kind of guy; it seemed he went out of his way to be cantankerous and disagreeable. At least that was my experience with him.

"Before Bob felt comfortable recommending Mark to others, he hired him to do a small job at the Thyme and Tide to test his skills."

"And Mark passed?"

"With flying colors. Following that, Bob sent a number of small jobs Mark's way for family and friends. Several people have thanked us. Mark is conscientious, and his prices are reasonable."

What she said was true. Over the last year, Mark had completed a number of projects for me and either met or exceeded my expectations. The only problem I'd had with him had to do with my rose garden, which seemed to have taken him an inordinate amount of time even before he broke his leg. The lengthy delay afterward was understandable. Still, I couldn't help feeling Mark's dawdling had been deliberate . . . although for the life of me I couldn't imagine why he would want to delay planting a rose garden. Perhaps the answer was as simple as the fact that he wasn't keen on gardening.

"Is there anything else you can tell me about him?" I asked. My voice must have been more animated than I'd intended, because Peggy's eyes widened.

"Any reason you're so curious?" she asked.

There really wasn't a reason except my curiosity. "No, not really," I admitted, striving to sound as nonchalant as possible. "It's just that he seems so . . . private."

"We all cherish our privacy," Peggy commented, without any censure. "Don't you think?"

"Well, yes, I suppose."

"What is it about Mark that intrigues you?" Peggy asked.

"I'm not intrigued," I returned instantly. "I'm curious. It seems to me he's hiding something." There, I'd said it.

"Mark?" Peggy said his name as if it were a joke, worthy of laughter.

"His home is . . . ?" I searched for the right word. "Spartan . . . there's nothing there that links him to anyone or any particular place. I asked him, as sort of a joke, if he was part of the Witness Protection Program."

"You didn't?" Peggy's eyes grew even rounder. "And what did he say?"

"He laughed it off." Actually, now that I mentioned it, Mark had made it sound like one big joke. My mind churned, coming up with other possible scenarios. "Maybe he's suffered some tragic loss and is running away from life." It made little sense to me that a man as talented as Mark would choose to be a neighborhood handyman.

"Jo Marie." Peggy, who had been amused just moments earlier, grew serious.

I looked up and our eyes met and held. "Yes?"

"I think it's important that you examine why you find it so necessary to know about Mark."

"Necessary?" That was a bit of a stretch.

"Yes."

She was actually serious; I could see it on her face. "Like I said, I'm just inquisitive."

"Have you asked yourself what it is about Mark that makes you want to delve into his life?"

"You're making more of this than warranted," I insisted. "I'm not interested in Mark . . . personally. Okay, I read a lot of mysteries and enjoy solving them. People behave the way they do because of something in their past. Trust me, when it comes to Mark, something is off."

"Something sinister?"

"Doubtful." As far as I could tell, Mark was as honest as a summer's day was long.

"Do you have feelings for him?" my friend asked, in that gentle way of hers that inspired confidence.

Mostly Mark irritated me. He was often cranky and ill-tempered, but buried beneath that outer crust was a decent human being. At times it was hard to believe, but most days we got along perfectly fine. Earlier that spring, I'd been grateful for his help in finding Rover, who'd run off. I'd been beside myself with worry. Mark had spent hours searching for him. I had, too, of course, but it'd been Mark who'd found him and Mark who'd brought Rover home. For that alone I owed him.

"Jo Marie," Peggy said, lowering her voice to a mere whisper. "Do you have . . ." She hesitated, as if unsure she should continue.

"What?" I prodded.

Sitting up a bit straighter, she plunged ahead. "Are you . . . falling for Mark?"

"For Mark?" Now it was my turn to hold back a laugh. "No way." I didn't need to think about my answer. "Absolutely not," I said, without the least bit of hesitation. "Half the time I'm not even sure I like him."

"A lot of wonderful romantic relationships start out that way."

I reached for my coffee and shook my head. "I suppose my curiosity about him might look like that," I said, wanting to downplay the suggestion as much as possible. My fear was that protesting too strenuously would only convince Peggy I was interested in Mark. "You need to know something about me," I added, figuring this was the best way to put a halt to this kind of thinking. "I love Paul Rose with all my heart. He was my husband and my soul mate. When we met, I'd more or less decided I would probably never marry. I doubted there were many decent men left in this world. I was cheated out of more time with him, but still, I had that year, that one glorious year that I will treasure the rest of my life. I don't want to fall in love again." Frankly, I didn't think my heart would survive another loss if something were to happen to another man I loved.

I raised both hands. "Maybe I am going a bit overboard with this thing with Mark. The only reason I asked is because I've seen him so regularly the past year and yet I know practically nothing about him. I can't help feeling that Mark has an interesting story. But whatever his story, it's clear he doesn't want others to know." In retrospect, it was probably best, as the proverb went, to let sleeping dogs lie. If Mark had a secret past he wanted to hide, then far be it from me to dig it up.

We changed the subject, talked business for a few minutes, and then it was time for both of us to get back to our day. For my part, I had a set of guests who were due to arrive sometime this afternoon.

The Porters: Roy and Maggie.

After thanking Peggy for the coffee, Rover and I walked back up the steep hill that led from the waterfront area to Rose Harbor Inn. As we rounded the corner and walked down the lengthy driveway leading to the inn, I paused and took in the three-story structure that was now my home. Seeing it never failed to stir me. The house had been built in the late 1800s and was one of the most prominent structures in Cedar Cove. It sat on a hillside overlooking the cove, with views of the Olympic Mountain Range and the lighthouse in the background. I remembered the first time I saw the inn. In that instant I knew this was home, the sense of welcome overwhelming me.

The first night there, after taking ownership, I'd keenly felt Paul's presence as if he'd stepped briefly back into life to offer his love and reassurance. It had been his way of letting me know that I'd made the right decision purchasing the inn.

As I stood admiring the inn, with Rover straining against the leash, a white SUV drove past me, toward the inn, pulling into the small parking area reserved for guests.

Simultaneously both the passenger and the driver's door opened and out stepped an attractive young couple.

Roy and Maggie Porter had arrived.

I started to call out a greeting but paused when Roy slammed the car door. Without a word, he went to the back of his vehicle and got out two suitcases and headed toward the inn without looking back.

When Maggie saw me, she paused and then offered an apologetic smile as though embarrassed by her husband's abrupt behavior.

I raised my hand. "Maggie?"

She nodded. "You must be Jo Marie."

"I am. Welcome to Rose Harbor Inn."

"Thanks." She glanced toward the inn. Roy was on the top of the porch and seemed to be waiting for her, although he stood with his back to us both.

"You'll have to forgive Roy's bad mood. He wasn't keen about taking this weekend off from work. But we've been planning it for such a long while and . . ." Her voice faded away. "We need time together."

"All couples do," I said, agreeing with her.

Maggie started toward the inn and I walked with her. Despite her reassurances, I had the strongest feeling something was very wrong between Maggie and Roy Porter.

Chapter 4

Maggie drew in a deep breath and followed Roy up the stairs to the room Jo Marie had assigned them. Roy had barely said a word the entire time they'd registered. Twice she'd been forced to bite her tongue and swallow her pride. Her husband couldn't make it any more obvious that he didn't want to be at the inn—or, for that matter, with her.

Roy used the key to unlock the door to their room and then swung it open, letting her go inside before him. It was a lovely room with a four-poster bed and dresser. A bouquet of roses rested on top of the dresser. Large windows overlooked the cove's blue-green waters. At the marina the boats gently bobbed up and down, the sailboats' masts tilting slightly. "It's beautiful," she whispered.

Roy didn't appear to agree or appreciate the beauty she saw. He remained stiff and silent. His resentment seemed to radiate off him

in waves. On the entire three-and-a-half-hour drive over from Yakima, Roy hadn't uttered more than a few words.

Several times Maggie had made a futile effort to break the silence, but it hadn't done much good. Roy responded with one-word,
clipped replies, if he answered at all. She tried not to think about her
husband's bad mood and forced herself instead to focus on the
scene outside the window. The beauty of it inspired and encouraged
her. Willing to try yet again, she turned back around to face Roy.

"Don't you think so?" she asked, doing her best to sound upbeat
and cheerful.

"Think what?"

"That the view is lovely."

Roy shrugged as if he hadn't noticed and furthermore couldn't
have cared less. He stood next to his suitcase with his hands buried
deep inside his pockets. The anger had gone out of his eyes, replaced
with hopelessness. His look nearly broke her.

"I know you don't want to be here," she whispered.

"You can say that again," he bit off.

Maggie had been looking forward to this weekend for months. It
was exactly the break they needed. Roy worked too hard. He left
the house before either of the boys was awake and often wasn't
home until their sons were ready for bed. One thing she would say
about her husband. He loved his children and was a good father. No
matter how tired he was, Roy took time to play with his sons, to
read to them or share in bath time. But right after they were down
he crashed, exhausted, from a long day of running the family's construction company. His father had recently retired, and since then
much of the responsibility for the business had fallen on Roy's
shoulders.

Fearing they were growing further and further apart, Maggie
had convinced Roy to take this time off, setting the date far enough
in advance that he'd be able to work it into his schedule. When her
in-laws had heard about this mini-vacation, they had offered to stay
with the boys and as a bonus had paid for the weekend. It couldn't

have worked out better . . . until . . . well, that was certainly a topic she didn't want to dwell on.

"I wouldn't be here at all if it wasn't for my parents," Roy reminded her. He walked over to the window and looked out.

Maggie had the strong impression he wasn't enjoying the view; probably he hadn't even noticed the beauty spread out before him like a masterfully designed patchwork quilt. The green and blue colors blended together, creating a radiant picture of the beauty of the Pacific Northwest.

"I know you'd rather be anyplace but here with me." He couldn't have made it any more clear.

He frowned and looked away.

Suddenly it felt as if this attempt to save their marriage was utterly useless. Tears sprang to her eyes. She'd managed to keep them at bay on the endless drive over Snoqualmie Pass and through the heavy traffic by Tacoma before they reached Cedar Cove, but no longer. Silently, wet tendrils rolled down her cheeks and she slumped onto the side of the bed and hung her head. It all seemed so pointless.

Although she didn't make a sound, Roy must have sensed her distress because he turned around and exhaled. After a moment he sat down next to her on the bed, the mattress dipping with his weight. He placed his arm around her shoulders and leaned his head against hers.

Desperate for his warmth and love, Maggie turned toward her husband and wrapped her arms around his middle, clinging to him. She buried her face in his shoulder and softly sobbed. Roy comforted her and stroked the back of her head.

"I'm sorry," he whispered.

Unable to speak for the emotion that clogged her throat, she nodded.

"I'm trying, Maggs."

"I know." Her words were little more than a whisper.

"Give me time, okay?"

Again she nodded. Lifting her head, she wiped the moisture from her face. She wrapped a strand of long dark hair around her ear and sniffled once.

Roy offered her a tentative smile and she responded with one of her own. "I'll unpack our suitcases," she whispered, thinking if she did something physical it would help ease the emotion that threatened to break down into sobs.

"Okay." He lifted both pieces of luggage onto the bed for her.

It took only a few minutes to hang up their clothes and set out what else they needed. She noticed that Roy had brought along a paperback novel. Maggie couldn't remember the last time she'd seen her husband reading for pleasure. For herself, Maggie read voraciously. It used to be they would talk about the books they'd read and would often read one at the same time, but that had been years ago, before Roy became so heavily involved in the construction company . . . before the boys were born.

"Are you ready for lunch?" Roy asked, as if he felt the need to lighten the mood.

"Sure." Actually, she wasn't the least bit hungry, and she doubted that Roy was, either. This was his way of letting her know he was making an effort. Maggie deeply appreciated the fact that he was willing to try.

"I'll ask Jo Marie for a suggestion. What are you in the mood for?" her husband asked.

Maggie had to think about it. "Seeing that we're close to salt water, how about fish and chips?"

He nodded eagerly. "Good idea."

Roy led the way down the stairs and into the kitchen, where they found Jo Marie. She was on the phone but smiled when she saw them and raised her index finger, indicating that she would be only a moment. Sure enough, she was off the phone a short while later.

"We're looking for a recommendation for lunch."

"Some place that serves fish and chips," Maggie added.

"Oh, there's a great place not far from the Pancake Palace—in fact, the two restaurants share the same parking lot. I don't think I've ever tasted better fish than Queen's." She handed them a brochure she'd had printed up with a list of local restaurants and circled Queen's.

"Thanks," Maggie said, as they headed toward the front door.

"My pleasure." The innkeeper offered Maggie a thumbs-up as if to say she was pleased that whatever was wrong between the two had been resolved. Oh, how Maggie wished that were the case.

Roy held open the car door for her, which was a surprise. Maggie forgot the last time he'd done that. Generally, they were both too busy ushering the boys to the car to see to those kinds of niceties.

"Thank you."

Roy then surprised her again by leaning down and kissing her. Once more, Maggie felt tears gather in her eyes but quickly blinked them away while her husband walked around to the other side of the vehicle. He started the engine and glanced down at the brochure Jo Marie had drawn. "It doesn't seem that far away."

"Fish and chips does sound good."

Roy reached over and gently squeezed her hand, and for just a moment, a very brief moment, Maggie could almost pretend that everything would work out between them. Even in the worst of it she had to believe Roy wanted their marriage to survive . . .

They found Queen's without a problem. It was a hole-in-the-wall sort of place without fancy furnishings or an extensive menu. The special for the day, fresh salmon, was listed on an erasable whiteboard close to the cash register. Once inside, a waitress with a name tag that said Nikki handed them plastic-coated menus. They were instructed to seat themselves. Seeing that it was a bit beyond the lunch hour, there were plenty of booths to choose from.

Maggie read over the menu and chose the two-piece fish and chips option. One piece would probably be enough—she hadn't enjoyed much of an appetite lately—but she wasn't sure of the size of the fish. When Nikki came for their order, Maggie asked for a two-piece combo and Roy ordered the three-piece plate, which offered coleslaw along with the chips.

It didn't take long for their order to come up. Right away, Roy dug into his meal. Maggie, too, but with less gusto. After her first bite, she had to admit Jo Marie was right. These were some of the best fish and chips she'd ever tasted.

"I was surprised at Collin," Roy commented, after he'd licked some ketchup off his fingertips. "He didn't cry when he saw that we were both leaving."

"I was surprised, too," Maggie admitted. Their three-year-old didn't like being left behind. To hear him sob, one would think he was being abandoned for life.

"My mother probably had something to do with that," Roy said, and reached for another french fry. "Knowing her, she might have told him he could have ice cream for dinner."

"She does love spoiling the boys."

"It's a grandmother's job, and my mother takes it seriously."

Maggie wished they had family closer. Roy's parents had retired and spent the winters in Arizona and the summer months traveling in their motor home. It was their goal to visit every national park in the country. They were well on their way to achieving their dream. Maggie's parents lived in California.

"How is Collin doing in his soccer?" Roy asked.

"Great. Just the other day, he asked me if his daddy was going to coach him the way you do Jaxon."

Roy smiled, and for the first time that day his smile reached his eyes. Her husband had coached Collin's older brother's team for the last two years. It was hard for Collin to stand on the sidelines when he was just as eager to play soccer as his big brother. During one game, Collin couldn't hold back any longer. Right in the middle of the game, he dashed from the sidelines and ran onto the field. It'd taken Roy and the referee to catch him.

Maggie reminded Roy of the incident. He chuckled and shook his head. "He's going to be a good little player."

"I think Collin might even be more athletically inclined than Jaxon."

Roy thought for a moment and then shrugged. "It's hard to tell, but what I do know is that Jax plays with heart."

"He does everything with heart." Their sons were true joys. Maggie loved being a stay-at-home mother. It was difficult to watch Roy work as many hours as he did. He was often gone twelve to fourteen hours a day. But she doubted that his hours would change if she worked outside the home. Lately . . . no, she wouldn't let her mind dwell on that; she couldn't, or she'd slowly go mad.

Roy was a man driven to succeed. Maggie felt it was her job to be his support, his helper, and to be at home for their children, especially in these formative early years. Thankfully, Roy's business enabled her to do that. Many times, especially recently, she didn't think that Roy understood her role in his home or life. From the outside looking in, it wasn't much. She didn't get a paycheck, didn't manage his schedule or handle the paperwork. Her role was to simply see to everything else so that Roy could go off to the job without worrying about what was happening at home. She took care of the house and the boys, and offered her husband encouragement and emotional support.

They talked nonstop about the boys while they enjoyed their lunch. Maggie found that she could laugh, and it felt amazingly good. She could almost forget . . .

All at once, Roy went quiet. "Do you realize all we've talked about are Jaxon and Collin?"

"We mentioned your parents," she reminded him.

"True," he agreed, "but only in relation to them staying with the boys."

He was right. "What would you like to talk about?" she asked, not understanding his concern. To her, the important fact was that they were communicating. They'd done far too little of that in the last few months.

"It's good, I suppose," Roy said. "I love my sons, and I know you do, too. You're a good mother, Maggie, a very good mother. Our sons are lucky to have you."

Roy didn't pay compliments easily, and his words meant a great deal. She nearly choked up when she spoke. "Thank you. And you're a wonderful father." It wasn't an exaggeration or a ricocheted compliment. She meant every word.

"We need to take the boys out of the equation for a few minutes," Roy suggested. "You wanted this time away for us to work on our marriage, right?"

"Yes."

"Then let's talk."

"Okay." The word stuck in her throat like a peach pit.

Her husband was silent for a long moment. "We've both made mistakes."

She looked away and nodded. "I don't want to focus on our mistakes. At this point, it isn't going to help. Instead of tearing each other down, I'd like to look for ways to build each other up."

Roy went silent, then pushed his half-eaten lunch aside. "You're right."

She smiled. It was far too infrequent for her husband to admit she was right about anything, especially lately.

"What's that smile about?" Roy asked. "And don't bother denying it. I saw you grin just now. Is it because I was willing to admit you're right?"

She blinked several times and, try as she might, couldn't squelch a smile. "Okay," Maggie said, "let's focus here. We agree; we love our children. This time is for us, though, just you and me. Talking about the boys is off-limits."

"Okay."

They smiled across the table at each other. Maggie thought to mention the work project that had taken up so much of Roy's efforts in the last three months. Unfortunately, that led to other, more sensitive, subjects she'd hoped to avoid. Katherine, for one. She bristled just thinking of the other woman. No, the subject of Katherine was definitely one to be avoided, and unfortunately the other woman was tied to the job.

Roy looked like he was about to say something important. He opened his mouth and then quickly closed it as if he, too, had thought better of it.

They sat in silence for a full five minutes. As each second ticked away, Maggie had the sad realization that while they deeply loved each other and their two sons, they had become strangers. Their relationship had dissolved to the point that they lived together and shared a bed, but they had become little more than roommates.

Maggie felt her heart swell inside her chest as the sadness nearly overwhelmed her. "You used to talk to me," she whispered, gazing down at her plate.

"Oh come on, Maggs, don't go there."

"Okay, fine, I won't."

"This is exactly what I feared would happen; you're going to use this weekend to remind me what a horrible husband I am and how badly I've let you down."

"No . . . I don't want that."

"Fine, I'll admit it. I'm a rotten husband, but the truth is, you haven't been much of a wife, either."

His words came at her like nails out of a roofer's gun, striking her squarely in the chest. The pain was so sharp and the hit so solidly on target that she could barely breathe.

Roy instantly looked contrite. "I didn't mean that the way it sounded."

"I think you did," she whispered, and reached for her purse. She was about to slide out of the booth when her phone rang. She hesitated, and reached inside her purse and froze. The phone chirped again, louder this time, more insistent, as if the message was highly important, urgent.

Maggie read the name on caller ID and then glanced toward her husband. "It's your mother."

Roy frowned and scooted from the booth. "She wouldn't be phoning this soon if it wasn't serious."

Chapter 5

After my conversation with Peggy, I had the feeling that I'd given my friend the wrong impression regarding my curiosity about Mark. I loved my husband, and that wasn't going to change. I thought about the letter I received from him, the one he'd asked a friend to give me in case something happened to him while he was on his tour of duty. I kept his last letter to me in the nightstand next to my bed. I read it shortly after I got definitive word that Paul wouldn't be returning from Afghanistan. His remains had been identified and returned to Washington, D.C., where he was buried in Arlington National Cemetery. I'd attended the ceremony early in June. I hadn't looked at the letter since that time. I simply couldn't bear to read Paul's last words, his love letter to me, again.

For a number of months after I learned Paul and several others had gone down in a helicopter I physically felt his presence with me.

He seemed close and so very real. It was almost as if I could reach out and touch him. In retrospect, I believe that was my mind's way of dealing with this overwhelming sense of grief. I so desperately wanted Paul to be alive that I conjured him up in my mind. At times I could almost hear him speak . . . not with audible words that I heard with my ears, but words that spoke to my heart. That hadn't happened in a long while now, not since I received his letter. I missed that. At times I desperately longed for another chance to feel him with me . . . and didn't. Instead, I was alone, so very alone.

In an effort to distract myself from thinking about Paul, I busied myself with projects I'd been putting off. Although it was summer, I tackled spring-cleaning chores that I hadn't quite gotten around to doing. Today it was the kitchen cupboards. I took the glasses down from a cupboard and set them along the countertop.

"Need any help with that?" I turned around to find Mark standing in the doorway leading into the kitchen.

I hesitated, standing on top of the step stool I kept in the kitchen. The time Mark found me on a ladder, he'd nearly gone ballistic. We'd had a terrible argument about it. He'd ended up walking off the job and I'd threatened to sue him. Thankfully, it didn't take long for the anger to cool on both sides. Since then, Mark had eased up on his dictatorial ways and I'd stopped making threats. We'd treaded pretty lightly with each other ever since.

"I'm tackling some spring cleaning."

"It's August," he reminded me. "It seems you've been doing a lot of spring cleaning lately."

"So I'm a tad bit late." I wasn't making excuses, although if he asked, I had several good ones. I didn't know why it concerned him, anyway. So what if I was behind schedule? "You know what they say: Better late than never."

He eyed the step stool and seemed to debate whether he should say anything. Apparently, he decided against it. He reached for a mug sitting on the crowded counter and headed toward my coffeepot. "Mind if I help myself?"

"Go ahead."

"Should I brew you one while I'm here?"

It seemed Mark had something on his mind; otherwise, he wouldn't be interested in coffee or in me joining him. If I knew anything about Mark, it was that he wasn't one to sit around and shoot the breeze. Nor was he one who indulged in idle conversation. If he had something on his mind, it didn't stay there long.

"Coffee?" he repeated, holding up a second mug.

I didn't realize that I hadn't answered him. "Sure, I could use a break."

After he brewed two cups he walked outside with his coffee, which led me to believe I was supposed to follow him, so I did. I found him on the back deck off the living area, where my guests most often congregated. He leaned against the railing with his elbows braced against the freshly painted surface. "It sure is a beautiful afternoon." His gaze scanned the waterfront.

"It is." August was often like this. The green trees and the crystal-blue waters never seemed more vibrant. I hadn't traveled extensively, but Paul had, and he'd reassured me that there was no place on earth as lush and gorgeous as Puget Sound when the sun was overhead.

I didn't figure Mark had come to discuss the weather; I had known him long enough to understand that he didn't like to be rushed. He'd tell me whatever was on his mind when he was good and ready.

"Did your guests arrive?"

"All but Peter McConnell."

Mark turned around, his face tightening. "Peter McConnell? Not the same Peter McConnell who lives in Cedar Cove?"

"Yes, one and the same. Peter phoned for a reservation earlier this morning."

Mark's gaze narrowed. "Peter has a house in town."

"Yes, I know. I believe this has something to do with some plumbing work he's having done on his house."

Mark made a harrumphing sound as if to say he didn't believe a word of it. "And you mean to say he hasn't got a single friend in this entire town who was willing to put him up for the night? Not even his own daughter?"

"I didn't ask him. Besides, I'm not about to turn away a paying customer."

Mark stood his ground. "In this case, I think it might be a good idea."

I could feel my ire rising. I inhaled a steadying breath and then, as calmly as I could manage, I said, "Mark, stop right now. You're stepping over the line."

"What line?"

"The one I just drew in the sand." I could feel my ears heating up, which was a good indication I was about to blow my cool. "Who I choose to accept as a guest in my inn is my business." I spoke slowly, making sure he heard and understood each and every word.

Mark looked back at the water view and didn't speak for several seconds. Tension seemed to vibrate between us. Finally, he exhaled and said, "I don't trust the man, and if you knew him better, you wouldn't, either."

I hadn't heard anything about Peter McConnell one way or the other. I glared back at Mark.

Apparently, he got the message, because he looked away first. "If I were you I'd collect my fee up front."

"He owes you money?"

"Just take my word for it, Jo Marie."

"I will," I promised, my irritation vanishing as quickly as it came. "Did you have something else on your mind?"

He returned my stare with a blank look, as if the reason he'd stopped by had slipped his mind. "Oh yeah. I have an estimate for the gazebo."

"You already gave it to me; I trust you to be fair."

He dug into his shirt pocket and withdrew a folded piece of

paper. "I got everything tallied here. The price of lumber went up in the last week, so I had to revise the figure I gave you earlier. If you want to hold off building the gazebo, I'll understand."

I read over the formal estimate. The earlier bid he'd given me was off the top of his head. This time he'd priced the materials, added the cost of his labor, and written me a formal proposal. From the look of it, he'd taken the better part of the morning putting it together. The bottom line was only a two-hundred-dollar increase over the estimate he'd told me earlier.

"It's fine."

"You want me to get started, then?"

"I do."

He grinned as if he was glad for the business, although to hear him, he had more work than he knew what to do with, which was probably true.

"Did you see the reader board at the hardware store?" I asked.

He gave me an odd look. "Yeah. What about it?"

"They're looking for an experienced sales associate. That kind of work would be right up your alley."

Mark frowned. "Why would I want to work at the hardware store?"

The answer should be obvious. "You'd be good at it, Mark. You know how to fix just about anything. You could help a lot of people."

He shook his head as if the very idea went against the grain. "I help a lot of people now."

"But you'd have a regular paycheck and benefits."

"I have all the benefits I need, thank you very much."

"Okay, okay, don't get bent out of shape; it was just an idea."

"A bad one." He scratched the side of his head and frowned as if I'd insulted him by the mere suggestion.

I heard a car door shut in the distance and figured that either the Porters had returned from lunch or Peter McConnell was ready to check into his room. Despite what I'd said, I'd take Mark's warning seriously, but I wasn't going to turn McConnell away simply because Mark didn't trust the man.

Mark walked around to the front of the inn with me. I'd guessed right. It was Peter. Right away, the Mark Taylor who I'd always known to be taciturn and short-tempered took on an entirely new persona. He raised his arm and waved to Peter, and called out a cheery greeting.

"Peter. How you doing, buddy?"

I looked at Mark as if seeing him for the first time.

My latest arrival stopped and looked as shocked as I was. Peter was in his late forties, I guessed . . . maybe early fifties. His hair was completely gray, and he was reasonably good-looking. I had to assume he lived alone, since he'd requested a room for one.

Peter looked from me to Mark and then back again. "Oh hi, Mark. Listen, if you're worried about what I owe you . . ."

"Forget about it," Mark cajoled, as if however much was due him was of little consequence.

Mark glanced over his shoulder and shot me a warning look. I wasn't entirely sure what his message was, but I could tell he wanted me to keep quiet.

"Jo Marie was telling me you're having some work done at the house."

"Plumbing. The water's been shut off and won't be turned back on until tomorrow morning."

"Better on the house than having a doc work on your plumbing," Mark said, and laughed as if he'd found himself highly amusing. Then he looked at me and whispered under his breath, "I wonder if he paid his water bill."

"I wouldn't know," I whispered back.

Mark turned his attention back to the other man. "Listen, old buddy, there's no need to pay for a night at the inn. You can spend it with me at my house. I've got a spare room."

Peter hesitated. "You sure?"

"Why not? We're friends, right?"

"Right . . . but I wouldn't want to inconvenience you." His look said he was skeptical, and frankly, I didn't blame him.

"It's no problem," Mark said, with a wave of his hand. "I'm glad to do it."

Still, Peter hesitated. "I guess that would be all right, and it would save me a couple hundred bucks."

No way did I charge that much for a room. I opened my mouth to contradict him but changed my mind.

"You okay with that, Jo Marie?" Mark asked, directing the question at me with narrowed eyes.

"Sure, that's no problem on my end." But I intended on letting Mark know I was onto his game.

"That your truck over there?" Peter asked, looking over his shoulder.

"Sure is. Go to my place and I'll join you in a minute."

Mark was silent until Peter was out of earshot, and then, before I had a chance to say anything, Mark spoke. "You can get upset with me later, and as for the money you're losing, you can deduct it from my bid for the gazebo."

"Why are you doing this?" I asked. The man made no sense to me. Clearly, he disliked Peter McConnell. By his own words he didn't trust the other man, and yet he'd invited him to spend the night in his home.

Mark didn't look the least bit pleased. "The hell if I know." He shook his head and walked away, leaving me to wonder if all common sense had deserted Mark Taylor.

I retrieved our coffee mugs and returned to the kitchen, where I found Ellie Reynolds looking a bit lost and nervous.

"Oh hi," I said. "Can I get you anything?"

"No. I've been waiting most of the afternoon for a phone call from Tom."

"And you're antsy."

She shrugged. "We've never met, you see."

She'd told me that earlier. "And you've come a long way to meet him," I added, and the implication was more than just the distance. From the small amount of information Ellie had told me I knew that she'd defied her mother in order to meet Tom.

"He can't have his phone in the shipyard. I have to wait until he's off work to hear from him, and that won't be for a couple more hours. I went for a walk and had lunch, but I'm so nervous now I don't know what to do with myself."

I wasn't sure what to tell her.

"I see you're cleaning out cupboards," she said, eyeing the glassware lined up along my countertop and the roll of shelving paper. "Would you mind if I helped you?"

She wanted to help me clean. "Ah . . ."

"That's what I do, you know."

I didn't know. "You're a housekeeper?"

"No, I'm a professional organizer. People call me to organize their basements and garages or the entire house. I'm actually good at that sort of thing. I always have been."

"And you've arranged kitchens?" I could use the help, but it wasn't in me to ask a guest for this kind of professional advice without being willing to pay for it.

"Oh yes, I've reorganized dozens of kitchens."

"I'd be happy to pay you."

"Nonsense. You'd be saving me from going stir-crazy." Without waiting for my approval, she looked at the cupboard where I'd stored the glasses. Right away I knew what she was thinking. "I store them here because they're close to the breakfast room."

"Makes sense, but my guess is, you carry them out on a tray, right?"

"Right."

"Why not put them in the cupboard above the dishwasher?" I looked across the room and realized it made perfect sense. My goodness, I should have thought of that myself.

For the next hour, Ellie had me switching things around the

kitchen in an order I would never have thought of doing. Like she claimed, she was good at organizing, really good.

We were so involved in our discussion that we almost didn't hear her cell phone. When she did, she took it out of her pocket and tapped on the surface. Her face broke into a huge smile.

"It's Tom."

Seeing the joy that lit up her face reminded me of the way I felt when I received a call from Paul half a world away. That sense of happiness, of being connected, of being loved. It did me good to see that in someone else and know that I had experienced that same contentment once myself.

Chapter 6

~

"Hello," Ellie said, gripping the phone and pressing it so hard against the side of her face that her ear ached.

"Hi," Tom answered, and he sounded as excited as Ellie was herself. "So you got into Cedar Cove okay."

"Yes. I'm at the Rose Harbor Inn now."

"Your flight was smooth?"

He was asking about more than just the time in the air, she realized. "No problems." She didn't mention the troubles with her overprotective mother.

"I know your mom was dead set against this."

"My mother doesn't rule my life." Not from a lack of trying, however.

"I was sincere about talking to her, reassuring her."

"No." Ellie was adamant. Experience had taught her that nothing Tom said or did would ease Virginia Reynolds's worries. Over the years her mother had ruined Ellie's dating prospects far too often. She'd lost count of the number of promising relationships that had gone down in flames, all because of her mother's fears. What angered Ellie was how she had let it happen. Well, not this time. Not with Tom.

"I'm excited to see you," Tom said, his voice dipping slightly.

"Me, too . . . see you, I mean," she said with a nervous laugh.

"I'll be off work in another couple hours, but I'd like to run home and change clothes before I come to the inn. I made dinner reservations at DD's on the Cove. We can walk there from the inn, but I'd rather drive in case we want to go somewhere after dinner."

"It's perfect. I walked down to the waterfront shortly after I arrived." After being cooped up on the plane and then the bus, Ellie had felt the need to exercise her legs. Walking had helped her burn off nervous energy.

"I won't be more than fifteen minutes longer than the time I gave you."

"No problem. I'm not going anywhere," Ellie assured him. The anticipation was all part of the excitement. Meeting Tom was like Christmas times ten. "Are you nervous?" she asked. They'd spoken frequently, and she knew the sound of his voice, and she could hear the unease in him now.

"Very."

"Me, too."

"I don't want to disappoint you," he said.

"That's my big fear, too."

"You couldn't . . . it isn't possible. You're beautiful . . . inside and out; more than I ever expected to find in a woman."

Ellie felt the same way about him. He made her feel cherished and loved. Compliments didn't roll off his tongue with practiced ease as if he'd said the same words to a dozen women before her. He seemed just as ill at ease about this first meeting as she was, which reassured her.

"Promise me one thing," Tom whispered.

"I will if I can," she whispered back.

"That no matter what happens this weekend, that you'll . . ." He hesitated, as if he wasn't sure how best to continue.

"That I'll what?" she urged, eager to reassure him nothing would change between them.

Again he paused. "I have to go. Personal phone calls are frowned upon. My supervisor is giving me the eagle eye. I'll be at the inn to pick you up as soon as I can manage."

"I'll be waiting, and Tom, please don't worry. Everything is going to work out."

"That's my hope. Bye for now."

"Bye," she repeated. She returned her phone to her purse and heaved a sigh, wondering what it was that had Tom this concerned. Despite reassurances, he seemed to think she'd be disappointed in him, and that wasn't possible. It simply wasn't possible.

Seeing that Tom was going out of his way to make sure he looked his best for her, Ellie decided she should do the same. Grabbing her purse, she headed down the stairs once again. The woman she'd met on the bus from the airport, Martha, had mentioned that her daughter owned a beauty salon on the main street running through Cedar Cove. Ellie had worn her hair straight and parted down the middle from the time she was in grade school.

She'd taken this first leap toward independence . . . and that gave her courage to take an additional step and then another. Her heart beat hard and strong. It felt good to venture beyond what she'd always known and always done.

Jo Marie remained busy in her kitchen, implementing the suggestions Ellie had given her. She stood on the step stool, placing taupe shelf-liner paper on the cupboard's flat surface, although Ellie thought the current liner didn't look old or worn in the least. In fact, it looked almost new.

"I'm going out for a while," Ellie told the innkeeper.

"Are you meeting Tom?" Jo Marie asked.

"Not quite yet. He's still at work. I thought I'd walk down to Harbor Street. There's a hair salon there . . . the lady I met on the bus mentioned that her daughter owned it."

"Marilyn?"

"Yes, that's Martha's daughter's name."

"She's fabulous. The salon is across the street from the bakery and next to the Veterans of Foreign Wars post; you won't be able to miss it."

Ellie was glad to hear it. Her sense of direction wasn't the best. "Do you know if Marilyn takes walk-ins, or should I call and make an appointment first?"

Jo Marie bit into her bottom lip. "I've always made an appointment, but I believe she takes walk-ins as well."

"I guess I'll find out."

"If you need to wait, do it. Marilyn's worth it."

"Thanks. I will." Ellie started to leave and then stopped. "I was thinking of changing my hairstyle."

"Change it how?" Jo Marie asked, cocking her head to one side as if looking at her with fresh eyes. "It suits you the way you wear it now."

"I'm looking for sexy," Ellie explained with a soft laugh. "Alluring and glamorous."

"You're all that and more already."

The innkeeper's words were sincere and took Ellie by surprise. She thanked her and then headed out the door. She walked down the very hill she had climbed shortly after her arrival. She'd crossed Harbor Street then and gone directly toward the waterfront, exploring the park and strolling along the marina, admiring the overflowing hanging flower baskets that lined the sidewalk. The wire-framed baskets were a colorful arrangement of summer flowers in yellow, red, and white. On this second trip onto Harbor Street, instead of heading toward the marina, she went left and down the city walkway. It didn't take her long to find Marilyn's, the hair boutique the woman on the bus had mentioned.

The salon was bustling. It seemed every chair was filled, every seat taken. Ellie almost turned around and walked out—clearly, Marilyn did a lively business and it wasn't likely she had an opening, especially on Friday afternoon on such short notice—but the receptionist looked up just then and caught Ellie's eye.

"Can I help you?" the blond woman asked, her smile warm and welcoming.

"I'm in town . . . meeting a friend, and I wondered if by chance there was an opening for this afternoon."

"Are you looking for a haircut or a shampoo and set?" the receptionist asked.

"Actually, I'm not sure." Ellie's fingers went to her hair, pulling it forward as if the thick locks would offer a suggestion. "I've worn my hair exactly like this since I was in third grade. What I'm looking for is a new look."

"Well"—the other woman placed her pencil sideways in her mouth and stared at the computer screen—"Marilyn would be the best one for the job, but I know she's booked solid today. She wanted to leave a bit early this afternoon."

Ellie knew the reason. "Her mother's just arrived and she's probably looking forward to visiting with her."

The receptionist looked up, surprise written on her face.

"I met Martha on the bus driving in from the airport. She's the one who mentioned Marilyn's to me and suggested I stop by."

"You know Martha?"

"Not really," Ellie clarified. She didn't want to give the wrong impression. "Marilyn's mother sat in the seat across from me."

The receptionist raised her index finger. "Let me talk to Marilyn a moment." She left the area and walked over to one of the stylist's stations. Marilyn was working on a woman who was having her hair colored. The woman in the chair had her hair sectioned off and secured with large clips. Marilyn stood next to her, wearing rubber gloves and holding onto a squeeze bottle filled with the hair dye.

Ellie couldn't hear what was being said, but whatever it was caused Marilyn to turn away and glance in Ellie's direction. Ellie resisted the urge to hold up her palm and wave.

Marilyn said something to the receptionist, who nodded and then returned to Ellie. "She said she'll do it."

"She will?" Ellie felt like cheering.

"She needs to finish the color job on Mrs. Weaver first, and—"

"I'll gladly wait," Ellie said, cutting her off. Two of the chairs in the waiting area had been vacated by the time she finished at the reception desk. She claimed one and reached for a copy of *People* magazine, flipping through the pages. Halfway through a second gossip magazine, the receptionist returned.

"Marilyn is ready for you now."

Surprised, Ellie looked up. "Oh." It seemed hardly any time had passed. She replaced the magazine and then followed the other woman to the far end of the salon.

Marilyn was a petite woman with frosted brown hair and steel-gray eyes. "You must be Ellie," she said, reaching for the plastic cape.

"I am." She thought it was a nice touch for the receptionist to mention her name.

"I was telling the woman at the desk that I met your mother this morning on the bus from Sea-Tac Airport," Ellie explained.

"Mom mentioned you."

"She did?" Ellie didn't bother to hide her surprise.

"I called at noon to check on them. Cameron, my son, was thrilled to pick her up. I wanted to make sure he hadn't frightened Mom half to death. He only got his driver's license recently," she added. "Mom told me all about your chat."

Ellie had appreciated the older woman's words of advice. "Your mother is wise and wonderful."

Marilyn smiled. "I think so, too. I'd hoped to leave a bit early today, but when I tell Mom I'm later than expected because you stopped by, she'll understand."

"She's the one who mentioned your salon. She talked about you with real pride."

Marilyn shook her head and grinned. "That sounds like Mom. You'd think I was the hair stylist to the stars to hear her speak." She wrapped the plastic cape around Ellie's shoulders and ran her fingers through her hair. Apparently, she liked what she saw. "Your hair is healthy, good and thick."

"I know." It sometimes took as long as twenty minutes to blow it dry.

"Monica said you're looking for something new."

"Yes, please."

"You'd look great with an inverted bob." Once more, Marilyn riffled her fingers through the hair at the back of Ellie's head.

"I like that style . . . but I don't know how it would be on me."

Marilyn stepped back. "The nice thing about hair is that it grows. If you find you don't like the cut, then give it a few weeks. My guess is that you're going to love it." She draped a towel over Ellie's shoulders and led her to the shampoo bowl.

Forty minutes later, Ellie stared at her reflection in the mirror and couldn't believe the difference a simple haircut could make.

"What did I tell you?" Marilyn gloated. "You're an entirely new woman."

"That's exactly how I feel." When Ellie had stepped into the salon, she hadn't believed this kind of transformation was even possible. It embarrassed her that she couldn't stop staring at her reflection in the mirror.

"It's going to be easy to manage, too," Marilyn promised.

Ellie paid the bill and left a generous tip for Marilyn before she left.

"Mom said you're a special young woman, and she was right," Marilyn said, as she walked Ellie to the door. "Good luck meeting your young man."

"Thank you. I have a good feeling about this."

"Life has a way of working out for the best," the stylist said, and gave Ellie's shoulder a gentle squeeze. She removed her apron and said, "Now I'm off to enjoy a long-overdue visit with my mother."

Ellie wished her own relationship with her mother was as emotionally healthy as the one Martha and Marilyn shared.

Walking back to the inn, Ellie found herself humming a song she'd heard on the radio. She couldn't remember the words, but the music had stayed with her. It felt as if her life had become a song. Tom had done that for her. It didn't seem possible that she could or even should feel this strongly about a man she hadn't met in the traditional way.

The thing was, she *knew* Tom. They might never have met in person, but it felt as if she'd known him her entire life. They shared a closeness, an easy intimacy. He might never have held or kissed her, but she swore she knew what it would be like to feel his arms around her and the taste of his lips on hers.

Whoa, she was getting ahead of herself. Way ahead.

Jo Marie was still working in her kitchen when Ellie returned. She glanced at her and said, "Can I help . . ." For one short second she stared. "Ellie, is that really you?"

She lifted her hand toward her head. "Do you like it?"

"I didn't recognize you at first. This is an amazing transformation. Unbelievable."

Ellie was thrilled by the innkeeper's reaction. "I'm so glad you like it."

"I do, but, more important, do you?"

"I love it. Marilyn was great. She took one look at me and knew right away what style would best suit me. I wasn't sure if I'd like my hair stacked in the back like this, you know . . . cut in layers."

Jo Marie ran her hand along the smooth edge of the back. "It looks amazing."

"Thanks so much . . ." Ellie said. "I guess I should go get changed. I bought a new outfit for my first date with Tom."

Ellie headed up the stairs to get ready, butterflies exploding in her stomach. This time would be different. In fact, she had the feeling it might end up being the most romantic night of her life.

Tom was different. She'd felt it almost from the first moment when they'd started communicating online. One thing was sure: Ellie wasn't about to let her mother's fears ruin this relationship.

The short conversation with Tom lingered in her mind. He'd wanted to say something, wanted her to make him a promise, but had stopped before he could ask. Ellie could only wonder what had held him back. Well, no worries there. She'd find out soon enough.

Chapter 7

After lunch, Maggie and Roy decided to take a walk along Harbor Street. When they'd left Rose Harbor Inn for lunch she'd noticed a number of antiques shops along the main street of the town and wanted to investigate.

"Would you mind checking out a couple of the stores?" Maggie asked her husband.

"Sure," he said, readily agreeing. "Who knows, we might find priceless canning jars or a discarded yarn project that's half knit."

Maggie glanced at him to be sure he was joking, and when she saw his smile, she returned it with one of her own. Shopping was one of his least favorite ways to spend time, but his willingness showed her that he was doing his best to recapture what they'd lost over the last few years. "I enjoy looking at old buttons."

"Buttons?"

"Some of the older buttons from the 1960s and before are lovely. I especially like the pearl ones."

"When I was a kid I used to collect baseball cards," Roy mentioned. "If I'd kept them, they'd probably be worth a fortune now."

He was right. "What became of them?"

He shrugged. "I don't remember. I traded off a few when I was twelve or thirteen and kept the rest in an old cigar box I got from my grandfather. I haven't thought about them in years. I haven't got a clue where they went."

As they walked down the hill, Roy reached for her hand, gripping it in his own. The simple gesture was like healing salve on a throbbing burn.

Even now Maggie wasn't sure how their marriage could have taken such a drastic detour when they continued to love each other. It had hit her all over again at lunch how far apart they'd grown. When Roy had suggested they leave the boys out of the conversation, she'd been shocked to realize they had nothing left to say to each other.

Finally, Roy talked about the job that had demanded so much of his time. She noticed how careful he was to avoid the subject of Katherine. The other woman, a high school flame, held a job with one of his plumbing suppliers. That was how they'd connected on Facebook and become "friends" again. Maggie was convinced it'd all started out innocent enough, at least in the beginning.

She stopped herself, refusing to dwell on Katherine. Roy had severed the relationship and she had to learn to trust him again in the same way that he had to put his trust back in her.

Still, the entire time he talked about the construction project, Maggie felt a burning sensation close to her heart. Her husband hadn't been unfaithful, at least not in the physical sense. But Katherine and Roy were emotionally involved, texting and communicating day after day, meeting for drinks and exchanging sexually explicit emails. It was when she found the emails that Maggie had blown up. The most painful one suggested Maggie was a cold fish in bed. Another was a cruel joke. How do you turn a fox into a cow? Marry her. Just thinking about the messages Maggie had read on his phone from the other woman was enough to fill her mouth with bile.

She couldn't allow her mind to dwell on all the lonely nights she'd gone to bed by herself because her husband was busy with paperwork or other business. He didn't have time to talk to her, but he'd spent copious amounts of time flirting with another woman. It hadn't gotten to the point of being physical, but it was clear to Maggie that that was exactly where the relationship was headed. Far too clear.

"I'm enjoying quilting," she'd told him at lunch. No doubt he found the subject of little interest, but he'd listened politely and suggested that for Christmas she might like a new sewing machine. She appreciated the offer and the fact that he felt their marriage would survive until the holidays.

The bile didn't settle well, and she had to deal with heartburn. The acid built up in her as they strolled down Harbor Street. "I need an antacid," she said, and noticed a pharmacy located a block down on the corner. "It must have been the grease from the fish."

They walked to the end of the street and went inside together. While she searched the aisle for what she needed, Roy looked over the magazine rack where the novels were positioned and picked out a paperback thriller by one of his favorite authors.

"I can't remember the last time I got involved in a book," he said. "The one I brought with me is months old, and I've forgotten the storyline."

Actually, she'd been thinking the same thing. She couldn't remember the last time she saw him reading, or doing anything that didn't involve his job. "That's part of the problem, don't you think?"

He frowned, as if the comment confused him. "Not reading?"

"Not taking time for ourselves." She didn't for herself, either. It was difficult, especially with two young boys who were constantly in need of care and attention.

"You quilt."

"That helps keep me sane." She had a minimum of an hour every afternoon while the boys went down for a nap, but Jaxon was fast outgrowing nap time. He'd start kindergarten in another month. The plan was for Maggie to find part-time employment once both boys were in school full-time. It wasn't necessary for the money as much as her emotional well-being. While Maggie enjoyed her role as a wife and mother, she needed to get out of the house and socialize with other women and develop her own interests.

Part of the problem, she realized, was that Roy didn't seem to understand or appreciate the role she had in their home. They'd once had a tremendous argument because he'd needed her to return a pair of jeans for him. She hadn't found the time. She'd been on the run all day. Collin had a dentist appointment, Jaxon's preschool needed cupcakes for a bake sale, and it was her turn with the car pool. She hadn't gotten groceries in two weeks. When Roy discovered she hadn't returned his jeans for the right size, he'd demanded to know what she'd done all day. To hear him talk, she'd been lying around the house eating chocolate-dipped strawberries all afternoon.

Again she forced herself to stop focusing her attention on the negative. It seemed her mind automatically lingered on old hurts. This was supposed to be a time to heal and rebuild, not stew over past slights or misunderstandings.

Maggie stepped to the counter and paid for their purchases. Right away she chewed two antacids.

As they exited the small pharmacy, Roy pointed down the street. "That shop looks interesting."

"It does," she agreed. This was exactly the kind of antiques store she enjoyed exploring most. The window display was of blue glass from the time of the Depression. No doubt it was priced beyond what she'd be comfortable paying.

"Look at that *Star Wars* lunch box," Roy said, pointing toward a second window display. "I had one just like that when I was in school."

"It's hard to think of it as an antique, isn't it?" she teased.

"I'm too young to be considered an antique," he insisted, shaking his head as if to dispel the thought.

"Way too young," she agreed, and resisted squeezing his cheek. "You've still got a baby face."

He rewarded her with a smile. "And you don't look a day over thirty."

"I'm barely thirty-three," she reminded him.

"Really? I thought you were still thirty-one."

"Time flies when you're having fun."

"So I've heard." As quickly as it came, the humor left his voice and he looked away. Oh, she'd had fun, all right, and turned up missing for nearly twenty hours. Tit for tat.

It appeared her husband held onto old hurts as well. Perhaps it was unavoidable, seeing the hit their marriage had taken. First Roy and then her. These missteps had the potential to destroy them both, if they let them. Neither of them wanted a divorce, if for no other reason than their children. The key was in their ability to learn how to forgive. Try as she might, Maggie wasn't sure that was possible.

"Let's go inside," Roy suggested, and held the door open.

They were both trying, Maggie realized. Trying hard. Perhaps too hard. It was possible that they might never be able to recapture what they'd lost.

Mentally she shook her head, refusing to give in to negative thinking. No, she couldn't, wouldn't, allow that to happen. Roy was her husband, the father of her children, and she was determined to fight to keep her marriage intact. They'd both made huge mistakes, but they'd vowed to start again and she wouldn't allow petty grievances to sabotage their intentions.

The store gave off a musty scent that reminded her of old books. It wasn't entirely unpleasant. They walked down the aisles and saw a woman standing at the counter. There didn't seem to be a lot of customers in the store.

"Feel free to wander around and explore," the clerk told them. "If you need help, let me know."

Maggie asked where to find old buttons, and the woman directed her to an area against the back wall. Roy followed, looking a bit bored, his hands in his pockets.

Maggie noticed an overstuffed chair close by. "This might take a while," she told him. "If you want, you can sit and relax."

"You don't need to handle me, Maggie."

She hadn't realized that was what she was doing. "I'll feel rushed if I know you're bored."

"Don't worry about me, okay?"

"Okay." He could be prickly at times, which led her to believe that he, too, continued to struggle with negative thoughts, old wounds, and fresh ones, too. Determined not to allow his mood to alter her own, she sorted through the buttons, searching out the ones that caught her attention.

Roy looked around a bit and then sat down in the chair and reached for his phone.

Maggie went completely still. If he was sending Katherine a text, she swore she'd walk out this door and not look back.

Roy must have read her thoughts, because he looked up and caught her eye. "I'm checking emails to make sure everything is running smoothly on the job site."

Rather than respond verbally for fear her voice would tremble, she nodded.

Ten minutes later, he was still responding to emails.

For once, just once, she wished Roy could leave work behind.

Roy stood. "I need to make a call."

"Now?" she asked without censure. "We're taking a weekend break, remember?"

"Maybe you are, but I need to see to this."

"Roy, you promised."

"Maggie, listen, I'm sorry, but the electrical foreman's run into a problem and the entire job site is about to be shut down. Time is money, and we can't afford to let that happen, not when it's within my power to prevent it."

"I . . ." He had a valid point.

"I know you're disappointed, but this won't take more than a few minutes, I promise."

"Okay."

He pushed a button on his cell and then swore under his breath. "I can't get good reception in here."

The clerk, who'd apparently overheard their conversation, called out, "If you step out and face the marina, you shouldn't have a problem."

"Thanks."

Maggie was upset. She didn't want to be unreasonable or difficult over this. They'd had more time together in the last twenty-four hours than they'd enjoyed all year. That alone said it all.

It used to be they made love three or four times a week. It'd dwindled down to once every other week, if that. Maggie didn't want to complain, didn't want to nag her husband. To be fair, she was equally neglectful when it came to the physical aspect of their marriage. The problem, she surmised, was their inability to get in sync with each other. When she was willing and ready, Roy was home late or overly tired. It was the same with her. Her husband would let her know what he wanted and she'd beg off. Neither one of them put up much of a fuss, all too willing to accept the other's weak excuses, which said a great deal, she supposed, sadly.

After a few minutes, when Roy didn't return, Maggie paid for her purchases and left the store. She saw her husband pacing the sidewalk alongside the marina, intent in conversation. He didn't seem to notice her approach.

Didn't seem to notice her at all.

No, she wouldn't go there, feeling sorry for herself, making up excuses for what happened, for her own role in the mess they'd made of their lives together. She had to think positively, look forward rather than dwell on all that had gone wrong. The past could bury them. They had to look ahead, not behind.

Roy saw her and waved. As she approached, she heard him speaking to the project manager. He ended the call and placed the phone back in his pocket. "It looks like that problem is squared away."

"Good."

"Did you find some buttons you wanted?"

"I did." She held up the small bag.

"Is it going to set me back a house payment?" he teased.

"It is if we're paying ten dollars a month for the mortgage."

He grinned and looped his arm around her shoulders, bringing her close to his side.

"I was just thinking we might want to take the boys to Disneyland," she said casually.

Roy mulled over the suggestion for a couple minutes. "Aren't the boys a little young yet for Disneyland?"

"Perhaps, but it will give us something to look forward to as a family."

She tacked on this last part so he'd understand she was looking to the future, their future as a couple. "If we get it on the schedule early, it'll be easier for you to get away." She bit her lip to keep from mentioning that the boys needed time with their parents. It was vital that their children know their parents loved each other. Roy was good about giving them attention at night, but they rarely were together as a family.

"Disneyland," he repeated slowly, as though considering the idea. "We could plan the trip around Christmas."

"Great." She was enthused now, and Roy seemed to be, too. "I'll get online and see what I can find."

"Yes, do." He leaned down and kissed the top of her head. It was the first romantic gesture he'd made toward her in longer than she wanted to remember.

Maggie scanned the waterfront and the marina. Everything looked inviting. What a charming community. All at once her stomach heaved and a wave of nausea hit her, taking her by surprise.

"What's wrong?" Roy sensed right away something wasn't right.

"I don't know," she whispered, and clenched her stomach. "All of a sudden I'm feeling sick."

"Do you think it was the fish and chips?"

Maggie didn't know. "Everything tasted so fresh and good. You're feeling okay, aren't you?"

"Yes. Fine. My goodness, Maggie, you've gone pale."

"We both ate the same thing, so I doubt this has anything to do with lunch." Her stomach heaved again then, and she clenched it tighter.

"Should we go back to the inn?" Roy asked.

Maggie nodded. "That's a good idea."

Keeping her close to his side, Roy led the way up the hill to the inn. Maggie had hoped that the walk and fresh air would help, but they didn't. If anything, she felt worse. By the time they arrived back, her face had broken out into a sweat and her hands felt clammy.

Rover barked just once when they walked in the front door, and Jo Marie came around the corner from the kitchen.

"Maggie isn't feeling well," Roy explained.

"Is there anything I can do?" Jo Marie asked.

Maggie shook her head. "No." At the moment, it was imperative that she get upstairs, and quickly. Reading the look in her eyes, Roy raced up the stairs and unlocked their room. Maggie made it into the bathroom in the nick of time, losing her lunch with violent heaves.

Roy stood just outside the bathroom door, and when she'd finished he handed her a wet washcloth. She wiped her mouth clean, and he gently led her to the bed.

"Oh Roy, I just can't have the flu. I just can't."

"Honey, don't worry."

She lay down on the bed and he covered her with a knitted afghan from the foot of the mattress and then leaned over her and tenderly kissed her brow. "Close your eyes and rest, and you'll feel better when you wake."

"What are you going to do?" she asked, feeling wretched that this would happen now. Oh why now? Why, why, why?

"I got a book to read, remember? I'll sit on the chair here and delve into a good story."

All of a sudden it was all Maggie could do to keep her eyes open. "Okay," she whispered.

She heard a gentle knock against the door. Roy answered, and it was Jo Marie.

"Everything's fine. Maggie's going to rest," she heard Roy whisper.

This was Roy, her husband, the father of her children, the man she loved with all her heart. Her eyes drifted closed and she remembered the first day she saw him walk across campus. They were college students, both young and eager to make their mark on the world, full of ideas and idealism.

So much had changed . . . so much.

Chapter 8

I felt terrible for Maggie Porter. She'd looked deathly pale when she'd arrived back at the inn. From the frantic way she raced up the stairs, I knew she was about to be sick. I'd hoped there was something that I could do. I'd suggested that I bring up a pot of weak tea, but Roy told me it wasn't necessary. Maggie appeared to be resting comfortably now. I knew she'd been looking forward to this weekend getaway with her husband, and I hated the thought of her coming down with the flu.

Currently, all was quiet upstairs. Ellie Reynolds was busy dressing for her first date with Tom. And I suspected that Roy had either joined his wife for a nap or found some other way to occupy himself.

The Porters were an attractive couple. My first impression of the two led me to believe there was trouble brewing in the relationship, but I'd since changed my mind. They seemed to have settled whatever was wrong. It'd probably been a small misunderstanding that had escalated but had since been resolved.

With everything under control, I sat down in my small office off the kitchen. A pile of papers cluttered my desk and needed filing. I kept paper backups, although everything I needed was on my computer. Once I dealt with the clutter on my desk, I worked on completing tax forms the state required from business owners each quarter.

When I finished I leaned back in my chair and sighed. My meeting with Peggy that morning had been a disappointment. I'd hoped that between her and Bob I'd be able to learn more about Mark.

It irritated me that he remained so tight-lipped. I thought we were friends, and friends should be open and honest with each other. Right? Well, not Mark. Oh no. The details of his life were like gold bars stored inside a bank vault.

I suppose I could bribe him with cookies. "What do you think, Rover? Should I bake Mark a batch of peanut-butter cookies and hold them hostage until he fills in the blanks?"

My faithful companion cocked his head and stared up at me as if to remind me that I'd basically tried that earlier in the day.

"Right," I mumbled under my breath.

Rover placed his chin back down on his paw but kept his gaze focused on me.

"Well, there's more than one way to find out what I want to know," I said aloud, fire stirring my blood. I'd worked in the banking business and there were ways of garnering information.

More determined than ever, I went onto the Internet and Googled Mark Taylor. Within a matter of seconds I had what I wanted . . . sort of. The Internet listed the information for two hundred and eleven men named Mark Taylor spread all across the country, from Nome, Alaska, to Key West, Florida.

"Oh great." What I needed was his middle name and his date of birth—otherwise, I'd be spending copious amounts of time and money shuffling through the lengthy list. And even then it would be little more than guesswork. I needed a lot more details if I was going to uncover anything of importance. And, really, was it worth all the time and hassle? That was the real question. I could always go back to my spring cleaning. I'd been meaning to check out what was up in the attic for some time.

I heard a car door slam and Rover was instantly on his feet. Fearing he might bark and wake Maggie Porter, I hurried to the front door. To my surprise, I found Mark parked outside. The bed of his pickup truck was loaded down with lumber.

The man never ceased to astonish me. It'd taken him weeks to get started on the rose garden. *Weeks.* Yet only that morning I'd given him the go-ahead on the gazebo. Already he'd purchased the lumber and seemed set on unloading it in the yard.

He had a long two-by-four balanced on his shoulder, and carted it from the bed of his truck to the lawn before he noticed me and Rover standing on the top step. He hesitated. "What is that look about?" he asked.

"What look?"

"The one you're giving me."

I had no idea he could read me that easily. "I'm surprised is all."

"About what?" He set the piece of lumber down and then removed his gloves.

"You're starting on the gazebo?"

His gaze narrowed. "I thought that was what you wanted."

"I do."

"Then how come you've got the look of a mounted bass?"

I wasn't keen on the analogy but let it pass. "I thought I'd need to wait."

"For what?"

He was being thickheaded. "For you to get started. By the way, where's Peter McConnell?"

"Don't know and I don't care." He didn't explain, and while I was curious as to what had happened to the other man, I had more pressing subjects on my mind.

"Do you want me to come back later?" he demanded.

"No, no, don't let me stop you."

He put his gloves back on and then shook his head as if to say he found me impossible to understand. "It sounds to me like you're complaining because I'm starting the job. Last time around you were upset because I delayed planting the garden."

"I'm not complaining," I shouted, louder than I intended.

"Women," he muttered, just loud enough for me to hear. He returned to his truck, shook his head, and reached for a second piece of lumber.

"I said I'm not complaining," I repeated.

"That's your mad voice."

"I am not mad," I insisted again, calmer this time, for fear of waking my guest. "I'm amazed. And pleased," I added.

"You make it sound like a bad thing."

"It's a good thing." Rover went down the stairs and parked himself halfway between the two of us, lying in the grass with his legs spread out, soaking in the coolness of the lawn.

"When's your birthday?" I asked.

He set the board down next to the first one. Either he didn't hear me or he chose to ignore the question.

"Your birthday," I repeated, coming down the steps.

"What about it?" he asked gruffly. He was on his third trip back from the truck, another long board balanced on top of his shoulder.

"You have one, don't you?"

"Most folks do."

"Mine's in February."

He shook his head as if to say it was none of his concern. "You expected me to buy you a birthday gift?"

"No." He twisted everything around. "When is yours?"

"My what?"

"Birthday!" I was fast losing my patience. He was purposely being obtuse in hope of exasperating me, and he was succeeding.

He stopped and planted his hands on his hips and glared at me as if I'd asked him if he had a prison record. "What do you want to know for?" he demanded, his words as hard as the lumber he'd carried.

That was a tricky question. To admit I'd been online seeking information about him was more than I wanted him to know. "I don't know . . . maybe I want to throw you a surprise party."

"Ha. Ha. Very funny."

"I'd invite Peggy and Bob and . . ."

"You aren't throwing me a surprise birthday party, and we both know it."

He frustrated me to no end. "Okay, fine. Forget the birthday party."

"Gladly." He was sweating hard now; hauling heavy lumber was strenuous labor. He paused and wiped his forearm across his brow. A dark strand fell across his forehead.

"You could use a haircut."

The look he sent me would have melted kryptonite. "Are we married?"

"Hardly."

"Are you my mother?"

"No. Okay, fine. I apologize." He was long overdue for a haircut, but far be it from me to mention it. I didn't know what was the matter with me. It was like I was going out of my way to irk him into an argument.

"You're getting on my nerves, Jo Marie."

I could tell. Seeing how badly I'd bungled this, I returned to the house and brewed him a fresh glass of iced tea and then carried it outside. "Here," I said, holding out the icy-cold drink for him to take. "It's a peace offering."

He hesitated and stared at the glass for a good five-second count before he deigned to reach for it. He made it seem like he was doing me a favor by accepting. Once he took the glass out of my hand, he drank down the tea in several large gulps and then returned it to me. The ice made clinking sounds against the side of the glass as I took it back.

Thinking I should make casual conversation, I mentioned Maggie Porter was feeling sickly.

"That's a shame. Flu?"

"Don't know. I hope not, for both their sakes."

He braced his hands against his hips. "I've got another load."

"You must be exhausted. Sit with me for a while."

He cast me a suspicious look. "Why?"

"So you can relax, unwind."

"Are you going to hound me with more questions?" he asked.

"No." Not because I wasn't curious, though. Getting Mark to admit to anything was like chasing after a dog with a bone. It was clear to me that I was going to need to be a whole lot more subtle if I was going to dig up information. I would have to trick him into giving me what I needed to know.

I poured another glass of iced tea for him and one for myself. We sat side by side on the top step of the porch with Rover resting between us.

We were silent for several moments, each lost in our own thoughts, I assumed. My musings went straight to Paul, as they often did, although I made an effort to remember the good times we'd had. I'd never laughed as much with anyone as I had with Paul.

I looked up and noticed Mark studying me. When I caught his eye, he frowned and asked, "You okay?"

I shrugged and then said the first thing I thought of, which in retrospect made no earthly sense. "Paul's sweatshirt has lost his scent."

"I beg your pardon."

It stunned me that I'd blurt this out. "Never mind."

"No," he said, frowning, refusing to let this pass without comment. "So that's it."

I was embarrassed now. Earlier I'd been feeling depressed and lonely and I'd gone into my room and taken Paul's sweatshirt out of the closet. I did that from time to time. I couldn't explain why, other than that I gained some comfort in an old Seahawks sweatshirt of his. We'd met at a Seahawks game and he'd given it to me to keep for him when he'd been deployed. I wore it myself on occasion, mainly because I felt close to Paul when I had it on. After I learned he'd been killed, I kept it in a special spot in my closet and periodically held it against my face. Then I would breathe in the scent of him. That afternoon I noticed the fragrance that was uniquely my husband had faded. I felt as if I was losing this last bit of Paul, and I wasn't ready to let him go, wasn't ready to give this up when I'd had to surrender so much else.

"Jo Marie?" Mark eyed me curiously. "Are you okay?"

"Of course I am," I blurted out, lost in my thoughts.

"You look like you're about to break into tears."

"I'm not, so don't worry." I leaped up off the step and rushed back into the house, and set the full glass of tea on the kitchen counter.

A few moments later, Mark followed me inside. He took his own sweet time setting his empty glass in the sink. "What's this about wanting to know my birthday?" he asked.

"It's nothing. I shouldn't have asked." I don't know why I'd bothered to Google his name. Wanting to resolve this mystery around Mark was ridiculous. "If you don't want to tell me, it's fine."

He started to walk out of the kitchen, hesitated, and turned back. "You're sure you're okay?"

"Yes," I insisted.

Again he paused as if at a loss at what to think. "I was born May eighth."

I stared back in surprise and blinked, hardly knowing what to say. I wouldn't go back to my computer search. It felt wrong now. Mark had given me a small bit of trust, and to search out his background like a bloodhound hot on a trail felt like I'd be abusing his confidence.

Another hour passed and I found myself dealing with the same restlessness that had plagued me recently. I heard footsteps and looked up to find Ellie descending the staircase, one hand on the railing. The change in her appearance was dramatic. The haircut was perfect for her. She wore a lovely sleeveless floral dress with a wide black belt and carried a thin white cardigan over her arm. Her purse hung from her shoulder.

On seeing me, she said, "Tom is on his way."

"You look fabulous," I said, and I meant it.

A smile appeared. "Do you really think so?"

"I do." She was going to knock Tom's socks off.

Her cell phone dinged, and Ellie glanced at it and sighed.

"Tom?" I asked, seeing the look that came over her. If this young man was messing with Ellie's tender heart, I swore I would find a way to make him suffer.

Ellie shook her head and ignored the call. "I'm going to pretend I didn't hear that," she said, as she tossed the phone back inside her purse.

Chapter 9

~

When Ellie heard Tom's car pull into the driveway at Rose Harbor Inn, she froze. It felt like her entire body had shut down. This was it. The moment she'd been waiting for all these months.

With all her heart she had to believe that Tom was everything he claimed and that he wasn't out to abuse or use her. She had to believe that their feelings for each other were genuine. Her heart told her he was sincere, and she needed to trust her heart and drown out her mother's dire warnings.

The porch steps creaked as Tom approached the front door. Ellie stood a few feet away on the other side, her heart racing like she'd just finished running a marathon. Rover came and sat on his haunches at her side as though standing guard over her.

The doorbell chimed and Ellie inhaled a deep breath, slowly

counted to ten, and then, as casually as she could manage, stepped forward and opened the door.

Tom looked exactly like his picture. He was tall, about six-three, but then she was tall, too. Her mother claimed she got her height from her father. Tom's eyes were a rich shade of brown as he steadily regarded her. It seemed they both held their breath. Ellie knew she did, waiting for she knew not what.

For the longest moment of her life, neither spoke.

Finally, Tom broke the silence. "Ellie?"

She nodded. "Tom?" Her voice squeaked.

He nodded and then whispered as if in awe. "You're even more beautiful in person." With anyone else that might have sounded like a well-practiced line. It didn't with him. If anything, he looked as nervous as Ellie felt. He continued to stand on the other side of the door. Her manners, it seemed, had completely deserted her.

"Would you like to come inside?" she asked, once she found she could speak without sounding like a high-pitched pond frog.

He glanced at his wrist, reminding her that he'd made a dinner reservation.

"Perhaps later, if you don't mind," he said.

"I don't mind at all," she rushed to assure him. He took her elbow as they descended the porch steps. Then he hurried to her side of the car and held open the passenger door. One of the text messages from her mother had cautioned her that she should beware of men who were overly polite or well mannered. The warning rang in her ears now, but she refused to listen.

Tom waited until she was inside and then closed the door for her. He raced around to the driver's side and slipped behind the steering wheel. Ellie couldn't help but think it was a rare man who saw to such details. He was like her, an old-fashioned kind of person.

The car's interior had been freshly detailed, she noticed. The dashboard gleamed and the seats felt slippery. It told Ellie that Tom wanted to make a good impression. Her mother had warned her about that, too. Once more, Ellie refused to listen to her mother's voice, no matter how loud Virginia Reynolds shouted in her ear.

"DD's on the Cove is the best restaurant in town."

"Jo Marie mentioned what a good restaurant it is," Ellie said. "She's the innkeeper. Do you know her?"

He started the engine and glanced over his shoulder while backing out of the driveway. Once he was on the road, he said, "I haven't met Jo Marie, but I've heard nothing but good things about her and the inn. I thought you'd feel most at home there."

"I appreciated the recommendation."

He waited until they were down the hill before he spoke again. "Your hair looks different now."

Automatically, her hand went to the back of her head. "Yes." She resisted asking him if he liked the new style. It might sound like she was fishing for compliments.

"It's a good look for you."

"Thanks."

When they arrived at the restaurant their table was ready. Tom held her chair out for her, and once they were handed the menus, he made a couple suggestions. "Their clam chowder is excellent."

Ellie lowered the menu to look at him and smile. "What's your favorite thing to order?"

"Fried oysters."

"I enjoy fried oysters, too, but the seafood Cobb salad is tempting me." Her decision was made. She was going for a cup of the chowder and the salad, then set her menu aside. The waiter returned and Tom ordered a white wine from New Zealand. Ellie enjoyed wine, but her knowledge was limited. Tom went on to explain about several varieties until their wine was delivered. The waiter took their dinner order and then discreetly slipped away.

"What shall we drink to?" Tom asked, raising his wineglass, holding onto the stem.

"To finally meeting," Ellie suggested.

He tipped his glass toward hers until the two goblets made a slight clinking sound. "May it be the first of many such meetings and dinner dates."

Ellie hoped that was true. Tom was exactly as she pictured him, and not just in the physical sense. He was as uptight about this dinner date as she was.

"Is your mother upset with you?" he asked, after their soup was delivered.

"A little," Ellie confessed. He had no clue, and she wasn't telling him. She tasted the chowder and Tom was right to have recommended it.

"Which means she's probably texting you every hour."

"Something like that."

He set his wineglass down and frowned slightly as if he was well aware of her mother's tactics. "It means a lot to me that you'd be willing to meet me."

That was the way Ellie wanted it. She had to be away from her mother for this first meeting. Tom had offered to come to Oregon, but Ellie had discouraged that for fear of what her mother would do to embarrass her.

"I'm sure she means well," Tom said, as if following her train of thought. "If you were my daughter, I'd want to protect you, too."

"Do I need protection from you, Tom?"

"No." His dark eyes widened slightly. "I'd never do anything to hurt you, Ellie, God as my witness."

His words warmed her. They talked for a while. A lot of their previous conversation had revolved around their families. With Ellie, there was little to tell. She'd been raised with her grandparents, homeschooled, and had taken a few community college classes. It'd been a friend's suggestion that she join a group of other women who shared a talent for organization. The four of them had started their own company, which had proven to be successful beyond their expectations.

Ellie knew Tom's father had died when he was young. His mother had remarried, and Tom and his younger brother, Earl, had basically been raised by their stepfather, although they both thought of him as their father and called him Dad.

"I know your mother is worried about us, and frankly I don't blame her," Tom continued. "Maybe we should call her and reassure her later."

"No." It wouldn't do any good and would quite possibly arouse her mother's suspicions. Knowing Virginia, Ellie accepted that there wasn't anything Tom could say or do that would appease her.

"Even now I miss my mother," Tom said, looking thoughtful. "She's been gone ten years now. I was in my late teens when she died. Her death changed the course of my life."

"I'm sorry." Ellie probably didn't appreciate her mother nearly enough, but lately that had been difficult. Virginia was much too refined to argue verbally with Ellie, but her disapproval was evident in nearly every way imaginable.

"For a long time my dad was an emotional mess. Mom died unexpectedly. One minute she was fine and the next moment, she grabbed her head and collapsed. She was gone within a few hours. We were all left in a state of shock.

"Dad blamed himself. Although there was nothing he could have done, he thinks he should have been able to help her somehow. He's filled with regrets, and it isn't just about what happened to Mom."

"I never knew my dad," Ellie whispered. She set her spoon aside as a deep sense of sadness settled over her. "He and my mother divorced before I have any memories of him."

"You never had any contact with him following their divorce?"

"Never."

Tom's face tightened.

"I think the marriage was so bad that he was looking to put it all behind him."

"By *everything*, do you mean you, too?" Tom asked this as though he found the suggestion seriously wrong.

In reality, Ellie couldn't blame her father, but she had missed knowing him.

"Have you ever thought about reaching out to him?" Tom asked.

When she was in grade school and later as a preteen she'd wanted to write him a letter, but her mother claimed she had no idea where he lived or how to reach him. "I did want to find him."

"Why didn't you?"

"Mom claimed he didn't want anything more to do with us. He'd moved on with his life and so had she."

Tom shook his head as if he found that hard to believe. "You must have missed having a father."

She lowered her gaze. It was as if Tom had read her heart. At various times in her youth, she'd yearned to know her father, dreamed of what it would be like to have him in her life. As young as she'd been when he left, she wondered if she might have been part of the reason. Perhaps she'd been a cranky baby. Her mother once told Ellie how she'd cried and cried with colic, keeping her parents awake all hours of the night.

"I think I might have been a difficult baby."

"So? What does that have to do with anything?"

Clenching her hands together, Ellie stared down at the table and tried to smile. "I might have turned him off fatherhood."

"To the point he'd abandon you?" Tom asked incredulously. "You're joking, right?"

Ellie lifted one shoulder in a shrug. "I don't know what else to think." The subject depressed her and she preferred not to discuss it. "Do you mind if we talk about something else?" she asked.

"Of course." He seemed to regret bringing up the subject.

Soon afterward their entrées arrived, and everything was delicious. The conversation drifted easily from one subject to the next. It helped that they'd become familiar with each other through email, phone calls, and social media. These first meetings could be awkward and uncomfortable, yet Ellie felt completely at ease with Tom.

After dinner, Tom suggested a movie and Ellie agreed. Because the next showing wasn't for more than an hour, they decided to walk along the waterfront. The night was lovely, with a slight breeze blowing off the cove. Earlier, Jo Marie had suggested Ellie bring a cardigan, and she was glad she'd taken her advice.

"Let me help," Tom offered, taking the sweater out of her hand and holding it while she slipped her arms into the sleeves. He brought it up to her shoulders and let his hands linger there. Of her own volition, Ellie leaned back, pressing her body against his, tucking her head beneath his chin. How well suited they were. She fit perfectly in his embrace and loved the feel of his arms around her.

"I've dreamed of kissing you," he whispered close to her ear.

Ellie smiled. "I've thought a lot about it, too."

He slid his hands down the length of her arms. "I can't believe you're really here." He turned her around so that they faced each other. His gaze delved deep into hers. After a lengthy moment, he broke eye contact and glanced around them.

The waterfront area was crowded. Another couple, lost in conversation, strolled past, followed by a little boy around five who chased after a seagull, laughing as his short legs pumped for all he was worth. A dog barked in the distance.

Tom expelled a harsh breath. "Later," he whispered, and then reached for her hand as they continued down the waterfront pathway.

"I took a long walk earlier this afternoon," Ellie told him. "It's so beautiful here with the cove and the Olympic Mountains in the background. I heard someone mention they'd spied a pod of killer whales close by. People hurried down to the marina, anxious to get a look."

"One of my greatest joys is being out on the water."

"I never have . . . my mother was always afraid something would happen to me."

"You've never been in a boat?" His look was incredulous.

"Not out so far that I couldn't swim to the shore."

"Would you like to go sailing with me?" he asked eagerly, his eyes bright with excitement. "I have a friend who owns a boat, and he offered to let me use it any time I want."

"I'd love that."

"Tomorrow, then. I'll pick you up first thing in the morning. Can you be ready by nine?"

"Sure. No problem."

"I'll take you around Puget Sound, and if we're lucky we'll see a few killer whales. But I have other plans for us in the afternoon."

"You do?" She made it a question, hoping he'd fill her in on what he'd scheduled. "You want to share what they are?" she asked, half pleading.

He briefly hesitated and then shook his head. "It's a surprise. You have to wait."

"You can't tell me now?" In his previous emails and text messages, he'd alluded to the fact that he had something special planned for her. To this point, he'd refused to tell her what it was. From his hesitation, he seemed to fear she might not enjoy his surprise, which made Ellie all the more determined to be grateful and reassuring, no matter what it was.

He shook his head. "You'll have to wait until tomorrow." His worried expression changed, and he teased her by bouncing his index finger against the tip of her nose.

"Can I guess?"

"Nope." He tucked her arm around his elbow as they lazily strolled toward the theater. It was an old-fashioned one with a single screen, unlike the multiplex Ellie had seen advertised in the *Cedar Cove Chronicle* with ten theaters.

He paid for their tickets. The movie was one Ellie had seen before, but it didn't matter if she'd viewed it a thousand times—it would be fresh and new because she was sharing it with Tom.

"Popcorn?" Tom asked, as they ventured inside the theater.

Ellie pressed her hand against her stomach. "I'm still full from dinner."

Tom grinned, and it struck her how attractive he was when he smiled. The truth was, he was appealing in every way, smile or no smile.

"What does it matter when we ate dinner? It's impossible to watch a movie without buttered popcorn, and they use real butter here, not that artificial stuff most theaters use."

"Real butter?"

"We're getting popcorn," Tom insisted. He purchased a small bag for them to share. By the time they found their seats the theater was dark and previews played across the screen. Holding her by the hand, he led her to the far right-hand side to the seat farthest from the door.

Ellie stumbled along, hardly able to make her way in the dark. Because she carried the popcorn, Tom held down the seat for her. She made herself comfortable.

"Remember what I mentioned earlier about this dream I've been having?"

"Dream?"

"About kissing you?" His voice took on a husky whisper.

"In the theater?" she whispered back, her smile so big it hurt her face.

"Honestly, Ellie, I don't think I can wait a second longer."

For that matter, neither could she.

Chapter 10

~

Maggie woke slowly, coming out of a dream so blissful she didn't want it to end. Luxuriating in the warm feelings, she kept her eyes closed. The dream revolved around when she'd first started dating Roy. They were both college students and deeply in love with the future, so bright and perfect, spread out before them.

At one time that idyllic happiness, that sense that nothing could ever tear them apart, had been real. Even now it was hard to believe that it had dwindled down to the point where the love that held them together was a slender thread.

As much as she wanted to linger in the dream, Maggie forced herself to pull back to reality. The blanket over her was warm and comfortable. Reluctant as she was to wake, Maggie accepted that while it was tempting, she couldn't nap forever.

Roy was in the room. She could hear him sitting on the other side of the king-size bed in a comfy overstuffed chair. Apparently, he was on the phone, because she could hear him whisper, although she couldn't make out the words. He kept his tone low.

She didn't want him to know she was awake, and she listened as intently as she could. Her fear, rational or not, was that Katherine was on the other end of the line. The thought of the other woman caused her to go instantly cold.

"No," Roy said, and then repeated it a bit more loudly now. "That won't work."

What wouldn't work? Maggie wondered. Was it possible after everything they'd been through that Roy was setting up a rendezvous with the other woman? Maggie hated the way suspicious thoughts immediately assaulted her. She couldn't allow herself to give in to these fears. They would destroy her and destroy their marriage.

At the same time, it helped her appreciate what Roy must be feeling about what had happened with her. She'd been so foolish, so stupid. It was hard to believe that she was capable of the crazy things she'd done after learning about Roy's emotional affair with the other woman.

She stretched, purposely letting her husband know she was awake. Right away Roy ended the telephone conversation.

"I have to go," he whispered. "No, I can't talk later." He was adamant about that, raising his voice.

Maggie swallowed hard. It definitely sounded like a conversation her husband didn't want her to listen in on.

"Maggie's waking up now. Good-bye."

Pretending to stir from sleep, Maggie raised her arms over her head and stretched again, arching her back.

"Hi," Roy said, coming to sit on the edge of the mattress. "You certainly did sleep."

She blinked up at him until she noticed the guilty look he wore. So it had been Katherine on the phone. Little wonder he hadn't wanted her to overhear the conversation.

Maggie had told him before and she meant it: Any contact with the other woman, no matter how innocent, would not be tolerated. Roy had given her his word that the affair was over. He'd severed the relationship and his ties with the business that employed Katherine.

One of the many reasons Maggie had married Roy Porter was because she felt he was a man of honor. He would abide by his word. Until recently, she'd had no reason to doubt him.

"How long did I sleep?" she asked, playing innocent.

Roy checked his wrist and cocked his eyebrows as though he, too, was surprised. "Almost two hours."

That shocked Maggie. "Two hours? My goodness . . ." She hardly knew what to say. It was unheard-of for her to take a two-hour nap in the middle of the afternoon. By now it must be close to dinnertime. She sat upright and rubbed the sleep out of her face.

"You were exhausted."

"I must have been." The truth was, she hadn't slept well in more than a month. Although she was physically drained at the end of each day, she found it almost impossible to sleep. No doubt that was due to the constant tension between them.

"How are you feeling?" Roy asked. He leaned forward and brushed the hair from her face, his look somewhat guarded.

Maggie studied her husband, fearing what she saw in him was guilt. She bit back the hard questions and accusations. As difficult as it was, she forced herself to swallow her suspicions and pretend she hadn't heard any part of his conversation.

"I'm feeling much better," she said, faking a smile. Physically, she felt fine, but her heart ached. She couldn't let this go. It would be easy to pretend, and frankly . . . maybe it was better not to know. If Roy had been talking to Katherine, Maggie would have an extremely difficult choice to make, and at the moment she didn't feel capable of choosing a dinner entrée, let alone the fate of her marriage.

She glanced at the digital readout from the clock on the night-stand. "It's after six. You should have woken me."

"It's fine, Maggie," Roy reassured her. "You needed the sleep."

"What about dinner?" To her surprise, she discovered she was hungry.

"Do you feel up to it?"

She nodded, and Roy looked mildly surprised. "Well, great." He stood and reached for his phone, which rested on the dresser top next to the chair where he'd been sitting. Maggie's gaze fell on it, too, and once again she was faced with indecision, with doubts and fears.

"I'll run a brush through my hair," she said, and climbed off the bed. She tossed aside the blanket, and to her amazement, Roy reached for it, folding it neatly and placing it at the foot of the bed. It wasn't like her husband to think of doing something like that. Right away, she sensed he'd done it in an effort to avoid eye contact.

Maggie closed the bathroom door and leaned against it while she tried to reason this out. If she allowed it, the conversation her hus-band had taken such pains to hide would ruin their weekend. She had to let it go or spoil everything these days away were meant to be.

She refreshed her makeup and, after taking a moment to com-pose herself and her thoughts, joined Roy. When they came down the stairs, Jo Marie was in the kitchen with Rover.

"Oh Maggie, you're up," Jo Marie greeted. "How are you feel-ing?"

She offered the other woman a reassuring smile. "Much, much better, thank you."

"We're going out for dinner," Roy said. "Any place you'd like to recommend?"

"Several," Jo Marie said, and opened a kitchen drawer. "The brochure I gave you earlier lists area restaurants along with their signature dishes. If you mention you're from the inn, you're likely to be offered a discount."

"Great." Roy took the folded sheet out of his hip pocket, read it over, and handed it to Maggie.

She glanced at it and then tucked it in the outside flap of her purse. They might be able to use it again later. They weren't scheduled to return to Yakima until Sunday afternoon, which gave them all day Saturday and part of Sunday. Their plans for the rest of the weekend were flexible. They could go into Seattle easily enough. Or drive to any number of local attractions.

"What suits you?" Roy asked, as they left the inn.

"Say again?"

"For dinner. Did you take a look at the list of restaurants Jo Marie gave us?"

"Oh." She should have realized what he meant. "Anything is fine."

His gaze narrowed. "What if I want sushi?"

That was a joke. Roy had gone to a sushi restaurant with a few guys from the job site. He'd taken a fancy to the wide variety of fish and flavors so unlike the meat and potatoes of his childhood. Maggie had given sushi a fair try but was unable to get over the fact that they were eating raw fish.

"I'd manage," she replied, as she got into the car.

Roy didn't bother to hide his surprise.

"What about Mexican?" he suggested, more serious this time.

"Sure. Whatever."

Again, her lackadaisical response seemed to catch him by surprise. "You're generally pretty picky about where we dine out."

"I'm not, either," she insisted, disliking his tone. "You make it sound like I insist upon having my own way, and that's simply not true."

"Whoa, hold on," he said, raising his hand in a defensive posture. "I didn't say anything of the kind."

"It was what you implied."

"It wasn't what I meant." Taking a moment, he went quiet and then exhaled before suggesting in a much calmer tone, "Mexican might not be a good choice if your tummy is queasy."

"My stomach feels fine. I don't know what happened earlier, but I'm feeling much better now."

"Okay, if Mexican food is what you want, then that's what it'll be." He started the car's engine but kept his hands tightly grasping the steering wheel. "Is something bothering you?"

"No," she returned, far more adamantly than she'd intended.

Her husband exhaled sharply as if he knew she was lying but was unwilling to get involved in an argument.

On the drive to the restaurant, Maggie kept her gaze focused on the scenery outside the passenger window, her head turned away from Roy.

Neither spoke. It seemed to take an eternity to find the restaurant on the list. When they did pull into the parking lot for the Taco Shack it was full and Roy was forced to circle around once before he found an empty slot.

"The food must be good for them to be this busy," he commented.

Maggie felt bad for the way she'd snapped at him. Reaching across the confined space, she placed her hand on his arm. "I'm sorry," she whispered. "I seem to be a bit out of sorts, don't I?"

For a moment, Maggie feared he wouldn't accept her apology.

"That happens with Jaxon, too, if he's slept too long. Extra sleep seems to have the opposite effect than what one would expect."

Maggie appreciated him inventing a convenient excuse for her less-than-charming behavior. It was almost as if she wanted to pick a fight so she could throw the telephone conversation in his face. She didn't know what was wrong with her to be this irrational. She had to credit Roy with keeping his cool; it couldn't have been easy.

To her surprise, there wasn't a waiting list and they were seated in a booth within minutes after their arrival.

"How about a margarita?" Roy suggested. "I know how you love licking the salt off the rim of the glass."

"Sure," she said after a short hesitation, doing her best to be agreeable. The last time she'd overindulged in alcohol the results had been disastrous. One thing was certain, there wouldn't be a second time. She'd sworn off drinking to excess ever again. One drink with her husband would be fine, though.

The waiter came for their drink order and within only a few minutes their margaritas were delivered along with a basket of tortilla chips and a small bowl of salsa.

The menu was several pages long, and Maggie took her time reading over the selections. She probably took longer than necessary. Roy made his decision almost right away and set the menu aside.

"You aren't going to order arroz con pollo?" he asked, which was what she generally liked.

"No." Again, the word came out clipped and abrupt. She tried to soften its effect with a halfhearted smile. "Not tonight. I'm in the mood for something different."

"Apparently so," Roy murmured under his breath.

She glanced up and found him studying her. Rather than meet his gaze, she quickly looked away. She reached for a chip, dipping it into the salsa. Right away, she noticed her husband's frown. Rarely did she allow herself to indulge in the chips. For her it was far too easy to fill up on the greasy carbs. It wasn't like her, and Roy knew it.

The waiter returned for their food order and she blindly asked for a number three without even knowing what the combination was.

Again, Roy frowned, and he gave the waiter his own choice. He waited until the other man was out of earshot. "Okay, Maggie, what's up?"

"I beg your pardon?"

"You heard me. Something is bothering you."

Her automatic response was to deny it, but she couldn't make herself do it. She spread the paper napkin across her lap and kept her head lowered. "You were on the phone when I woke."

"Yes. So?"

"You were going to read, remember?"

He stretched out his arms and took hold of his drink with both hands, giving the impression he was relaxed. Maggie knew otherwise.

"I got tired of reading."

She took a moment to digest his answer. While she could get lost in a novel, it wasn't that way with Roy. He was accustomed to physical activity. Sitting for any length of time was foreign to him, which was one reason he found traveling by plane uncomfortable.

Looking up, Maggie held his gaze. This was the very conversation she'd wanted to avoid. Her husband knew her far too well and wouldn't allow this to pass. He was determined to force it out of her.

Keeping her back straight, she boldly met his eyes. "Who was it on the phone?"

Maggie watched as his fingers tightened around the margarita glass until it was a wonder it didn't snap in half and send the alcohol and ice sliding across the tabletop.

"What makes you ask?" His question was deceptively calm.

"I heard part of the conversation."

"Did you, now?"

She swallowed hard. "Yes . . . the part about you not being able to talk later and how that wouldn't work."

"And you automatically assumed I was speaking to Katherine."

Refusing to answer him, Maggie lowered her gaze.

"I wasn't. That was Alex on the phone, the project manager. There's another problem on the job site. Alex did what he could, but he needed my advice. He offered one suggestion, but I know what it's like to deal with these labor unions, and quickly realized his idea wouldn't work and told him so."

"Oh."

"As for the part when I told him I wouldn't be able to talk later . . ." His voice was tight and barely controlled.

When she did look up, Maggie noticed how he'd clenched his jaw. "Yes," she urged, needing to know.

"It was about preserving this weekend with you. He wanted to call me tomorrow, and I told him he couldn't. I'd promised you I'd do my best to leave the job behind."

"Oh." Maggie felt horrible. A hard knot formed in her throat and her bottom lip started to quiver. She bit into it in order to keep it still until she regained her composure. "I owe you an apology . . . again."

"Why didn't you ask me right away?" he demanded.

Her voice wobbled when she spoke. "I . . . was . . . afraid."

"Afraid? Of what?"

Surely he knew, surely he understood. "Of the decision I would be forced to make if it was Katherine."

He reached across the table and took hold of her hand. "I'll say it again, Maggie, but this is the last time. It's over. I will never speak, text, Facebook, tweet, or use any other form of communication with Katherine again. You have my word of honor."

Unable to speak, she nodded several times.

"Can we put this behind us? Please?"

Again she nodded, but frankly she didn't know if it was possible. She could forgive him and could only pray that in time she would learn to forgive herself.

Chapter 11

~

The inn was empty and silent. My guests were out for the evening and the house felt cavernous. I felt a bit lost and out of sorts with nothing pressing to occupy my time. The incident with Paul's sweatshirt lingered in my mind. As if that wasn't enough, I realized I'd forgotten what Paul's voice sounded like. *No. Not that, too.* Determined to try, I closed my eyes and strained to remember, yet as hard as I tried I couldn't pull the memory of his voice back into my head. His scent was gone, and his voice was no longer part of my memory. It hit me then as strongly as the moment I got word that my husband's helicopter had gone down in a fiery crash: I had lost Paul. He was gone from me. Never again would he be a part of my life, this side of heaven.

I was accustomed to living without my husband. When he was deployed we communicated every day. Although he was literally half a world away, we were together in spirit and in heart. His death had come as a harsh blow, nearly crippling me with grief and heartache. I clung to each memory, to every detail, treasuring each one, holding onto them, clenching them in my fist, determined to keep them as close as I could, and now they were slipping away despite all my efforts.

As the months progressed, I'd found a fragile peace with my husband's death. But now I realized it was a lost cause. His sweatshirt, the sound of his voice. This was more than I could bear, more than I dared let my mind dwell on—otherwise, I'd break into tears.

As I did most evenings, I walked through my small flower garden, checking on my roses. I needed the distraction more than ever. I clipped a few and arranged them in a vase for the inn's foyer. When I finished, I watered my vegetable patch. My tomatoes were coming along nicely, and the pumpkins, although green, showed promise for later in the fall. The snap peas and green beans were coming into their own. Both the spinach and leaf lettuce grew in profusion. I thoroughly enjoyed my small garden space along the south side of the house.

I had Mark to thank for it. He was the one who'd turned up the earth for me. It'd been no small task, especially with his leg in a cast. It'd taken several days and patience on both our parts.

I found a few ready-to-eat tomatoes, so I picked those, plus a large batch of spinach, and brought both vegetables into the kitchen. I hadn't eaten dinner and decided to make a batch of Italian wedding soup. I had most of the ingredients on hand, and what I couldn't find I'd substitute with something else.

Thirty minutes later I added the small meatballs I'd made and frozen weeks earlier into the simmering soup. The chicken broth had come from the freezer as well. I preferred to make my own. Seeing how well it was simmering, I placed a lid on the soup, and I decided to sit on the porch, giving the ingredients and flavors time to meld.

In other circumstances, I would have shared the bounty with

Mark. When he'd worked on preparing my vegetable garden, I'd promised that I'd give him a portion of whatever the land yielded.

The sad fact was, I wasn't sure Mark would appreciate seeing me for a while. After he'd delivered the lumber for the gazebo, he'd conveniently disappeared. Not that I blamed him.

If past history was anything to go by, I might not see him again for a week or more. Mark generally stayed away for a few days when I got emotional about Paul or when I drilled him for information about himself. One of the things I appreciated most about Mark was the fact that he didn't hold onto hard feelings for long.

Rover let out a bark and then raced down the porch steps, running to the very edge of the property.

"Rover," I shouted after him. For the most part, my rescue dog stayed close by my side. After losing him that one afternoon not so long ago, I kept close watch over him.

It wasn't long before I realized what had gotten Rover's attention. His tail started to wag and Mark Taylor rounded the corner of my property. He looked disgruntled, his face marred by a barely disguised frown.

"Hey, what's up?" I asked him.

"I'll tell you in two words: Peter McConnell."

I'd forgotten the other man was making himself at home at Mark's place for the night. I'd been surprised when Mark had made the offer to house Peter, seeing how protective Mark was of his privacy. Even now I wasn't entirely sure what had prompted the generosity. One thing was evident: My handyman didn't consider Peter a friend. My guess was that Mark had been looking to protect me, and I suspected it was from more than the other man's inability to pay for the night's stay.

I was surprised to see him and at the same time grateful. I hadn't been looking forward to spending the evening alone. "I thought you told me you didn't know where Peter had gone."

"I didn't," he grumbled.

"I take it he's returned."

Mark snickered loudly, making his feelings clear. "He settled right down in my favorite chair, reached for the television remote, and ate his way through the contents of my refrigerator."

"In other words, he drove you out of your own house."

"Not exactly."

"Oh?" Clearly, more had taken place that Mark wasn't telling me.

"Okay, if you must know, I left because otherwise I was going to punch him. He had the gall to tell me I should go buy him a six-pack. As far as I'm concerned, he's lucky he's in full possession of his teeth. The man doesn't lack for nerve."

I hid a smile and changed the subject. "I've got a kettle of soup on. Most everything in it came from the garden. Are you interested?"

"You serving anything else with that soup?"

"Like what? A sandwich? Cookies?"

"No, interrogation?"

I smiled, wanting to reassure him. "You're free to enjoy your soup without me hounding you with questions."

He studied me skeptically, as if he wasn't sure he should believe me. "What kind of soup is it?"

"Your favorite."

Again, he frowned. "How do you know? I like more than one kind of soup."

"You told me."

"When?"

"I don't remember. Good grief, talk about looking a gift horse in the mouth."

He broke into a rare wide smile, his eyes twinkling.

I didn't know what his game was. "Do you want the soup or not?"

The smile made him look almost boyish. "Guess you don't like being hounded by questions any more than I do."

He'd made his point. "Touché."

He followed me into the kitchen, and when I removed the lid

from the kettle, he took an appreciative sniff. "It's that spinach-and-meatball concoction you make, right?"

"Right. I picked the spinach just an hour ago, and it's called Italian wedding soup."

"I know; I just don't happen to like the name."

"That's ridiculous."

"The soup's good," he assured me, "but the reference to weddings is enough to turn off most men."

"Oh, for the love of heaven." I shook my head and brought down two deep bowls. I had a loaf of Asiago cheese bread I'd picked up earlier in the day at the bakery when I met Peggy and planned to use for breakfast. It went really well with poached eggs, but even better with soup. I could easily change my breakfast menu to stuffed French toast, another favorite. I cut off a couple thick slices and set them aside.

"How about eating outside?" I suggested. Early in the summer, I'd purchased a small wicker table with two chairs for the deck. I ate out there most evenings. It was perfect to sit in the fading sunshine with a view of the water and the mountains and absorb the beauty and shadows of the setting sun, reflected on the water.

Mark regarded me as if I'd suggested we do something illegal. "What's wrong with the kitchen table?"

"Nothing, but why eat inside when it's such a lovely evening?"

His frown darkened. "Are you going to light a candle and put on music, too?"

"Hardly." He couldn't seriously believe I wanted to make this meal of soup and bread into some kind of romantic interlude.

Still, he hesitated.

"Fine, you eat in the kitchen, but I'm going onto the deck." I picked up my bowl and bread and headed toward the porch. Faithful companion that he was, Rover followed me. I'd taken my seat and had reached for my spoon when Mark appeared.

"Don't look so worried," I chided. The truth was, I enjoyed teasing him. "You have nothing to fear from me."

He grumbled under his breath, but whatever he said was indecipherable. After his first taste of the soup, he nodded appreciatively. "This is good."

"Thank you."

"It comes as a real surprise what a good cook you've turned out to be."

"Oh?" He had the most backhanded way of giving a woman a compliment.

"You being a former banker and all," he added.

It took restraint on my part not to roll my eyes. "What does that have to do with anything?"

"It only makes sense," he argued. "Women in high-powered positions don't have time to cook."

"Mark," I said, holding up my hand, "stop. You don't know what you're talking about, and you're only digging yourself in deeper."

"Okay, fine, whatever."

"Thank you." It was times like these that I wondered how I could consider Mark a friend.

"Mary Smith," he said.

I glanced up, uncertain I'd heard him correctly. "What about Mary Smith?" She'd been a guest earlier that spring.

He shrugged one shoulder. "She's an example of a high-powered businesswoman. I knew the minute I met her that she'd be the type who couldn't find her way around a kitchen with a road map." He must have recognized the fire in my eyes, because he quickly added, "Just as an example. I've said my piece; I won't say anything more."

"That's probably wise on your part."

"What did you do the rest of the afternoon?" I asked Mark, making a determined effort to change the subject.

"You mean after I delivered the lumber?"

I nodded and tore off a bit of my bread to dip in the soup's rich broth.

"We both know I couldn't go in the house with Peter taking over and eating everything in sight. A plague of locusts leaves more behind."

"It might be a good idea to count the silverware tomorrow morning." I was joking, but Mark took me seriously.

"I will."

He'd already eaten the entire bowl of soup. "Mind if I help myself to seconds?"

"By all means." Most of the time the leftovers got tossed anyway.

He excused himself. Rover lifted his head and watched him go but stayed at my side. Mark disappeared into the kitchen and returned in short order. "I could eat that entire kettle."

"Take some home with you," I offered.

He chuckled and shook his head. "Trust me, it would be gone by morning."

I'd forgotten about Peter. "Right. I'll save it for you."

"I appreciate it."

His attention centered on the soup and then out of the blue he said, "I worked on the cradle."

Mark had completely lost me.

He must have read the question in my eyes, because he explained. "You asked me what I did this afternoon."

"You and that cradle," I muttered. The man remained a complete mystery. He had paying customers clamoring for his services, and yet he chose to work on a project no one had commissioned or paid him to build. He'd started on it shortly after we met and worked on it off and on whenever the spirit moved him.

He wagged his finger at me. "You've got that look again."

"What look?"

"That disapproving one when I say or do something you don't agree with."

"I don't have a look."

"Yes you do. You got it just now when I mentioned the cradle."

"Okay, fine." I wasn't about to argue with him.

"It's a big project and I'd like to get it finished." He seemed to feel the need to justify how he spent his time to me, and he was right.

"But don't you have other jobs, ones people are actually paying you for?" I argued.

"Yes. *So?*"

"*So,* people are waiting."

"I'll get to them all in good time. It's nothing you need to worry about."

"I wasn't chastising you."

"Yes you were. You might not have said anything, but you were thinking it."

The man drove me to the edge. "So now you can read my mind?"

"In this instance, yes."

If he wasn't so right I might have argued further. I brushed off his comment and said, "Think what you want."

He returned to his soup. "The cradle relaxes me."

"I beg your pardon?"

"You might not have noticed, but I get uptight every now and again."

"No way." I made sure my tone mocked him.

"I'm not joking, Jo Marie. I don't know what'll happen to that cradle or where it will go, but I enjoy working on it."

Over the months, I'd seen that cradle several times. Mark had designed it himself. The headboard was intricately carved and was sure to be a showpiece for whoever purchased it.

"Like I said, working on it settles my nerves, and there was a lot that needed settling after you started hounding me for information. Playing host to that bloodsucking Peter McConnell isn't helping any, either."

"You didn't need to invite Peter to spend the night, you know."

Again he muttered something I couldn't understand.

"What did you say?" I asked.

"Nothing."

"Yes you did," I pressed.

He seemed to be weighing his response. "I don't trust McConnell and I wasn't comfortable with him being at the inn."

"I can handle myself, Mark."

His look said he doubted it. "McConnell's a sleazebag, and I didn't want him anywhere close to you."

"Ah," I said, and placed my hand over my heart. "You actually care."

"I care about a lot of things."

"So you do care about me?" I was beginning to enjoy this.

"Sure I do," he said with a frown, "but not the way you're suggesting."

"I'm crushed."

"Yeah, right."

For a moment, I wasn't sure if he was teasing or not.

His wagging finger reappeared. "You've got another look."

"Another one?"

"I can't read this one as easily as the first, but I've seen it before; I just haven't figured out what it means yet."

"When you do, let me know."

He nodded, taking me seriously.

I'd eaten about half of my soup and all of the bread. Carbohydrates were my downfall, always had been and probably always would be. Leaning back in the wicker chair, I sighed, taking in the scenery around me. It was nights like this that I missed Paul the most. He'd been heavy on my mind all day. Despite my best effort, a deep sense of loss filled me.

Mark grew silent, too, gazing off into the distance. It came to me that I owed him an apology. "I'm sorry about earlier."

"I know."

"You know?"

"You're sorry about a lot of things, Jo Marie. You think I can't read that in you?"

He was beginning to worry me with his ability to see through me.

"You're sorry you don't have your husband with you any longer. He died much too soon."

He was right about that.

"You're sorry you won't have children."

How he knew that was beyond me. "Anything else?" I asked, a bit defensively.

He nodded. "Nothing that needs mentioning. If you look into your heart you'll recognize more. We tend to do that, you know, when we've suffered a significant loss."

We sat in silence for a long time. The only sounds were those drifting up from the waterfront and the birds overhead. And then there was an occasional snore from Rover.

After a few moments, I broke the peace. "I'm glad you stopped by," I told him.

Mark didn't say anything right away, and then, in a low voice, said, "I am, too."

We looked across the table at each other and smiled.

Chapter 12

~

By the time Ellie Reynolds arrived back at the inn she was walking on a cloud; her feet hardly felt like they touched the ground. For the movie with Tom, she'd silenced her cell phone. Because her mother was sure to make a nuisance of herself, Ellie had kept it off the entire night. They'd kissed several times during the movie and afterward, too. It'd felt natural and good to be in his arms. She experienced none of the awkwardness she had with other relationships. Tom was polite and sweet. She treasured that he was as nervous about meeting her as she'd been about seeing him for the first time. He couldn't seem to stop looking at her as if she was the most beautiful woman in the world.

It was after midnight before she got back to Rose Harbor Inn. Everyone else had settled down for the night. Being careful not to wake the others, Ellie let herself in the front door, locking it behind her, and then headed up the stairs to her room.

She'd been with Tom the entire evening, and the hours had sped past. When it came time to part, he'd been as reluctant as she was to say good night. It helped to know they'd be meeting again in the morning, right after breakfast. Tom wanted to take her out on Puget Sound in his friend's sailboat. Ellie looked forward to the excursion but not nearly as much as she did to seeing Tom again.

This weekend, her visit to Cedar Cove was a test. After spending time together they'd decide if they wanted to pursue this relationship. Ellie already knew what she wanted, and she was fairly certain Tom felt the same things she did. Even now she felt like she needed to pinch herself to make sure this happiness was real and not part of her imagination.

Sitting on the edge of her bed, she closed her eyes and sighed. This was destined to be one of the most incredible nights of her life. And she had a full two days more to be with Tom before she had to return home.

Home.

The word alone was enough to cause her shoulders to droop. No doubt by now her mother was frantic with worry because she hadn't heard from her. Knowing her mother, Ellie felt sure Virginia would assume that Ellie had been abducted and she'd never hear from her again.

With only a slight hesitation, Ellie reached into her purse and looked at her phone for the first time in several hours. Sure enough, there was another message from her mother. Ellie didn't bother to read it. It wasn't necessary; she already knew what it said.

Forcing herself back into the real world, she selected her mother's number. No doubt her mother would be sitting up in bed, awaiting Ellie's call. Virginia would be afraid to fall asleep until she was assured her daughter was safe and secure.

Sure enough, Virginia answered on the first ring. "Eleanor? Oh thank God. You don't know how worried I've been."

"Yes, I know." She kept her voice flat, devoid of emotion.

"Why didn't you answer my text?" her mother demanded, as though it'd been a matter of life and death. "If you'd sent me a simple *I'm okay* it would have made a world of difference."

"Sorry, Mom."

"Well . . . tell me how your date with Tom went," her mother said, slowly releasing her breath as though a heavy burden had been lifted from her heart. "Is he everything you expected?"

"Yes." Ellie purposely kept her responses as brief as possible.

"Sweetie, I want details."

"Oh Mom . . ." Ellie didn't want to dilute the magic of the evening by relating the specifics to her mother, who was sure to dissect the evening into tiny parts.

"Did he kiss you?" her mother asked, her voice dipping slightly, as if this was a fact to be shared in confidence.

"Mom! I'm twenty-three years old. You make it sound like I'm thirteen and just went to my first boy-girl party."

"I know, I know, sorry," Virginia apologized. "I guess no matter how old you are, you'll always be my little girl."

That was the problem in a nutshell. Her mother continued to treat her like a child in need of care and protection. "I like him, Mom, so much. Tom is kind and thoughtful and funny."

"Your father was all those things, too," Virginia whispered, her voice tightening.

Ellie tensed. "So I should be cautious, right?"

"No," her mother protested. "Well, yes, you should be cautious, but then you should do that with any man you meet. What I meant was that it's very easy to fall in love with a man when he's all the things you mentioned."

"But there's a dark side to him, too," Ellie murmured, not wanting to hear yet another forewarning, "one that most likely won't show itself until after we're married."

"Ellie, sweetheart, quit putting words in my mouth. I didn't mean to imply anything of the sort."

"But you were thinking it." Ellie was only voicing the very comment her mother had made previously when she'd first learned about Ellie's growing relationship with Tom.

"Well, yes," her mother confirmed. "Everyone has faults, and character weaknesses. When we first meet others we tend to put our best foot forward, so to speak. I'm sure you did, and Tom, too. You both want to make a good impression, right?"

Ellie had no option but to agree.

"It's only later that our faults become apparent."

"And by then you're married and pregnant and you're stuck in a relationship that makes you miserable and he doesn't understand your needs or love you the way you feel you deserve to be loved and you're so unhappy you don't know if you will survive," Ellie said in one long breath, stopping only when she needed to breathe again.

A shocked silence reverberated from the other end of the line. "You're putting words in my mouth again."

"What I'm doing, Mom, is repeating all the warnings you've given me through the years."

"I said all that?" Virginia asked, sounding as if she found it impossible to believe.

"That and more." The truth was, Ellie had heard the story of how her father had done the family wrong so often she could repeat it verbatim.

"Oh dear," Virginia murmured in a rush, as though stunned.

"Can I go now?" Ellie had fulfilled her obligation and called to reassure her mother. It was late and she'd had a long day.

"Well, yes, of course," Virginia said, with such deep disappointment that Ellie felt instantly guilty. "But you really didn't answer any of my questions," her mother added.

"It's late, Mom."

Her mother hesitated. "Is there something you don't want me to know about Tom?" she asked, in a gentle way that lent itself toward expressing confidences. "I am your mother, and, sweetie, there isn't anything you can't tell me. Did he try to get you into bed?"

"Mom, no. He's not like that. You raised me, so why don't you trust my judgment?"

"I do, but when I met Scott my head was in the clouds. All common sense deserted me and—"

"And then it was too late."

"Eleanor, please don't."

Her mother's tone told Ellie she was quickly growing impatient with her, but Ellie couldn't make herself stop. For once she refused to allow her mother's unfortunate past to cloud her own future. "Good night, Mom," she said, letting her know the conversation was over. She'd done her duty as a daughter, and while she loved and respected her mother, she was more than ready to become her own woman and make her own decisions.

"Good night, sweetie," she said, and then, as if she had to know, she rushed the question, "Are you seeing Tom tomorrow?"

What did her mother think? Ellie hadn't come this far to spend the weekend in her room reading a romance novel, although she often devoured books in the genre.

"Yes, Mom, I'm seeing Tom on Saturday." And then, for shock value, she added, "He's taking me boating on Puget Sound."

Her mother sucked in a breath. Ellie paused, awaiting a tirade of dire warnings, but thankfully, and to her amazement, none came.

"You aren't going to remind me of how many people drown every year?" she asked, half in jest. This was commonly how her mother approached the subject of Ellie being on the water.

"No. Tom's boat has life jackets, doesn't it?"

"Mom!"

"Okay, sorry, you're right. You're an adult and capable of taking care of yourself."

"Thank you!" The least her mother could do was credit her with some intelligence. Ellie had never been a daredevil and had no desire to drive fast cars, leap out of airplanes, or go bungee jumping. Probably the most dangerous task she'd ever undertaken was opening a tin can with a handheld opener!

"Will you be out on the water all day?"

"No. In the afternoon, Tom said he has a surprise for me."

"What kind of surprise?"

"It wouldn't be a surprise if I knew what it was, would it?"

Her mother gave a small, halfhearted laugh. "You're right, it wouldn't."

"Night, Mom." Hadn't she wished her mother that once already?

"Night." Her mother's voice was heavy with reluctance.

At the last moment, Ellie thought of something important she wanted to say. "Mom," she said urgently.

"Yes, honey." How eager she sounded, how excited.

Ellie felt a little uneasy with the fib. "I thought you should know I'll be out of cell phone coverage all day."

That laugh again. "Very funny, Ellie."

"I'm serious, Mom."

"Okay, message received. I'll wait for your call and I won't bother you."

Ellie was grateful. "I appreciate that. Now, for the third time, good night."

"Good night."

Ellie ended the call before she or her mother found yet another reason to stay on the line. As she went to plug her phone into the charger, she noticed another text message. If it was from her mother, Ellie would be tempted to scream.

Instead, the text was from Tom. Thank you for a lovely night. Morning can't come soon enough.

It couldn't come fast enough for Ellie, either! Her phone alarm woke her at seven, and it felt like she'd been asleep only a few minutes. As happy and excited as she'd been, it'd taken her a long time to fall asleep. Her inclination was to pull the sheet over her shoulders and go back to sleep. She might have given in to the temptation until she remembered Tom would be picking her up in less than two hours.

Leaping out of bed, she headed for the shower, eager to dig into her day. Another day with Tom.

By the time she'd showered, dressed, and fussed with her hair—and fuss she did—breakfast was ready.

With a smile as bright as the August morning, Ellie practically floated down the stairs. She wore a pair of cropped white pants and a blue-and-white loose-fitting tank top with a blue pair of Toms shoes. She hoped Tom would find it amusing that she'd chosen that brand of shoes. Then, in case it was chilly on the water, she brought along a white cotton cardigan, which she had draped over her shoulders.

She found Jo Marie in the kitchen.

"I'm not early, am I?"

"Not at all," the innkeeper assured her. "Are you ready for a cup of coffee?"

"More than ready." Ellie didn't feel like herself in the morning until she had a cup of coffee.

"There's fresh-squeezed orange juice set out on the table, along with blueberry muffins."

"My favorite," Ellie said, heading in that direction. Happy as she felt, she nearly skipped into the other room.

"I'm fixing cream cheese–stuffed French toast this morning," Jo Marie called out after her.

"Juice and muffins are all I need," Ellie said. It wasn't a good idea to go out on Puget Sound with a full stomach. She wasn't sure if she was prone to seasickness or not, but it wasn't worth taking the chance.

After a couple moments, Jo Marie joined her in the breakfast room. "I suspect the Porters won't be down for quite some time yet," she said.

Ellie sat and poured herself a glass of orange juice.

"Did everything go well last night?" Jo Marie asked.

Ellie couldn't have held back a smile any more than the little Dutch boy could have held back the water from a leak in the dam. "It was an amazing night. After dinner we went to a movie and then we walked along the waterfront and went for coffee at the Pancake Palace and talked and talked and talked. We've spent part of nearly every day communicating in one form or another; you'd think there wouldn't be much left for us to say."

"But you did?"

"Yes. It shocked us both when we saw it was midnight."

A faraway look came over the innkeeper, as if her thoughts had drifted to another time and another place. "It was like that when Paul and I first met."

Ellie remembered hearing, although she couldn't remember who'd mentioned it, that Jo Marie was a widow. Perhaps it was the handyman she'd chatted with briefly the day before.

"So you know what it's like to meet someone and know right away that he might possibly be the one?" Ellie asked.

Jo Marie nodded. "I do. Paul and I met at a Seahawks game."

"Do you enjoy watching football?" Ellie asked. She had never been excited about the sport until she'd learned that Tom had played football in high school and college. He was on the wait list to get Seahawks season tickets. It went without saying that if their relationship continued—and she prayed it would—she'd need to learn the basics of the game. Already Tom had volunteered to tutor her.

"Both Paul and I were football fanatics," Jo Marie said, and then, as if it was painful to talk about the husband she'd lost in Afghanistan, she changed the subject.

"The Sounders are Seattle's soccer team, and a lot of folks attend those games as well. I've never been, but I've heard it's quite an experience."

While talking over coffee the night before, Tom had mentioned the Sounders and his hope that one day they'd be able to see a game together. Ellie was willing to give it a try, never having attended a professional sporting event.

"Tom's athletic," Ellie said, taking the first bite of her muffin. It was delicious, far and away better than any she'd ever tasted. "Wow, these are great."

"Oh thanks. I got the recipe from a friend of mine, Peggy Beldon. The blueberries came from her garden, which reminds me, I need to pick up blueberries at the farmers' market today."

Ellie would love to visit the market, with its booths displaying homemade crafted goods, fresh fruit, and vegetables. She hoped they'd be back in time from their boating trip so she'd get the chance. She'd ask Tom about it.

Glancing out the window, Ellie saw Tom's car pull into the parking area by the inn. She looked at her watch and saw that he was a few minutes early, which told her he was as eager to see her as she was to see him.

Rover must have heard the car door close, because the dog hurried to the front door.

"It's Tom," Ellie explained. "He's a bit early."

"Invite him in for breakfast," Jo Marie told her. "I've got plenty."

What a thoughtful thing to do. "I will, thank you."

Tom hadn't made it up the front steps before Ellie opened the door. For just an instant they stood and stared at each other as if even now it was impossible to believe they were together.

He broke the trance first. "Morning."

"Good morning. Come on in. Jo Marie invited you to have coffee and a blueberry muffin. They're really good."

"Great. I was in such a rush to get here and didn't take time to eat breakfast."

Ellie had felt that same happy anticipation.

Tom joined her at the table, and she noticed that he had dark lines beneath his eyes. "Didn't you sleep well?" she asked.

"I didn't," he admitted. "I was up practically the entire night."

"Is something troubling you?" she asked.

His smile seemed forced as he shook his head. "Not a solitary thing." Then he wrapped his hand around the back of her neck and touched her forehead to his own.

Something was troubling him, something he didn't want to tell her, and Ellie didn't have a single clue what it might be.

Chapter 13

Roy was still asleep when Maggie woke Saturday morning. Their argument from the afternoon before kept circling in her mind. Years ago, while they were college students, Roy had written her a love letter. She'd kept it all these years and reread it from time to time. His letter had been the turning point in their courtship.

At the time they'd been dating steadily and were deeply in love. Maggie could easily see them marrying one day after she graduated. Roy had met her parents and she'd met his. The future seemed pretty much decided for them. Then Roy had gone out with some friends from his frat house. He'd told her it was a poker match and that he needed "guy time."

It wasn't a big deal until pictures of Roy with a couple of nearly naked women had turned up on the Internet. Apparently, there'd been very little card playing that night, and then through the grapevine Maggie learned that this little "get-together" with the guys had happened at a local strip club. And it wasn't the first time.

As far as Maggie was concerned, the incident settled their future. Roy wasn't the man she'd thought he was. When the Internet photos made the rounds on campus, Maggie had been deeply embarrassed and equally saddened. She really didn't feel she could marry a man who got his thrills in strip clubs. The fact that he'd lied to her about what he'd be doing raised a huge red flag.

They'd argued. Roy claimed it was all in fun and didn't mean anything. As for the lie, it was a little white one he told so she wouldn't get upset. In actuality, he was protecting her. It didn't mean anything; he was letting off steam after cramming for his finals. He downplayed his role as if it meant nothing and she was making an unnecessary fuss. His friends weren't having problems with their girls, so Maggie should be willing to let it go, too. Yes, the photos were embarrassing, but all the hoopla would die down soon enough.

Maggie had been shocked by his attitude. He simply didn't get it. In his eyes, he'd done nothing wrong. It was all supposed to be in fun. His rationalization had stunned her. Rather than argue, she knew what she had to do, and that was to end the relationship. To that point, it was the hardest decision she'd ever made. With tears in her eyes, she broke up with Roy.

At first he didn't believe she meant it. He sent her flowers and met her after class, sang to her in public, and bought her a huge teddy bear. It took almost a month for him to realize she was serious. It about killed her to walk away, but she felt she had no choice. Roy had showed her a side of himself that she could never condone or accept.

Then Roy's letter arrived. He didn't use flowery language or attempt to convince her to reconsider their breakup. He'd basically written to say good-bye.

Dear Maggie,

I hope you'll read this letter. It's taken me nearly a month to write it. I've forgotten what version this is, not that it matters. What is important is that you believe me when I tell you that I mean every word.

When you broke up with me, I couldn't believe it. I wasn't sure what I thought. You were angry. I understood that. Frankly, I was angry, too. Those pictures embarrassed me, but I didn't let anyone know because it was too important for me to be cool about it. So I pretended it wasn't any big deal, only it was. It was a very big deal.

It took me a couple weeks to realize you were serious about breaking up with me. We were finished. That made me angry, too, and then sad and sick with what I knew I'd lost. I wasn't easy to live with during that time. In fact, if it wasn't so close to graduation, I think I might have gotten kicked out of my fraternity.

You're well aware of everything I did to get you to change your mind. You stood by your word, though, and that took courage and determination on your part. I assumed, at first, that you were simply being stubborn. It took me far longer than it should have to realize there was much more involved than your pride.

When all my efforts to convince you to take me back failed, I was at a loss. It was time for soul searching. I spent a lot of time in my room, basically feeling sorry for myself, before it hit me what you'd been trying so hard to get through this thick head of mine.

You love me . . . loved me, past tense. I screwed that up for good and I don't have anyone to blame but myself. I know you've moved on and are dating other guys now and I accept that. It's what I deserve.

The point of this letter is to say I get it now. I understand

*why you made the decision you did, and I realize it couldn't
have been any easier for you than it was for me. I lied to you
about where I was and what I was doing. Not just that one
night but multiple times. It'd seemed innocent enough. What
you didn't know wouldn't hurt you. I was with the guys and we
were doing what guys do, which is stupid, I know. But it's far
more than me misleading you into believing I was playing
poker. It's a matter of character. You expected more of me and
I failed us both.*

*In a few days I'll graduate and be leaving WSU to join my
dad in his construction business. Thank you for everything,
Maggie, and I mean that. You've encouraged me to be a better
man, a man of integrity and principle. The kind of man who
would make a good husband and father, the kind of man you
deserve. You are wise not to accept anyone less.*

*These have been painful lessons because of the high price
I paid to learn them. They cost me losing you.*

*It's unlikely that we will see each other again, and that's
probably for the best. And while it's hard to accept your
decision, I want to thank you. It might not mean anything to
you now, but it's important that you know I genuinely love
you. I will always love you. If at any time you need help,
I'll come. You can count on me.*

*If you've gotten this far in reading my letter, then I want to
thank you for taking the time.*

Good-bye, my love.

*Forever yours,
Roy*

When the letter had first arrived, Maggie had read it through
four or five times without stopping, taking in every word, soaking it
into her heart. Then she'd started to weep. Her friends didn't know
what had happened or what Roy could have said to cause this reac-

tion. He had no idea how miserable she'd been, how heartbroken. Maggie had contacted him and they had sat in Starbucks for two hours talking. Following their talk, Maggie felt that Roy had been sincere. He'd meant what he'd said in his letter. Even then, Maggie wasn't sure reconciling would be right for either of them, and said so. When they left the Starbucks, they'd gone in opposite directions. As she left Roy, Maggie had a change of heart. She loved Roy and he loved her. She wanted them to try again. By the time she reached Roy, she was astonished to find that he had tears in his eyes. He didn't speak, and she didn't, either. They simply reached for each other and hugged, both weeping, overwhelmed with emotion. By the end of the summer, following graduation, they were engaged.

Roy's letter had changed everything. If ever she needed reassurance of his love it was now, which was why she'd brought the letter with her on this trip.

Her husband stirred and he rolled onto his back and stared up at the ceiling.

"Morning," Maggie whispered, and bent down to kiss him.

He moved his head so that her lips bounced against his cheek instead of his lips. So that was the way it was going to be. She stiffened and climbed out of bed.

Bracing herself, she decided she had no option but to face this head-on. "You told me yesterday that you didn't want to talk about what happened."

"You're right, I don't." His words were unyielding, as if written in stone.

"I don't, either . . ."

"Good, then it's a closed subject." He rolled over and presented her with a clear picture of his back.

Maggie debated how far she should press the matter. It was clear that unless they addressed this open wound, their marriage would never heal, never recover. It would be only a matter of time before it disintegrated entirely.

"What time is breakfast?" Roy asked, tossing aside the covers and sitting on the edge of the mattress. Again with his back to her.

"Not until eight or nine, I believe."

"Then we should get downstairs, don't you think?"

"No," she breathed, keeping her voice low for fear it would tremble with emotion. "I think we need to air this once and for all."

Roy pretended she hadn't spoken. "Any idea of where you'd like to go today? I was thinking we could drive to Mount Saint Helens and visit the site of the eruption."

She decided to change the subject entirely. "Do you know I kept the letter you wrote me in college after we broke up?" she asked.

Roy glanced over his shoulder at her.

"In fact, I brought it with me."

"Here?" he asked, frowning. "Why would you do that?"

She walked around the bed so she could face him. "I read it every now and again when we're going through a rough patch just to be reassured you still love me." To her, every word of that letter had vibrated with love. She hesitated, wanting a confirmation of his love and at the same time fearing his answer. Still, she'd rather know his feelings now than waste time by kicking a dead horse, or whatever that saying was.

"I wrote that years ago." He said it as if to discount the letter.

"Do you still mean what you wrote, Roy, or did my . . . mistake ruin that forever? Do you love me?"

His short hesitation nearly destroyed her. "Of course I do. I'm here, aren't I?"

Maggie slumped back onto the bed next to him, struggling not to break down as she buried her face in her hands.

He tentatively touched her shoulder and she heard the regret in him as he spoke. "Maggie, please, don't. It rips my heart out to see you cry. I meant what I said in that letter, then and now. It's just hard for me to accept . . . to think of you being with another man."

Pulling herself together, Maggie inhaled a deep, calming breath and forced herself to be still. "You won't talk to me."

"What are we doing now?" he demanded, none too gently.

"Let's go back to that night, please, just this once, clear the air . . . we need to do this, Roy, please."

"No," he all but shouted at her. "I want to put it behind us."

"We can do that," she murmured, "but one day it'll catch up with us, and my guess is that it won't take long. Burying our feelings, our pain, will soon devour our marriage and destroy us. If you won't do it for me, then do it for Jaxon and Collin. More than anything, they need the security of a mother and father who love each other."

Roy stood and walked to the far side of the room, keeping his back to her. "You have no one to blame but yourself, Maggie. What you want is for me to step forward and accept the blame, but it wasn't me that got so drunk and ended up in bed with someone I met in a bar. That was all you, sweetheart. All you. You're the one who stepped over the line. Way over the line, I might add."

"Really?" she asked, not bothering to hide the sarcasm. "All me? I find that interesting from the man who was carrying on an affair with some old girlfriend he hooked up with on Facebook."

"At least I never slept with her."

"No, but you might as well have. You gave her everything you vowed to give me."

"See what I mean?" He spat out the words as if he was a dog chewing meat off a bone. "Our little talk, as you call it, is merely an excuse to throw blame on me."

Maggie went still and quiet. Raising their voices, arguing, wouldn't help matters. "After our blowup, after I found out about Katherine, I figured our marriage was over, so what did it matter what I did. I'd never been more devastated in my life.

"I'll be the first one to admit that what I did was beyond stupid and wrong. I'm horrified that I would drink myself into oblivion to the point that I would sleep with another man. You of all people should recognize how much out of character that was for me."

Roy didn't answer.

"He made me feel attractive and desirable . . ."

"Of course he did. He wanted to get you in bed, and he succeeded, didn't he?"

Maggie wasn't sure how much more of this she could take. "You want to blame me, and that's understandable, but I think you should take a long, hard look in the mirror."

Once more Roy went silent. He didn't understand, and Maggie wasn't sure she could explain what she'd felt that dreadful night. In her eyes, her husband had betrayed her even if the relationship with Katherine hadn't gone to the point that they were having sex. Clearly, that was where the two were headed. Maggie needed Roy to do more than apologize, to admit he'd wronged her and their children. What she needed was for her husband to realize that she'd been hurt and what she sought was to be healed.

"I don't need a crystal ball to look into the future, Roy," she said, doing her best to remain calm. Cruel, thoughtless words would soon demolish everything they'd spent the last ten years building. "Every time we have a disagreement you're going to throw that night in my face."

"You mean the way you throw Katherine in my face?"

"Yes." She couldn't be any more direct than that.

He frowned and rammed his fingers through his tousled hair. "So what do we do?"

"I love you, Roy. Heart and soul love you. This has the power to destroy us, destroy our family, destroy our future. We have to learn to forgive each other."

It took him a moment to agree and nod. "It isn't easy."

"No, it isn't," she said. "We've both been badly hurt."

He turned his head and looked away. For the longest time, he said nothing and then seemed to reach a decision. He turned to face her. "I'm sorry, Maggie, so sorry. I could never have believed accepting Katherine as a Facebook friend would lead to this. It seemed so innocent at the time. Forgive me, please."

"And I'm sorry, too, so, so sorry. Can you find it in you to forgive me?"

Her husband came across the room and reached for her then, bringing her into a tight embrace, his arms hugging her close. "I love you. I've always loved you and I'll go to my grave loving you."

Maggie wanted to weep but held the tears at bay. "You're a good husband and a wonderful father and God knows I love you."

Roy exhaled as though he'd released a heavy burden from his heart. Maggie felt the weight lift from her shoulders, too. Roy hadn't wanted to have this talk, and, frankly, she would've liked to have avoided it as well, but it was necessary. There was only so much pain and disillusionment they could ignore before it damaged them both beyond repair.

"I'm hungry," Roy announced all at once, and he headed into the bathroom to shower.

Maggie smiled. She was hungry, too, and had bright hopes for a new day. It felt as if they were starting over. It wouldn't be easy, but it was a start in the right direction. They'd both made an effort to forgive the other, each accepting blame for their part in this mess.

Roy was in and out of the shower in ten minutes, and by then Maggie had dressed and was applying her makeup.

"What do you think of driving out to see Mount Saint Helens?" he asked, and placed his hands on her shoulders and kissed the side of her neck.

Maggie shrugged, not overly excited to return to the site of the 1980 volcanic eruption. "We were there once before, remember?"

"True, but it's an amazing site."

She agreed. "I think I'd rather go someplace we haven't been or go into the city."

"Okay by me. Let's ask Jo Marie for a few recommendations."

"Perfect."

When they came down the stairs, Jo Marie had homemade muffins and orange juice laid out in the breakfast room. She offered them a feast, and both Roy and Maggie took advantage of the fried bacon, stuffed French toast, and eggs.

Jo Marie offered a variety of ideas as to how they could spend their day. "Bremerton has a lot to offer and it's close by," she suggested first, listing a number of tourist attractions and museums that were a short foot-ferry ride away.

"Then there's the Olympic National Forest. Did you know Washington State has the only rain forest in the continental U.S.?"

"No." Maggie had lived her entire life in Washington State and didn't have a clue.

"Some of the hikes inside the forest will take your breath away," the innkeeper mentioned.

Roy looked to Maggie as if to say he was interested in a short hike if she was.

"Speaking of museums, there's a Museum of Glass in Tacoma that displays Dale Chihuly's work. Really breathtaking, or so I've heard," Jo Marie continued. "I haven't visited yet myself, but I plan to make an excuse to go soon. I've heard nothing but raves about it, and there's a car museum close by as well."

Maggie noticed how Roy's eyes lit up at the mention of the car museum. He had a long-standing love for cars.

"That gives us several options," Roy said, and reached for another slice of bacon.

"Take a light sweater," Jo Marie said, as she refilled Roy's coffee mug. "It's overcast this morning, and according to the weather, there's a chance of rain later in the day."

"Will do."

Maggie's stomach felt a bit queasy. "I'll get our jackets," she told Roy as he went over a map with Jo Marie. Hurrying up the stairs, Maggie reached for her purse and what else they'd need for the day, when she stopped cold.

All at once she felt dreadful and rushed into the bathroom just in time to lose her breakfast.

It hit her then like a two-by-four slamming into her midsection.

The only other time in her life when she'd thrown up like this, outside of the time when she was sick with the flu, was when she was pregnant with her sons.

Slumping onto the bed, Maggie felt the blood drain out of her face. *Dear God in heaven,* she prayed fervently, *please don't let me be pregnant.*

Chapter 14

~

Once Roy and Maggie headed out to explore and enjoy the day, I brought the dishes and leftover food back into the kitchen. Rover sat next to his dish, reminding me that in my eagerness to feed my guests I'd overlooked him. That happened, but rarely. My mind seemed to be on other matters lately, most of which revolved around Paul.

"Sorry, Rover," I said, and bent down to pat his head. He luxuriated in the attention and lifted his chin. He enjoyed it when I stroked his chin and neck, and seemed to sigh. "I spoil you rotten." I brought the bag of dog food from the pantry floor and filled his bowl. Rover quickly dug into it, spilling the nuggets over the sides of his dish in his eagerness. He seemed to think if he didn't gobble it up right away someone else would nudge in and cheat him out of his meal.

I'd just tucked the bag back inside the pantry when the phone rang. It was the business line instead of my cell.

"Rose Harbor Inn," I said, making an effort to sound as crisp and professional as a corporate reservations operator.

"Jo Marie?"

It was my mother. "Hi, Mom. You're calling on the reservation line for the inn."

"I am? You have so many phone numbers I hardly know which one is which. It baffles me that I can have two children and between them they have six or seven phone numbers. I don't know if I consider this progress or not."

I couldn't help but laugh. She was right. I had three phone numbers and I knew Todd, my brother, had that many as well. In addition, Jennifer, his wife, had her own cell, and it wouldn't be long before his two children had their own phones, each with individual numbers. By all that was fair, Mom was onto something.

"I'm calling about Sunday afternoon," Mom said, getting right to the point of her call. "You wouldn't by chance happen to be free, would you?"

"Let me check." I got on the computer and brought up my calendar. Unfortunately, I had three sets of guests due to arrive midday. "What do you have in mind?"

"I was thinking it's been a while since we last saw you."

It really hadn't been that long. A month, maybe. Since Paul died, my parents had been keeping close track of me.

"Can't you break away for just one afternoon and come to Seattle for dinner?" Mom asked, her voice soft and pleading.

With guests leaving and others checking in, it would be almost impossible to take time off. One of the downfalls of owning the inn was the lack of free time. Peggy Beldon had warned me about this and suggested I make contingency plans in case of emergencies. I'd taken her advice and hired a couple local girls to help. They were good, but I wasn't confident they were up to taking over for me entirely.

"Sorry, Mom, I don't think I can make it." I hated letting my family down, but I really didn't feel comfortable leaving the inn.

"Oh, that is disappointing."

I had a suggestion, though, and I hoped it would work. "Could you have dinner in Cedar Cove?"

"Yes, I suppose," she said, after a short hesitation. "Todd and Jennifer are free, and you know how hard it is to get the family together these days. Brian's involved in soccer and Shauna's constantly on the go."

That was true. My nephew and niece, although young, were already involved in a number of activities. Shauna was a Brownie and took piano lessons, and Brian played soccer and had recently joined Cub Scouts. And this was in addition to all their church activities.

"I could host the dinner." To me, this was the logical solution.

"But, Jo Marie, that's a lot of work when you've already got your hands full."

"Mom, please. I cook for a crowd nearly every day. I'd enjoy hosting the family. Besides, it would give me an opportunity to show you how far my culinary skills have come along."

"Are you sure?" Mom sounded hesitant.

"I'm positive. I'm a good cook." I don't know what Mom thought I did all day. But in the last year I'd learned more about putting meals together than I had in my first thirty-seven years.

Still, she hesitated and I could almost see her chewing on her lower lip, a habit she had when uneasy about making a decision. "This is a dinner, remember, not breakfast."

"True." No argument there, and while I was an old hand when it came to breakfast, I wasn't as adept at dinners. "I'll look through my cookbooks and come up with something wonderful."

Mom chuckled. "You amaze me, Jo Marie."

"Does that mean you'd be willing to come my way?" On second thought, I might have been a bit hasty in asking the entire family over for a home-cooked meal. Before I took over the inn, I would have either taken them out to a local restaurant or brought in take-out.

"I'll need to check with Todd and Jennifer, but seeing that this may be the only way we'll get a chance to see you, I doubt they'll have any objection."

My mind was abuzz with ideas of what I might serve. The farmers' market was in session and fresh fish were often sold from one of the fishing boats that docked at the marina. My dad especially enjoyed fresh salmon. I could steam clams as well. I'd bake the salmon, put together a green salad loaded down with vegetables from my garden, and pick up bread from the bakery. For a side dish, I'd serve Dad's favorite rice, a recipe handed down in his family, made with raisins and pine nuts. In a matter of seconds I had the entire menu.

"That'll be seven of us," Mom reminded me.

My table would easily seat seven and often up to twelve. That was when it struck me. "Would it be all right if I invited some-one?"

"Who, dear?"

I could be opening up a can of worms. Still, I couldn't resist. "Mark Taylor."

"Who?"

"Mark. He's my handyman."

"The one who put in the rose garden? Oh, and wasn't it Mark who crafted the sign for the inn?"

"That's him." I should have thought of this earlier. My mother had a gift, a knack for reading people in the most natural, non-threatening way. I would love for her to get a feel for Mark. I couldn't think of a better way than to have her sit across from him at dinner. My mother was wonderful with people, and if anyone could get Mark engrossed in conversation, it would be her.

My mother went suspiciously quiet.

"You wouldn't mind, would you?" Perhaps I'd misjudged the

intention of this family dinner. I'd assumed it was just another get-together because it'd been a while. Apparently not. It seemed there was an agenda at play that I knew nothing about.

"Do you like . . . Mark?" Mom asked in a small, quiet voice that wasn't quite like her.

"Like?" I was beginning to get the picture. "Mom, there's nothing romantic between us. Mark's a friend."

"Are the two of you involved?"

"No," I said automatically. *What was I thinking?* By suggesting I invite Mark I'd given my mother the wrong impression about my relationship with him. "No way," I repeated for emphasis.

Mom spoke softly, as if she was dealing with a child. "You seem to talk about him a great deal, Jo Marie."

I wasn't aware of that and would make a point of keeping him out of any future conversations. If I did mention Mark, it was no doubt in reference to something he'd done to irritate me, which he often did.

Now I was forced to own up to the truth. "I have a specific reason for wanting him to join us for dinner."

"Oh?" Mom's interest was instantly piqued. I could hear it in her voice.

"I see quite a bit of Mark." I shouldn't have admitted that. It would only add fuel to Mom's suspicions. "That didn't come out right," I amended quickly. "The only reason I see Mark as much as I do is because he's been working at the inn on a variety of projects."

"I thought he did a lovely job with the rose garden, and you did mention you planned to have him build a gazebo."

"I might have said something about that in passing." I feared I was digging myself into an even deeper hole every time I opened my mouth. "Mark's starting on the gazebo now, but the point is, Mom," I said, not wanting to get sidetracked with her questions and comments. "I don't really know him."

"What do you mean?"

"Mark rarely talks about himself, and you have such a great rapport with people. You connect easily with others, and I thought you might . . . you know."

"Get him to talk . . ."

"I guess, but in a natural, nonthreatening way. Get a feel for him, that sort of thing."

"Because you're curious?"

"I . . . yes, I suppose," I admitted reluctantly.

"Why do you want to know more about him, Jo Marie?"

My mother could get right to the point when she felt the need.

"Well, because . . ." I struggled to find the right words. "He's a friend, and I know practically nothing about him. I don't want to hound him with questions." Heaven knew I'd already tried that and failed miserably. My mother's talent was equal parts being genuinely interested in others and being a good listener. If Mark would open up to anyone, it would be my sweet-natured mother.

"W-e-l-l," Mom said, dragging out the word, "in that case, invite Mark for no other reason than I'd enjoy meeting him, and I know your father would as well, as often as you've mentioned his name."

Mom and I discussed the time for dinner and she promised to get back to me regarding the availability of my brother and his family. We hoped it would all work out.

We ended the conversation and Rover stood by the kitchen door, letting me know he wanted out. As I suspected, Mark had arrived with another load of lumber for the gazebo.

"Morning." I stood on the front porch and called out to him while Rover wandered about the yard, carefully choosing the exact blade of grass to water.

"Morning," he returned. He'd apparently been at work for quite some time, because the bed of his truck was nearly empty.

"How about a cup of coffee?" I asked.

He hesitated, as though he needed a bit more convincing in order to pull him away from his task.

"I baked Peggy's blueberry muffins this morning."

He paused, a long two-by-four balanced across the top of his shoulder. "Are the blueberries out of Peggy's garden?"

"They are."

He nodded, but without a lot of enthusiasm. "I suppose I could help you out and eat a couple of those muffins."

Help me out. "Your generosity knows no bounds," I said, and rolled my eyes.

While he set down the last of his load I returned to the house and poured us each a cup of coffee and then set two muffins on a plate. I carried both outside, where Mark stood waiting. When he saw me, he walked over to the porch, sat on the top step, and removed his work gloves. I settled down next to him with Rover between us.

"I have an invitation for you," I said, and handed him the plate with the muffins.

"Oh?"

"How would you feel about having dinner here with me on Sunday?" I thought it best not to mention that my family would be joining us, at least not right away.

He considered the invite. "What are you serving?"

"Salmon, I think. I'll walk down to the farmers' market in a bit and see what the fishing boats have to offer."

"They had tuna last week," he mentioned.

"Yes, I know." It'd been fresh and snatched up before I made it down to the marina. Not that it really mattered—I wasn't keen on tuna, fresh or otherwise.

"This time of year you can get Hood Canal shrimp, too."

The shrimp season was short, and while expensive, they were worth the price. The same with Copper River salmon, which was available only in spring.

"Salmon," Mark repeated. "I like salmon, but I thought it wasn't your favorite fish."

"It isn't, but it is my dad's." The minute the words were off my lips I wanted to snatch them back. I didn't want Mark to know my parents would be at the dinner and yet the first thing I did was blurt it out.

Mark reached for a muffin, and his hand paused in midair. "Your father's coming?"

"I'm not sure yet." A slight exaggeration; Mom had said she'd be getting back to me.

"Will anyone else be there that I should know about?" he asked innocently enough before he bit into the muffin. Crumbles fell unheeded onto the second step down. Rover lowered his head and quickly devoured what had fallen and then looked up, eager for more.

"Don't know yet," I said.

"Okay, let me rephrase that question," Mark said. "How many other people have you invited?"

I would make a terrible covert spy. The very thing I'd hoped to hide until I'd gotten a commitment I'd inadvertently blurted out in the first few minutes.

"Jo Marie?"

"Six. I invited my family to dinner."

Mark sipped his coffee and reached for the second muffin. He broke off a small portion and fed it to Rover. "Why do you want me to join this family function?"

"Why not? They admire the work you've done around the inn. I thought it was time they met you."

"Why?" he pressed again.

"Because." I could feel the blood filling my face, reddening my cheeks.

He stared at me as if I'd spoken in a foreign language.

"Wouldn't you like to meet my family?" I asked, turning the tables on him.

"Not necessarily."

I laughed and shook my head. "Tell me how you really feel, why don't you?" I joked. I could see my entire plan falling to pieces right before my eyes.

Mark frowned. "I'm not good with social situations."

"This isn't social; it's family."

"Your family," he reminded me.

I ignored that. "You attended my open house."

He squinted his eyes as if his attending the event I'd held last spring had nothing to do with our current conversation.

"That was a social event and you did fine."

"If you remember," he said stiffly, "I'd recently broken my leg and was on heavy pain medication. I wasn't myself."

"That's ridiculous." I was losing my patience with him. "Now, are you going to accept my invitation or not?"

"Not," he said, without even blinking an eye.

I was sorely disappointed and tried hard not to show it. As silly as it sounded, my feelings were hurt. In rejecting the invitation it felt as if he was rejecting me. After all these months I'd counted him as a friend, but I could see that I was wrong. I might consider him that way, but he held no such feelings for me. I was a job with the benefits of cookies and muffins tossed in.

"Don't take it personal."

"I'm not," I lied. He must have read the disappointment in my eyes.

"Like I said, I avoid this kind of situation."

I looked away and nodded. "It's all right, I understand."

"It's not my thing, Jo Marie," he reiterated.

"It's no big deal," I said, doing my utmost to be as chipper as possible. I stood and brushed off the stray crumbs that had fallen onto my pant legs. Rover was instantly there to lick them up. "I better get back to work."

"Yeah, me, too," Mark said, but he didn't make an effort to move away.

As I headed inside the inn, my shadow and constant companion, Rover, chose to remain with Mark.

As the screen door closed I heard Mark murmur to Rover, "Thing is, I don't know that I'd fit in with Jo Marie's family."

I wanted to reassure Mark, but hesitated. Just maybe I was the one in the wrong, looking to use the dinner invitation for my own purposes.

Chapter 15

"I appreciate how far you've stepped out of your comfort zone for me," Tom said, as he manned the helm of the sailboat. The wind helped them slice through the waters of Puget Sound. He pointed out Vashon Island, which was off in the far distance. They'd sailed all the way around Blake Island as he did a quick tutorial on the techniques of sailing.

Ellie listened intently and wished she could be more help, but this was an area with which she was completely unfamiliar. Being with Tom helped calm her pounding heart. At first Ellie had felt ill at ease sailing, but he'd been more than patient and encouraging. While being on the water was foreign to her, it didn't take long before she was able to relax and enjoy the sun, the wind, and the boat.

"I can't believe we're actually sailing," she said. The thing that struck her was how smoothly the vessel moved, gliding through the green water. The only sound was the flapping of the sails when the wind changed direction. No wonder Tom loved sailing. The day was perfect, the weather ideal, or so he had explained.

He had her sit close to his side, and he placed his arm around her shoulders. The sun felt good on her skin, warming her. Every now and again it would hide behind a billowing white cloud, and Ellie was grateful she'd thought to bring her sweater with her.

"Are you going to tell me about my surprise?" she asked, eager to discover what it was he had for her. He seemed a bit apprehensive about it, and she hoped to convince him to share his concern.

"Not yet." He didn't give her the opportunity to question him further. Instead, he bent down and kissed her, his mouth lingering over hers. His kiss was deep and hungry, and left her breathless with wonder that this could actually be happening to her.

When the kiss ended, Ellie rested her head against his shoulder. "Thank you," she whispered.

"For the kiss?"

"Yes," she said, content and happy, happier than she could ever remember being. "For everything, really."

"I hope I won't disappoint you," Tom said, so low that at first Ellie wasn't sure she'd heard him correctly.

"Disappoint me?" she repeated. "That would be impossible. You're everything I could ever have hoped for and beyond."

"I'm better-looking than you thought, right?" he teased.

"Indeed."

"Indeed?" he chided. "That's an old-fashioned word, isn't it?"

"I'm an old-fashioned kind of girl, I guess."

Tom rubbed his chin across her crown, and the wind whipped tendrils of dark hair against her cheek. "You've lived a sheltered life."

She couldn't deny it. "My mother and grandparents saw to that."

"Didn't you ever wonder why they felt it was so important to keep you protected?" he asked.

She hadn't, not really. To Ellie, that was the way it was; she didn't know any different. "No, actually, I never thought much about it."

"You're right, you probably wouldn't."

Although she couldn't see his face, Ellie heard the frown in his voice. "I was the only grandchild, and my grandmother lived in fear that something bad would happen to me," she said, thinking back over her youth.

"Like what?"

Ellie sighed, nestled into his warm embrace. "I never knew exactly, but I'm pretty sure it had something to do with my father."

"You're joking?"

"I'm not," Ellie assured him. She recalled comments about her father that were abruptly cut off the instant she walked into the room. More than once she could remember hearing her father's name mentioned in furious whispers.

"What did they think he would do?" Tom asked, and it sounded as if he was offended, although it didn't make sense that he should be.

Ellie wasn't entirely sure. "I can't say. In retrospect, it seems rather odd, doesn't it?"

"It does. Maybe they were afraid your father might come and take you away. That would explain why they decided you should be homeschooled."

Ellie automatically shook her head. "There were more reasons than that."

"Like what?" he asked.

"You have to remember, my grandparents were older. Once when I came down with the flu, I very generously shared the bug with my grandmother and she ended up in the hospital. Everyone was deathly worried about her."

"And you felt guilty."

"I was in preschool at the time. I still recall feeling bad that my grandmother would be so sick because of me." Naturally, she'd been too young to understand that a childhood ailment would hit an elderly woman much harder.

"In other words, homeschooling you was protection in case you inadvertently brought home a virus?"

"Yes, but being taught at home wasn't a bad thing, Tom. My grandmother was my teacher because Mom worked during the day. We went on all kinds of field trips, and lessons were always fun."

"She didn't worry about getting sick when she took you around? Did she think your being with her would ward off any bugs?"

"You're being silly."

"No, I'm serious. Wasn't she worried?"

"Apparently not." That didn't make a lot of sense to Ellie, now that she thought about it.

"What about your social development?" Tom asked. "Were you allowed to have friends?"

"A few. It wasn't bad, Tom. You make it sound like I was in prison. It wasn't like that."

"What happened once you were old enough to date?"

This was harder to explain. "You seem to think I didn't date, but I did," she said, somewhat defensively.

"Did your grandparents and mother have an approved list of boys they considered acceptable?" he asked. Again, she detected a slight hint of derision in his voice, as if he was angry on her behalf. And, really, it wasn't necessary. She had been loved and sheltered from many of the pitfalls of life.

"By the time I was old enough to date, my grandparents had both died."

He didn't ask about either of them passing, and Ellie was grateful. She and her mother had both taken their deaths hard.

"Tell me about your first date," Tom urged.

Ellie laughed, and Tom joined her, chuckling himself. "What's so funny?" he asked.

"Nothing."

"Tell me," he insisted.

"I was in braces and my mother insisted I wear a dress and I was so terribly shy I don't think I said two words the entire evening.

Thankfully, we went to the movies and a lot of conversation wasn't required."

"How old were you? Thirteen? Fourteen?"

"Sixteen."

She felt his arm around her tighten ever so slightly. "Sixteen," he repeated.

"I went to a dance once when I was fifteen, but no one asked me to dance."

"Were the boys in Oregon blind?" he asked incredulously.

Ellie smiled, loving the way he seemed to be annoyed on her behalf.

Then, because she wanted to change the subject, she asked, "What's your earliest memory?"

"My earliest memory," Tom repeated slowly. "Let me see. Ah, yes." He kissed her temple before he continued. "I was with my parents on a picnic. Mom spread out a blanket and we had a wonderful lunch. There was a lazy river close by, and I'd gone down to look for minnows with a cup in my hand, intent on going fishing."

"With a cup?"

"It's the best way," he insisted.

"How old were you?"

Tom shrugged. "I must have been three or four. I remember seeing a small fish and I wanted to catch it in my cup so I could show my dad what a good fisherman I was. I made the mistake of stepping into the water."

"And slipped?"

"It might have been a lazy river, but the current knocked me off my feet and down I went. I remember hearing my mother scream and my dad racing out into the water. He made a tremendous splash and caught me under my arms and scooped me up."

"Did you lose the fish?" she teased.

"And the cup. I was more upset about that than anything." He kissed her again and then asked, "What's your first memory?"

"I read once that almost always a first memory involves something that frightens us."

"Were you frightened?"

"I was, but it wasn't by being swept away in a current. My mother put me down for a nap and I wasn't tired."

"How old were you?"

"I don't know, but I was still in the crib. The only reason I know that is because I can remember seeing the bars as I pressed my cheek against the sheet."

"So young."

"Really young," she agreed.

"What happened?"

Ellie closed her eyes. It was as if it'd happened only a few years ago; the memory remained vivid in her mind. "For whatever reason, my mother had a picture of my father on the dresser. She'd taken it out and looked at it and hadn't put it away . . . that's the only thing I could guess."

"Do you think she loved him?"

"I do, in her own way, but she was afraid, I think."

"Of what?"

"Don't sidetrack me, I'm still in my crib."

"Right, sorry."

Ellie enjoyed this. It seemed there wasn't anything she couldn't talk to Tom about. "I wanted to see my father's picture. Mom had this crocheted runner my grandmother made for her across the top of her dresser. I thought that if I tugged on the runner, I might be able to reach to the photograph of my father."

"So what happened?"

"Mom had a vase on the dresser, too, an antique that she loved and—"

Tom broke into her story. "The vase fell and shattered into a thousand pieces."

"Hey, this is my story," she said, and elbowed him in the ribs.

"That's what happened, though, isn't it?"

"Yup." To this day, Ellie could remember looking at that broken vase through the slats of her crib. Eventually, she fell asleep the way she was meant to, but as she drifted off her mind was full of doom and gloom and the expectation that she was going to get a spanking.

"And you were afraid," Tom said for her. "So what happened?"

"I don't remember anything after that."

"So what you read is true in both our cases. It was a frightening moment for each of us."

"Yes, it was."

"Did you get to see your father's photograph?"

"No. As young as I was, I was afraid if I tugged on the runner again that something else might fall and break."

"Even at three or four you were one smart cookie."

Ellie could see that Tom had turned the sailboat around, and they started back toward the cove.

"I spoke to my mom last night after I got back to the inn," she mentioned, hoping to sound as though it was nothing to talk to her mother after midnight.

"I bet she was worried."

"Understandably so." She didn't want to paint a picture of her mother as a control freak, although in some ways Virginia was.

"Right," Tom concurred, but he didn't sound convinced. "You were meeting a stranger. Someone not on her approved list, someone she didn't know."

"You weren't a stranger to me," Ellie reminded him. "I want you to meet Mom one day, and I don't want you to think badly of her. She's been a good mother."

"Overprotective."

"Yes."

"Domineering."

"To a certain extent, yes, but in the gentlest of ways."

"She's chain-linked her life to yours, Ellie."

He spoke the truth, and while Ellie had never heard it said in exactly those terms, Tom was right. It was as if she couldn't make a decision without her mother making her own wishes known.

"Other than meeting me, have you ever done anything your mother disapproved of you doing?" he asked.

"Of course I have," Ellie insisted.

He chuckled like he found that hard to believe. "Like what?"

"Well, for one thing, on my first date she wanted me to wear my white dress and I insisted on wearing my pink one."

"Why not the white one?"

"Because I looked like I was in a wedding party."

Tom laughed. "Who won that disagreement?"

Ellie sighed. He would ask that. "Mom."

"So you were dressed as a bridesmaid on your first date."

"Wrong," she was quick to correct him. "I resembled the flower girl more than a bridesmaid."

As the marina came into view, Tom stood. "Do you think you could hold on to the helm for a couple minutes?"

"Me?"

"Don't worry. It'll be fine. I'm going forward to lower the sails, but I'll be back before you even notice I'm away."

Ellie sincerely doubted that. "Okay." Talk about being out of her comfort zone. She grabbed hold of the helm with both hands. Earlier he'd shown her how to make sure the wind was in the sails by keeping an eye on a small piece of yarn attached to the mast.

True to his word, Tom had the two sails lowered within a matter of minutes, and then they motored toward the marina.

Ellie glanced up. The waterfront was alive with activity. The sidewalk was crowded with those enjoying the park. Off to one side was the farmers' market, and it seemed to be doing a brisk business.

Tom moored the boat in the same slot from which they'd left. With only a minimum of effort, he leaped onto the dock and secured the craft. Then he took extra care to store the sails and leave the boat in the same condition in which they'd found it.

When he finished, he looked up and hesitated before glancing back at her. "Are you ready for your surprise?" he asked.

"Sure." That odd look was back in his eyes. She read uncertainty and something else she couldn't quite identify.

Taking her by the hand, he led her up the ramp to the waterfront park. "There's someone here I want you to meet," he said. His hand tightened around hers.

"Who?"

Tom didn't look at her. "My dad," he said.

A middle-aged man stepped toward them and a chill ran down Ellie's arms.

"This is my dad," Tom said. "My stepdad," he amended.

"Hello," Ellie said, smiling at the other man. He was attractive, with silver hairs at his temples adding to his appeal. His eyes were dark and serious, and in them she read doubt and that same uncertainty she'd seen in Tom. "I'm Eleanor," she said.

"You're Ellie," the other man said. "And I'm your father."

Chapter 16

~

Maggie's mind was in absolute turmoil. This couldn't be happening. She couldn't be pregnant, she just couldn't. A pregnancy would ruin her life, her marriage, her future.

"You okay?" Roy asked, as they left Cedar Cove, driving around the cove. After reviewing their options, they'd decided to take the Bremerton ferry into Seattle and spend the day on the waterfront. It'd been several years since they'd visited Pike Place Market and enjoyed the multitude of tourist activities the city had to offer.

"I'm fine," Maggie assured her husband, smiling for all she was worth, but at the moment, that wasn't much. As it was, she couldn't be sure how long she would be able to hide her fear and terror from her husband. One thing was for certain: She couldn't, she wouldn't blurt everything out the way she had before when she confessed what she'd done. That had proved disastrous. Their marriage had barely managed to survive one hit. Another in such quick succession was sure to do them in for good.

Roy was in a chipper mood, whistling along to the Katy Perry song playing on the radio. Following their heartfelt discussion, he appeared lighthearted . . . almost happy. Maggie couldn't remember the last time she'd seen her husband behaving this carefree. It was as though he didn't have a concern in the world.

The same couldn't be said for Maggie. It felt as if her arms and legs were weighted down in concrete. Doubt and dread made it nearly impossible to breathe. She was in a panic, her heart racing, her stomach pitching. She had to know before she went crazy.

"Honey, would you mind looking for a drugstore?" she asked, as evenly as she could manage. "I left the antacids we got yesterday at the inn."

His concern was immediate. "Is it your stomach again?"

"Yes, it's a bit queasy." But not for the reasons he assumed. She pressed her hand to her abdomen.

"I hope you're not coming down with a flu bug. If you want to go back to the inn, just let me know."

"No, no, I'm looking forward to being in Seattle." At least if she was busy she might be able to take her mind off the potential nightmare she could be facing.

"Riding the ferry will be awesome," he said, sounding almost boyish in his enthusiasm.

"It will be fun," she agreed. She'd always enjoyed a trip on the ferry. It was so picturesque, especially now that the sun was out. The weather couldn't be any more perfect.

"I think I see a drugstore on the next corner," Roy said.

"Good."

Roy made the turn into the parking lot. Even before he found a parking space or turned off the engine, Maggie had released her seat belt. "I'll run in and be back in a jiffy."

"I can go if you like," he offered.

"Thanks, but it's no trouble." She didn't need the antacids—she wanted a pregnancy test. She had to find out, and soon, or she'd go insane. Roy couldn't know the real reason she needed to stop at a drugstore.

She was halfway to the store when her husband rolled down his window and called after her, "Pick up a couple bottles of water, if you would."

"Will do." Once inside, it took her a moment to find the right aisle for the pregnancy test kits. She grabbed one and two plastic bottles of water, and in her rush nearly forgot the antacids. All in all, it took her less than five minutes. Before she joined her husband she hid the pregnancy test kit in her oversized purse.

They arrived in Bremerton with time to spare before the ferry arrived. Roy paid the fee and they joined the long queue of cars waiting for the next boat. Within a matter of minutes they were able to view the ferry turning into the cove.

An eagle soared above them, its wings outstretched, making a lazy circle in the cloud-dappled sky. Roy saw it first, which was no surprise, seeing how distracted she was.

"Do you see it?" Roy asked, pointing toward the horizon.

Maggie looked up and shaded her eyes, spotting the bird's white head, which was a sure indication. That and the massive wingspan. A few crows chased after the eagle, but they didn't have a chance of catching the bigger bird.

"I've never understood why they're named bald eagles when they have a full head of white hair," Roy said.

"Me neither."

"Wow, look at this," her husband whispered, as he made a sweeping gesture with his arm over the blue-green water. "It doesn't get any more beautiful than that, does it?"

The scenery was spectacular, but Maggie was unable to appreciate the splendor of the view. She couldn't begin to imagine what a pregnancy would mean to the newly established commitment Roy and she had made to their marriage. Nor could she bear the thought of what Roy would do when she was forced to tell him there was a baby. She couldn't know if the father of this child—if there was a child—was the result of her one night of infidelity or if it could possibly be Roy's.

Keeping the pregnancy a secret would be impossible for long. Roy was bound to guess . . . Oh goodness, she was jumping ahead of herself. She didn't have proof positive yet, but in her heart . . . in her heart, she knew.

What astonished Maggie was that she hadn't thought of the possibility earlier. She knew the risk . . . with their infrequent lovemaking, she'd gotten lax about taking her birth-control pills. She wasn't opposed to having a third child. At one point she'd discussed adding to their family with Roy.

A baby.

What in the name of heaven was she going to do? With the boys, each time she'd been thrilled and excited. Roy, too. The joyful anticipation he'd felt had spilled over in the most loving and tender of ways. Maggie recalled when they learned she was pregnant with Jaxon, their older son. Her husband had wrapped his arms around her and lifted her off her feet, swinging her around and around, all the while laughing. The joy in him was palpable.

Roy couldn't wait to tell his parents and sister. Jaxon was the first grandchild, and Roy's parents had been as excited as Roy and Maggie themselves. A short fifteen months after the birth of their first son, Maggie discovered she was pregnant with Collin. This second pregnancy wasn't planned, but that didn't diminish her husband's pleasure. He was just as thrilled by the news of this second child as he had been the first. Although after Collin had been born, Roy secretly admitted he'd been hoping for a little girl.

The ferry docked and a long line of vehicles filed off. Soon it would be their turn to board. When possible, Maggie would find a women's restroom and take the pregnancy test in with her. Once she had confirmation, she would decide when and how to tell Roy.

As crazy as it sounded, she wanted to run away, or bury her head under the covers and never get out of bed again. It seemed impossible that she hadn't once, not even one time, considered the possibility of a pregnancy.

How stupid could she get?

Anyone who knew her would be shocked to learn of her behavior that night. Maggie had always been the obedient daughter, the perfect wife and mother. Until that night, she felt she made wise choices. Her mother would find it unbelievable that Maggie was even capable of adultery. Actually, Maggie found it hard to believe herself.

After her terrible fight with Roy that night over Katherine, she'd believed her marriage was over. They'd tossed hateful words at each other, words that cut like knives, viciously stabbing at each other with insults and accusations until she felt the very lifeblood of their marriage drain away. After what she'd read in his texts to the other woman and the hateful words they'd exchanged, Maggie flew out of the house. She'd been convinced there was no repairing the damage, no going back.

Sobbing uncontrollably, she took off without a single idea of where she would go. She didn't want to run home to her parents. Telling them of Roy's emotional affair and that she was sure they would divorce was too humiliating. It would have been natural to seek out a friend, and hindsight being what it was, she wished she had. The fact was, it was simply too embarrassing and demeaning to have to admit to anyone that her husband had been involved with another woman.

When she ran a red light and narrowly escaped slamming into another car, Maggie realized she was too upset to drive. The parking spot she found was directly in front of a bar, and if ever she needed something to calm her nerves, it was then. After all, why not? She'd lost count of how many nights Roy had come home too late to eat dinner with her and the boys. Now she knew that on many of those nights he'd met Katherine for an after-work drink. Her husband would rather spend time with an old girlfriend than with her and their sons.

She'd gone into the bar and ordered a fruity drink, tossing it back as if it was no more potent than cranberry juice. When she finished the second drink, she recognized this was her limit. No more. Already her head was spinning.

Then a guy named Steve bought her another drink and had it delivered with his compliments. Shortly afterward he joined her at the table and they talked and talked. He sat next to her and he said all the things she wanted to hear from her husband but hadn't in a very long time.

She was beautiful and funny. The more she drank, the wittier she got. After four drinks, Steve No-last-name kissed her. And Maggie let him. It was a sweet kiss, a gentle kiss, and she'd nearly broken down in tears. It'd been so long since Roy had kissed her like she was the most precious gift he'd ever received.

The kisses felt incredibly good. After several such kisses and a few slow dances, Steve suggested they go somewhere more private. Right away Maggie knew this wasn't a good idea, but she was in no condition to drive. To her credit, she declined, and Steve was fine with it. He knew she was married, and he told her that he was as well. They were both lonely, hurting people.

Steve offered to buy her a cup of coffee. There was a diner just down the street, and that sounded like the thing to do. Unfortunately, they never made it to the diner. As soon as they were out the door, Steve was kissing her again. He claimed he found he couldn't resist her. There she was up against the side of the building, making out with a man she'd met only a few hours earlier, convinced her marriage was over.

After a token attempt to end the foreplay, Maggie surrendered. Why not feel loved and attractive and sensual? And wanted. Roy could have Katherine. As far as Maggie was concerned, she was tired of taking second place in her husband's life.

She spent the night with Steve in a hotel room and woke the next morning alone. Her head pounded with a hangover and she was sick to her stomach with what she'd done. After showering and scrubbing her entire body until her skin was red, she checked her phone and saw ten text messages and voice mails from Roy. Her husband was desperate to know where she was. He'd been forced to take the boys to his sister's house. He wanted to talk. He was sorry. He needed to hear from her. Please, please call.

She agreed to meet him. When they sat across from each other, Maggie was defiant and angry. Roy regretted everything. Maggie was right to be upset. He promised it was over between him and Katherine, and he vowed never to be in contact with her again. He even went so far as to sever the relationship with the company that employed her.

With tears in his eyes, Roy asked Maggie to forgive him and made her promise never to leave him like that again. For most of the night he'd paced the floor, worried sick about where she could be. And why in the name of heaven hadn't she answered her phone?

When she woke that morning, Maggie had had no intention of ever telling her husband what she'd done. But after his tearful apology, she couldn't keep it to herself. She wasn't so innocent herself, and she was sorry, too, so very sorry, and so she'd blurted out everything that had happened.

For the longest time Roy didn't say anything. Not a word. He just stared at her as if he refused to believe what she'd told him. And who could blame him? She would be the last person anyone would suspect of having a one-night stand. Even now she couldn't comprehend why it was called that. As far as she remembered, she'd done very little standing.

And until just this morning her husband had refused to even talk about that night.

She heard the car's engine start, and that pulled her back to the present. Her husband followed the car in front of him onto the ferry. They were directed onto the second level and parked near the stairwell that led to the observation level and the cafeteria.

He turned off the engine and said, "You seem a million miles away."

Debbie Macomber

She smiled, hoping to reassure him that all was well.

Roy reached for her hand, gently folding it in his own. "I didn't want to talk about what happened . . . and the aftermath of it. You were right when you said I wanted to sweep everything under the rug."

She hung her head. "I can't blame you . . . I wanted to do the same thing, too."

"But eventually it would have destroyed us. I feel better than I have in weeks."

Maggie forced a smile. With everything in her, she wanted to assure him she felt that same sense of peace, but it would be a lie. A very big lie. In all her life, Maggie had never felt less like putting on a happy face.

"Let's go up front," Roy suggested.

Maggie's legs felt like they wouldn't support her as she climbed the stairwell to the observation deck. The ferry had upholstered beige booths against both sides of the windows and chair seating in rows in the middle. Roy led her toward the doors leading outside.

As they stepped onto the deck, the wind whipped Maggie's hair about her face as the sun shone down bright and warm. The ferry released a loud honk as it glided away from the dock and toward Seattle. Seagulls followed, looking for handouts from the passengers. A teenager stretched his arm high above his head, holding on to a french fry. To the passengers' delight, a large gull swooped down and grabbed it from his fingers.

Maggie looked down at the waves slapping against the sides of the huge boat. The dark green water mesmerized her. How easy it would be to jump from here and disappear in the deep waters of Puget Sound. That way she'd never have to face the future. Never have to face the consequences of a single indiscretion. She didn't deserve this misery. It took all the restraint she possessed not to rant at God that this was unfair. It was all wrong.

Roy came to stand behind her, his hands on her shoulders, protecting her from the wind. Leaning close, he whispered, "I love you, Maggie, heart and soul, I love you."

She leaned back and tucked her head beneath his chin and closed her eyes. Right now his love was secure, but she wondered how long he'd love her once she told him she was pregnant.

"You asked me earlier if I still meant the things I wrote in that letter back when we were in college," Roy continued. "I shouldn't have hesitated. I knew then and I know now, every word was true. We were meant to be together. You're my soul mate."

Maggie turned around and buried her face in her husband's chest as he hugged her close. She found it difficult not to break down in tears.

"I'm going inside to use the restroom," she told Roy. She needed a definitive answer.

"I'll come inside with you. Do you want a cup of coffee?" he asked.

"Tea," she said, wanting to keep him occupied if this test took longer than she expected. "You know how I like it."

"I'll find us a seat."

"I won't be long," she promised.

Thankfully, the restroom wasn't crowded. Maggie went into the narrow stall and removed the pregnancy test from inside her purse and quickly read the instructions. Five minutes. That was all it would take either to reassure her or for her world to implode.

Five short minutes.

Only they weren't short minutes. They ticked by in agonizing seconds, one by one, until she thought she would go mad, waiting.

In truth, it didn't take the required time. The test strip confirmed her suspicions long before the final seconds of her cell-phone timer ticked off. It was blue.

She was pregnant.

Chapter 17

⌇

"This is . . . my father," Ellie repeated, when she found she could speak again.

The man standing in front of her looked as awkward and uncomfortable as she felt. Frowning, she turned to Tom, waiting for him to explain. None of this made sense. He'd mentioned a surprise for her, but surely this couldn't be it.

"Hello, Ellie," the other man said.

She didn't return the greeting. Instead, her gaze held Tom's, and when she spoke, it was to him. "I don't understand."

"I know this is something of a shock . . ."

"Something?" she repeated, incredulously.

"Give me a chance to explain."

"Please do."

Tom gestured toward a picnic table, silently suggesting they all sit down as if this was a big family reunion and everyone should be hugging and greeting one another.

Ellie shook her head. "No . . . no . . ." This wasn't a family outing where she'd whip out a tablecloth and set down a few plates while he cooked hot dogs on the barbecue.

"After your mother and I divorced, I married Tom's mother," the man who claimed to be her father said.

Ellie stretched out her arm as though to ward him off. "I asked Tom. He should be the one to tell me what this is about."

"I . . . wanted to find you for my dad," Tom said.

"Find me?" she repeated. "Find me?" All at once everything started stacking up in her mind in neat, orderly columns. The book-club friend request on the social-media platform, the skillful strategy as he introduced himself and kept the communication open, carefully wooing her. Bit by bit, day by day, a little at a time gaining her confidence. Their meeting hadn't been accidental or a quirk of fate but carefully orchestrated. He'd sought her out, discovered her interests, and then manipulated their meeting.

Ellie backed up two steps. "You planned this from the start . . . you hid who you are and used me. Was he in on this as well?" she demanded, nodding toward her father.

"This is as much a surprise to me as it is to you," Scott Reynolds murmured. "I didn't know anything about it until just recently . . . this morning, in fact."

No wonder he looked so ill at ease and uncomfortable.

In other words, her father had never had any intention of contacting her. Meeting her wasn't his doing, his wish. He'd walked out on her and her mother and found a new family, a new life. Countless times Tom had talked about his stepfather, whom he always referred to as Dad. Dad this. Dad that.

Her father. Tom had been raised by *her father*. Tom had no real feelings for her. He didn't love her. It was *her father* he cared for so deeply.

"It's only right that you know the man responsible for your life,"

Tom said. "You told me so yourself. Please, Ellie, give me a chance to explain."

Tom had taken the confidences she'd shared with him and used them against her. "Let you explain?" she repeated, her mind whirling like the blades of a helicopter, only she wasn't being lifted off the ground and taken away. Instead, she was left to face . . . she didn't know what.

"Scott is a good man. At least give him the opportunity—"

"No," Ellie cried, and for emphasis, shook her head. She turned on Tom, her voice shaking with emotion. "You used me."

"No," he protested, quick to defend himself. "It wasn't like that."

Ellie refused to believe him. "It was no accident that you sought me out on Facebook. You said so yourself."

"Okay, in the beginning. Dad talked about you and your mother with such regret and sorrow. I felt it was only right that he have a chance to know his own flesh and blood."

Ellie wasn't willing to listen to any of this. She noticed her father had nothing to say, which was just as well. "I find it interesting that it was you who went in search of me and not him." She pointed at the older man. "He couldn't be bothered with me, right?" She glared at this stranger, accusing him with her eyes. All the years she'd been without him, all the years she'd yearned to know her father, and all there'd been was silence.

Even now he had nothing to say for himself. He seemed to find it difficult to even look at her. He was ashamed of himself, as well he should be. He abandoned his own flesh and created a home for other children.

Almost right away another realization hit her between the eyes, this one more painful than all the other neatly compiled facts coming together in her brain. Tom had urged her to come to Cedar Cove, but it wasn't because he cared for her or wanted to make her part of his life. He had an agenda. Getting her to love him was a means to an end. His means; his end.

Once more she retreated, backing away from the two men.

Tom had involved her heart, gained her confidence for his own selfish purposes. He didn't care about her; he didn't love her. Almost everything her mother had warned her against was happening. Her big leap of faith, her single act of independence, had turned around and bitten her in the face.

Tears filled her eyes. "I don't believe this . . ."

"Ellie, please. Please, listen, give me a chance to explain."

"No." She glared at Tom and then her father. "I don't want to see either one of you again. Ever." With that, she took off in a rush, unable to get away fast enough.

Tom hurried after her. "It isn't like that, Ellie. Please listen. Okay, okay, you're right. Finding you was calculated, but then I fell in love with you."

She wanted to laugh. "Do you honestly expect me to believe that?"

"Yes. In the beginning my goal was to set up a meeting between Dad and you, but as time went on and we became more involved I realized I wanted you for myself."

His face was a blur as she glared at him through the moisture filling her eyes. "Then you should have told me who you were."

"You're right, I should have. Give me another chance. Please."

Ellie wrapped her arms around her middle as if to ward off a chill. "I need to think this through. And for now I need you to go away."

"I can't," he pleaded. "I can't leave things between us like this."

"Give me time," she insisted. "I need time to process this."

He hesitated and then asked, "How long do you need? An hour, a day?"

Ellie couldn't give him a timetable. "Let me put it like this: I'll call you, don't call me."

"No," he insisted, and stopped her, gripping hold of her by the shoulders. His eyes bore into hers, demanding that she pay attention. "You're right," he said. "I went about this all wrong, and for that I apologize. I'm sorry; I would never purposely do anything to hurt you."

Distressed as she was, Ellie wanted to push him away, but her heart desperately yearned to believe him. She'd already made a fool of herself once because of Tom and she was terrified of making the same mistake again.

"I fell in love with you, Ellie." His eyes were intent, serious. "I'm not making this up; I'm speaking from my heart."

How badly she wanted to believe him, but she was afraid.

When she didn't respond, he tried again. "Put my feelings for you aside. Your father loves you."

Ellie had no proof of that, none whatsoever. She tried to jerk her arms free, but Tom held on tightly.

"It's true," he insisted. "I didn't know about you until after my mother died."

That fact alone belied everything he'd just said. "My father loved me so much that I was constantly on his mind, right? He couldn't stop talking about me." If Tom thought he was proving his point, he'd achieved the exact opposite.

"He told my mother."

"That makes me feel worlds better," she murmured sarcastically.

"After Mom died, Dad said he had a lot of regrets in his life but the biggest regret was not knowing his daughter."

"It's a little late, don't you think?" She was unable to hide her sarcasm. "Somewhere along the lines of twenty years too late."

"He showed me your baby photo. He still carries it in his wallet."

"He could have called me. He could have written me letters."

"He tried countless times to reach you, but your grandparents made it impossible," Tom insisted. "If you don't believe me, ask your mother."

"I intend to do exactly that."

"Talk to him, Ellie," Tom pleaded. "At least give him a chance to tell you what happened between your mother and him."

"No."

"Do you think it was easy for him to come down here today? Don't you think it was as difficult for him as it is for you?"

Ellie shook her head. "I thought you said his one regret was me . . . If what you say is true and you had to practically drag him here, then he couldn't have wanted to meet me that badly."

"I didn't have to drag him. He came of his own free will because he loves you."

She snorted with disbelief.

Tom dropped his hands, releasing her. "He told me that this would happen. That you would hate him . . . that your grandparents and your mother would have turned you against him, and he was right."

"My mother has been there every day of my life, supporting and encouraging me. My grandparents were decent, honorable people who loved me."

"They suffocated you and dictated your every move," he challenged.

Ellie was too confused to think straight. "You don't know what you're talking about," she insisted, backing away from him.

"Go ahead," Tom said, "run away. Turn your back on your father and on me. You say you need time, then great, take as long as you need. If you want to talk, I'll be here, and so will your father. Hate me if that will make you feel better. I've no doubt that I'm exactly the kind of person your mother warned you against. But if you walk away from your father now, I promise you, Ellie Reynolds, you'll regret it the rest of your life."

He left her then, rushing back to the waterfront and her father. Ellie watched for just a moment and saw him join the father she'd never known. Scott Reynolds sat on a park bench with his shoulders hunched forward as though he wore a mantle of steel.

Ellie hurried back toward the inn. By the time she arrived, she was breathless from the steep climb and so badly shaken that every part of her body started to quiver.

Because she didn't want Jo Marie to see her when she was this upset, Ellie stayed outside. She made her way onto the porch and sat down in one of the chairs lining the deck, and looked out over the waterfront. From this viewpoint she could see the park, but she forcefully kept her gaze away from where she'd left Tom and her father.

A rogue tear wove its way down her cheek and was quickly followed by another. She wanted to believe Tom cared for her, but she was afraid to trust him, and who could blame her? The tears refused to stop, and her nose started to run.

Reaching for her purse to search for a tissue, Ellie was surprised to find that Rover had joined her, resting at her side, his chin on his paws.

"You won't believe what happened," she whispered, as she found what she needed and blew her nose.

"Rover?" It was Jo Marie.

Ellie grabbed a fresh tissue and wiped the moisture from her face, although she couldn't avoid sniffling.

"Ellie?" Jo Marie said, as she approached her. "My goodness, what's wrong?"

Not wanting to talk, Ellie shook her head, indicating that explaining anything at the moment was beyond her.

Jo Marie gave her shoulder a gentle squeeze. "I have just the thing," she said, and disappeared back into the house. To Ellie's surprise, Rover didn't follow the innkeeper. Instead, he remained steadfastly at her side, going so far as to place his chin on top of her foot. She found the action of great comfort.

"Have you ever loved someone who bitterly disappointed you?" she asked the dog.

A few minutes later, Jo Marie returned with a tray containing a big pot of tea, cups, and a small plate of cookies. She set it down on the table. "I can't think of a single thing more comforting than tea with cookies."

Despite everything, Ellie managed a smile. The other woman

poured; steam rose from the delicate china pot and then the teacup as Jo Marie prepared to hand it to Ellie.

"Milk or sugar?" she asked.

Ellie declined and took the cup. She held on to the saucer and blew into the steaming liquid. "I never knew my father," she whispered. "My parents divorced before I had any memories of him."

"You had no contact with him. Not ever?"

"No, until now . . . He was just here . . . down by the waterfront."

"Here in Cedar Cove?"

Ellie nodded. "He's Tom's father."

Jo Marie tried to swallow a gasp but didn't quite succeed. "Tom's your half-brother?"

"No, Tom is my father's stepson. He raised Tom and his brother, Earl, as if they were his sons. The only reason Tom . . ." She paused, hardly able to say the words. "He wanted to reunite me and my father," Ellie finally managed.

"Oh, Ellie, I don't think that's the only reason."

Tom had said as much, but Ellie didn't know what to believe.

"I saw the way he looked at you this morning," Jo Marie said gently. "Tom's crazy about you."

Ellie shook her head, dismissing the other woman's words of reassurance. "My father didn't know what Tom was doing any more than I did. He could barely look at me . . . Tom said my father had tried to contact me through the years but my mother and grandparents intervened and wouldn't allow it . . . but he could have gone through the courts. If he'd really wanted me in his life, he would have moved heaven and earth to make it happen."

"Yes," Jo Marie agreed, as she settled into the chair beside Ellie. "We all have regrets, though, don't we?" she asked. "I imagine you would have welcomed the opportunity to know your father."

"As a kid, I would have done anything to hear from him, to talk to him. I needed my father and he wasn't available. I was an inconvenience."

Jo Marie sipped her tea. "What's so different now?" she asked.

Ellie turned to look at her. "What do you mean?"

"He's here now. It must have taken a great deal of courage to meet you, after all this time, knowing how deeply he's failed you."

Tom had said basically the same thing. He'd gone so far as to claim if she turned her back on her father now she would always regret it.

"Don't you think you should give him a chance?" Jo Marie asked.

"But Tom . . ."

"Deal with Tom later," the innkeeper urged.

"My mother warned me about him . . . she told me I shouldn't trust him."

"Oh, Ellie, your mother's been hurt, badly hurt, and while her intentions are good, she's tainted your view of men and life. I don't mean to bad-mouth her, and I hope I haven't spoken out of turn."

What Jo Marie said was true, and Ellie immediately recognized it.

"You're right," she whispered. "I should at least give my father a chance to explain . . . we should talk."

"I don't think you'll regret it."

Ellie reached for her phone and sent Tom a text message. I'd like to talk to my father. Tell me where I should meet him. But you need to stay away.

Chapter 18

Poor Ellie. I wanted to wrap my arms around her and tell her it would all work out in the end. Mostly I wanted to give Tom a piece of my mind for pulling this trick on her. It didn't take me long to forgive him, though. After Ellie and I talked a bit and I returned to the kitchen I was less perturbed with him. Instinctively, I knew he meant well, although I questioned his methods.

It was apparent Tom cared deeply for his stepfather. After meeting Tom and seeing him with Ellie, I had to believe he held some deep affection for her. I said as much, which I think helped Ellie.

What was that saying? *Oh, what a tangled web we weave when first we practice to deceive.* I was fairly certain it went something like that. My guess was that Tom had gotten himself in deeper than he'd ever intended.

I noticed Mark wasn't working on the gazebo, and I suspected

I'd chased him off with my invitation to Sunday dinner. It seemed most every effort I made to get to know him better backfired. Clearly, meeting my family put him on edge. I wanted Mark to realize that I considered him a good friend, a prickly one, but still my friend. Even more, I hoped that he'd consider the invitation to meet my family as a roundabout way of showing him I genuinely wanted us to know each other better.

Until that morning, I didn't realize how close I felt to Mark. Not in a romantic way but as a friend. Why else would I have told him that I felt I was losing my grip on my memories of my dead husband?

The oddest look had come over Mark, and, really, who could blame him? It embarrassed me that I'd chosen to blurt it out. One look at him told me how uncomfortable the information had made him.

He wasn't someone who shared confidences, and it appeared he didn't know how to deal with it when others did.

Mark was on my mind a good deal lately, and that made me uncomfortable. Mostly he frustrated me, and at the same time he was my friend. We saw each other nearly every day, especially if he was working on a project at the inn. I'd come to rely on him, probably more than I should.

The door off the porch opened and Ellie came in carrying the teacup and saucer.

"Are you feeling better?" I asked, taking the china from her and placing it on the kitchen countertop.

She nodded. "Much better. Thank you for listening, Jo Marie."

"Anytime." I resisted the urge to hug her. She'd endured a shock, and while my tendency was to comfort and mother her, that wasn't what she wanted. From what I knew about her, Ellie had been nearly mothered to death. She had to reach this decision about her father and Tom all on her own. I didn't want to influence her one way or the other.

"I'm going to my room," Ellie said. "I can feel a headache coming on, and I think I'll feel better if I lie down for a few minutes."

"Call me if you need anything," I told her, wanting to be helpful but at the same time give her the space she needed.

"I will, and again, thank you." Ellie headed toward the stairs leading to the second floor.

Once more I felt the urge to do something physical and decided I needed to check out the attic, which was accessible from the third floor. It'd been on my to-do list for quite some time and I kept putting it off. First the cupboards, now this. I'd straightened out my drawers the night before, burying Paul's sweatshirt in the bottom of my dresser. If it wasn't going to comfort me as it had so often in the past, then I'd put it where it was out of the way.

I'd never explored the attic. When I purchased the inn from the Frelingers, they'd mentioned that they'd stored a number of small pieces of furniture and other items there. I wanted to take an inventory in case I decided to have a garage sale. I might put the items I didn't need on consignment, too. Of course, it depended on what was stashed up there.

I made my way up to the third floor, where three of the smaller bedrooms were. A rope dangling from the ceiling pulled down a ladder that granted me access to the upper area. I'd stuck my head into the attic to look one time but hadn't given it more than a cursory inspection. It was long past time I did.

Getting up the ladder wasn't a problem, and, luckily, I wasn't a tall woman. As it was, I had to hunch over in order to move about. If I ran into rodents or saw evidence of their presence I wasn't sure I'd be able to handle it.

Thankfully, the Frelingers kept everything in an orderly fashion. I found a couple of oak nightstands; a few lamps; a chest, which turned out to be empty; and three or four oil paintings. The artwork was actually pretty good.

I remembered Mrs. Frelinger mentioning that she'd taken an art class and wondered if these paintings were her own work. Although the light, a single bulb that dangled from the rafters, wasn't great, when I picked up one of the paintings I saw that it wasn't her name on the seascape.

None of the items I found were of any use to me. While a garage sale was a good idea, I didn't have enough goods to warrant all the effort that would entail.

My gaze skirted back to the seascape. It wasn't all that bad. The walls of the inn were full of artwork, mostly from local artists. The Frelingers had started the collection, and I'd added to it until there wasn't a single wall for this seascape unless I moved something else. It was a shame, because it really was quite lovely and deserved to be hung prominently.

Then, out of the blue, an idea came to me.

The walls in Mark's home were barren, bereft of anything personal, as if he didn't want to encumber himself with anything or anyone.

To me, however, artwork was important. A single painting could change the entire feel of a room. With that in mind, I decided I would offer this painting to him. Friend to friend, no strings attached.

Getting the framed oil painting out of the attic proved to be something of a challenge. I managed with difficulty. When I came down the ladder, Rover was patiently waiting for me. He'd lain on the floor at the bottom of the steep ladder and cocked his head up at me. When he saw the painting, he moved away and barked, letting me know he wasn't pleased with my disappearing into that hole in the ceiling.

"The painting is for Mark," I explained.

Right away, Rover raced down the stairs. By the time I joined him, he sat at the door next to where I kept his leash. He seemed to understand that I intended to walk to Mark's place.

Instead of hauling the picture all the way to Mark's only to discover he wasn't home, I phoned first.

The handyman answered on the fourth ring, just before his cell went to voice mail. "Hi," he said, "and before you ask, I haven't changed my mind about dinner on Sunday."

"Okay, fine. No problem. I didn't call about that. I had another reason entirely."

"Which is?"

"I have something for you."

He hesitated. "You're okay with me not meeting your family?" He sounded like he didn't believe me and had anticipated an argument.

"I'm fine with it," I assured him, doing my best to sound ever so understanding. If my voice was any sweeter, he'd be swimming in a bowl of honey.

He hesitated again. "Then what did you want?"

While he dawdled when it came to getting a job finished, he was far more direct with phone calls. "I already told you. I have something for you," I said, a bit annoyed by his attitude. The least he could do was be more gracious.

"What?" The question was filled with suspicion.

"An oil painting I found in the attic." I was about to describe it for him when he cut me off.

"A what?"

"Honestly, Mark, is something wrong with your hearing?" He was doing this on purpose and it annoyed me. The honey was quickly melting away.

"Why do I need a painting?"

"Because you don't have one," I snapped.

"I don't want one."

"It's a gift," I insisted, growing more agitated by the moment. You'd think I was the unreasonable one by offering him a very nice piece of artwork. To hear his tone of voice, I should be dragged out of town to be tarred and feathered.

He went quiet, as if deciding if he wanted to be troubled or not.

"Fine, whatever," I said. "If you don't want the painting, it isn't going to hurt my feelings." Well, to be accurate, it was going to irritate me, but I wouldn't tell him that.

The line went silent and seemed to hum as if we didn't have a good connection, only I knew we did.

"What's the painting of, anyway?"

I'd have happily explained earlier, if I'd been able to get a word in between his protests and accusations. "It's a seascape."

"Hmm . . ."

"What does that mean?" I demanded.

Rover grew impatient waiting at the door. His chin was raised, looking toward the leash, eager to get going on our walk.

"Listen," I said, doing my best to hide my frustration, "I'm taking Rover for a walk and I'll swing by your place and you can take a look at it. If you want it, fine, it's yours free of charge, and if not, no biggie, I'll bring it back to the house."

"How big is it?" he asked.

"Not big, and it isn't that heavy. Will you be around?"

"I'll be here."

"Great, then Rover and I will see you in a few minutes." By now I was more than eager to get off the phone. Blast the man, but he was difficult.

"It isn't necessary, you know."

I'd been about to disconnect. "Sorry, I didn't catch that," I said, gritting my teeth. I should have pretended not to hear him and hung up.

He exhaled. "I wanted to be sure you understood that I wasn't going to change my mind about that dinner . . ."

"Mark, honestly, I found the painting in the attic and thought you'd like it. This isn't about dinner, my family, or anything else."

"How'd you get it down from the attic?" he asked, sounding deceptively calm.

I wasn't fooled. Mark had a thing about me climbing ladders. "I brought it down. I'm safe; don't worry about it." I made sure my voice cooled considerably.

"Okay, fine."

A couple minutes later, I started out of the inn, hauling the painting. It wasn't heavy, but no more than a block away I wished I'd driven my car instead of carrying it myself. Rover was accustomed to walking faster and didn't take kindly to the slower pace. He tugged at his leash, pulling me with him.

"Slow down," I muttered, as I shifted my weight. Holding on to the painting and the leash made for a cumbersome walk.

I went a few more steps, and once again I was forced to stop for fear I was about to drop the artwork. The leash had wrapped itself around my fingers, squeezing off the blood flow.

"Jo Marie . . ."

I peeked around the top of the frame to find Mark walking toward me at a clipped pace. "What in the name of heaven are you doing carrying this?"

I had to agree it wasn't the brightest idea I'd ever had, and while I didn't appreciate the lecture, I had to admit I was glad to see him.

He mumbled something under his breath, and it was probably best I didn't ask him to repeat himself. As soon as he reached me he took the oil painting out of my hands. Together, we started to his house.

"Thanks," I murmured, feeling a bit sheepish for being so foolish.

"I assumed you'd be delivering it by car until I remembered you saying something about walking Rover."

So that was what caused him to meet me. He'd gone far more than halfway.

"Aren't you even going to look at it?" I asked. In the light of day, the picture was lovelier than I'd realized. The sun, the sand, the waves crashing against the shoreline, with seagulls flying against the backdrop of a robin's-egg-blue sky.

"I already did."

Sometimes getting him to communicate was like attempting to milk a billy goat. "And what did you think?"

"It's okay."

As he did with the cookies and muffins, he made it sound like he was helping me out by taking this lovely picture off my hands. The man really did perturb me at times.

"Where are you going to hang it?" I asked next, half skipping in order to keep up with him. Rover loved the quicker pace and trotted along with his head held high, as if he knew exactly where we were going.

"Don't know yet," Mark answered.

"Would you like a suggestion?"

He laughed softly. "I have the feeling you're about to give it to me whether I want it or not."

"True." His living room wall would be perfect, and I told him as much.

"Why there?"

"You need something to say 'This is a home.' Your house looks like the Sierra Desert."

He didn't bother to disguise his amusement. "You're joking, right?"

"No." I was completely serious, and I let it show.

"I suppose you're about to suggest I hire a decorator next."

"No. But this is your home, Mark. It should at least feel like one instead of a . . ."

"I don't need stuff."

"I agree."

"Stuff holds down a person."

"Are you planning on moving anytime soon?" I asked, and instantly felt a sense of loss. If Mark decided to leave Cedar Cove, I'd miss him. As much as he irritated and frustrated me, I would miss him. Over the summer, especially since he'd broken his leg, I'd come to rely on Mark's friendship. I'd lived alone the majority of my adult life and wasn't accustomed to depending on anyone, but I'd come to depend on Mark, and the realization shook me.

"I won't be leaving anytime soon."

I was glad to hear it. "But you will move on?"

"Probably. I generally get bored with a town after a while."

"Oh." I didn't know that about him.

He stopped walking and gave me an odd look. "You okay?"

"Of course." I immediately brushed off his question.

"You got a funny look just then. I've sort of gotten to think of Cedar Cove as a good place to settle down for a while, though."

I grinned. "Me, too."

We didn't talk the rest of the way to his house. Mark led me through the kitchen door, which he apparently kept unlocked. I followed him into the main area of the house, which looked almost identical to the way it had the last time I saw it. He had a sofa, a recliner, an end table, and a television, and that was it.

"I take it Peter McConnell is back in his house again."

"Yes. Good thing, too, because I'd had about as much of him as I could take."

I couldn't keep from smiling.

"That amuses you?"

"No. You do."

"Very funny."

With my hands on my hips I appraised the bare walls, but really there wasn't any question where it belonged. The wall on the opposite side of the television was perfect.

"What do you think?" Mark asked.

"There," I said, pointing to where I felt the picture was best suited.

He shrugged, and if he agreed or disagreed I couldn't guess.

"Do you want me to help you hang it?" I asked.

"You mean now?" He made it sound like an unreasonable demand.

"Yes," I insisted. "Otherwise, you'll put it off for another six months or longer." I could easily see it leaning against the wall at Christmas, exactly where it was now.

"I guess." He disappeared and I heard the back screen slam

closed. A good five minutes passed before he returned with a hammer and a couple nails.

Within a matter of minutes he had the painting hung, and I had to admit it was perfect.

"Well," I said, stepping back to admire it. "It looks really good, don't you think?"

He shrugged.

"Oh come on, Mark, admit it. The painting adds ambiance to this place."

"Okay, okay, you're right. It's a nice touch."

It surprised me that he was willing to admit it.

"I appreciate it, Jo Marie."

I was even more surprised when he thanked me. I must have done a double take, because he took one look at me and started to laugh.

"What's so funny?" I asked.

"You." He grinned and seemed to struggle not to break out in laughter a second time. "You should have seen the look that came over you just now." He scrunched up his own face, mocking me.

"Very funny."

"I suppose you're going to demand that I pay the piper," he said, growing serious all of a sudden.

"Pay the piper?"

"You want me to meet your family on Sunday."

I hoped he would, but if not, I'd accept that, too. "Not this time," I said. "You'll meet my family sooner or later."

His eyes narrowed slightly, as if he wasn't sure he believed me. "You're a rare woman, Jo Marie. Sometimes I wonder if I appreciate you near enough."

Chapter 19

The Bremerton ferry docked on the Seattle waterfront and Roy followed the line of cars that motored off the boat. Within a matter of minutes he located a parking lot only a few blocks away from the dock.

The secret of what Maggie had discovered weighed on her like the heaviest of yokes. She didn't know how she was going to get through the day, let alone the rest of this getaway weekend. The next eight months seemed like an eternity.

He paid for the parking with his credit card, set the slip on his dashboard, and then reached for her hand. It'd been a long time since they'd held hands. Instinctively, Maggie knew he wouldn't be nearly this caring or loving when he discovered she was pregnant.

"Where shall we head first?" Roy asked.

"I don't know," she said, and smiled at him, hoping he wasn't paying too close attention to her. Her mouth trembled slightly with the effort to appear happy and carefree. "What interests you?"

"Let's visit the market," he suggested.

"Sure." Pike Place Market was a staple for anyone visiting Seattle, right along with the Space Needle, the monorail, the waterfront, and the aquarium.

"I hope we get to see one of the fishmongers toss a salmon," Roy said, and gently squeezed her hand.

They made the climb up the steps leading from the waterfront to First Avenue, stopping now and again at vendor stalls along the Hill Climb. The market was a mixture of fresh fish, garden-ripened vegetables, myriad floral bouquets, figurines made from ash from the volcanic eruption of Mount Saint Helens, and just about everything else. Roy purchased a jar of honey, and Maggie found a photo of the Space Needle in the middle of an electric storm. The camera captured a bolt of lightning just as it struck the Needle. She was instantly drawn to it because that was how she felt, as if she, too, had been struck. But like the Space Needle, she would withstand this lightning bolt.

The original Starbucks was directly across the street from the market, so they stopped in for a latte, decaf for her, and picked up a pound of cheese from a local cheesemaker, along with a loaf of bread and fresh green grapes.

"We'll feast later," Roy promised.

Once they'd deposited their goods in the car, Roy said, "Okay, what next?"

With her mind in turmoil, Maggie couldn't think of a single thing to do. "I . . . I don't know."

"There's so much to choose from," Roy said, and looped his arm around her shoulders. "Would you like to have lunch at the Space Needle?"

"Do you think we could get a table without a reservation?" Notwithstanding the very real possibility she wouldn't be able to hold food in her stomach.

"Good point." Roy turned toward the waterfront.

The day was amazing. The sun was out, and the area was alive with activity. A boat pulled a parasailer, with a parachute the colors of the American flag. Sailboats sliced through the green waters of Puget Sound. White-and-green ferries hauled cars and passengers to a number of islands that dotted the Sound. A Ferris wheel was a recent addition, and the line of tourists waiting for a ride was amazingly long.

"What about a tour of Underground Seattle?" Roy suggested.

"Seattle has an underground?"

Roy nodded. "I read a brochure about it on the ferry. Apparently, Seattle had a large fire in 1890 and most of the buildings in town burned to the ground. When the city was rebuilt, the local government decided to elevate the waterfront area by one floor because of flooding problems with the change in tides."

Maggie vaguely remembered reading about the Seattle fire years ago in her Washington State history class. "And there are underground tours now?"

"That's what the brochure said."

Still, Maggie wasn't sure. "Is there anything to see . . . I mean, if the city burned down, what was left?"

"I can't say, but I think it might be worth checking into, don't you?"

"Sure, if that's what you'd like to do," she said, but at this point she was willing to agree to anything in order to keep her husband's mind occupied. Roy could so easily read her that it wouldn't take much for him to realize that something was terribly wrong.

Her husband pulled the brochure from his hip pocket and opened it across the hood of their vehicle for her to read. "It says here that we purchase the tickets in Pioneer Square." The brochure also listed the times of the tours.

Roy checked his watch. "We'll have plenty of time. It'll be fun just to walk around a bit and explore the city."

"It will," Maggie agreed.

They headed in the direction of Pioneer Square. Roy was in a talkative mood. Maggie did her best to pay attention, but her mind drifted to what she was going to do about this pregnancy. Sooner or later, she'd need to tell Roy. But when? If she held off as long as she could, she feared he'd think of it as an even greater betrayal. If she let him know right away, it would ruin this newfound communication and recommitment to each other. After weeks of this horrible tension between them, Maggie yearned to hold on to his love and goodwill for as long as possible.

". . . What do you think?" Roy asked.

The first part of what her husband said was completely lost on her. "Sorry, I didn't hear that."

"My goodness, Maggie, you seem preoccupied. Is everything all right?"

"It's fine. Wonderful." She pasted on another big smile.

"You're not feeling sick again, are you?"

"Not in the least."

"Good." His leaned over and kissed her.

Pioneer Square wasn't nearly as busy as the market or the waterfront area. Small cafés and restaurants outlined the square.

"That must be close to where the Seahawks play," Roy said, pointing toward CenturyLink Field. "I'm hoping to get us tickets for a game this year."

"I'd like that," Maggie said.

"One day I'll take the boys."

"Give them a couple years so they can fully appreciate it." At the price of the tickets, plus the three-hour drive from Yakima, it became an expensive weekend excursion.

"They'll love it," Roy said. "Now that the kids are five and three, it's a whole new world. Before long, they'll both be in school."

"Let's not rush it," she said, thinking that there were more diapers in their future, only Roy didn't know it yet. And she wasn't about to mention the pregnancy now.

"You said not long ago that you might look for a part-time position once Collin is in school."

"I will," Maggie said, and silently realized that that, too, would now be delayed for a few years. Unless she was forced to find a job in order to support herself . . . if she was no longer married. It was one thing to seek her husband's forgiveness for an indiscretion but another to expect him to love, accept, and raise a child that might not be his. A chill went down her arms at the thought of Roy leaving her. She swallowed a sob, which caught Roy's attention.

"Sweetheart?"

She managed another phony smile. If she made it through this day without giving herself away, it would be a miracle.

"Are you sure you're feeling okay?" he asked, looking concerned.

"It's just that I'm a little overwhelmed by everything."

He frowned, as if he found that hard to believe.

They purchased the tickets for the Underground Seattle tour and then, because they had almost an hour to wait, Roy suggested they eat lunch. The restaurant he chose seemed to have a wide selection of entrées.

"No more fish and chips for you," her husband teased.

"I'm more in the mood for soup," Maggie said.

"Soup?" her husband repeated, and seemed surprised.

Then Maggie remembered that when she was pregnant with both boys the only thing she'd been able to keep down the first few months was soup. It wouldn't take much for him to put two and two together.

"On second thought, the crab cakes sound good." They didn't, but she needed to steer him away from any suspicion that she might be pregnant. Somehow she'd manage to keep the crab down.

The waiter came for their order and Roy asked for a French dip. Oh dear, this was going to be difficult. The smell of cooked beef always caused her problems when she was pregnant. It might not have been as bad before she had proof positive, but every symptom she'd ever suffered was sure to make itself apparent now.

When she looked up, Maggie noticed the waiter was ready to take her order. "The Dungeness crab cakes," she said.

"Excellent choice," he said, as he wrote it down and left them.

Roy's phone rang and he automatically reached for it. Maggie froze, fearing it was Katherine. She already knew that the other woman hadn't taken kindly to having their relationship abruptly severed and had tried a couple times to reach Roy.

"Who is it?" she asked.

His gaze met hers, and his look told Maggie that her suspicions were well grounded.

"Don't worry, I'm not going to answer it."

"I thought you blocked her number."

"I did, but she isn't calling from her cell. This is the landline from her house." He pinched his lips together, revealing his disapproval. "I don't know when she's going to get the message; we're finished. I'm sorry, sweetheart, but you know it's over, right?"

Maggie believed him and then was left to wonder if her news would drive him back to Katherine's more-than-willing arms.

As soon as the call went to voice mail, Roy spent a few minutes on his phone, blocking the other woman's home number.

"I don't want you to have a single doubt about my commitment to you," he said, reaching across the table and gripping hold of her fingers with his own. "I feel better about us than I have in months. I don't know what I was thinking ever getting involved with her."

Maggie looked away. "Thank you for loving me," she whispered.

"I'll always love you, Maggie. I knew it when we were in college, which is one reason I wrote that letter. I'm glad you kept it all these years."

"Me, too. I love you . . . I'll always love you, Roy. Always. No matter what happens in the future. Remember that, okay?" Moisture filled her eyes and spilled down her cheeks before she could keep them at bay. Maggie quickly wiped the tears away. "Look at me, getting all emotional," she said, attempting to laugh at herself.

It seemed Roy was about to say something more when the waiter returned with their entrées. "Enjoy," he said.

Maggie took one look at Roy's sandwich and nearly gagged. If he noticed, he didn't say anything. Then, as if he hadn't eaten in weeks, Roy wolfed down his lunch while she picked at her crab cakes.

The waiter noticed her lack of appetite when he came to clear away their plates. "Was there something wrong with the entrée, Miss?" he asked.

Maggie assured him with a quick shake of her head. "I guess I wasn't as hungry as I thought."

He removed her plate, and Maggie made a show of looking at her wrist. "It's just about time for the tour," she said, more than grateful for the distraction.

Roy stood and paid their tab. Then, together, they walked over to where a small group of tourists had assembled, awaiting the tour.

The guide collected their tickets and then led them through a restaurant and down the stairs to the underground area.

As Maggie suspected, there wasn't a whole lot to see, but the guide was full of stories regarding Seattle's early history, telling anecdote after anecdote that had the group entertained and laughing.

"That was great," Maggie heard the woman in front of her comment as they left the tour.

"Really good," someone else said.

"What did you think?" Maggie asked Roy.

"It was okay."

"Roy, it was wonderful." Like the others, Maggie had been amused and educated at the same time. And, bless her, the guide had helped Maggie keep her mind off how unsettled her stomach felt.

"I think it's time we got back to the inn," Roy surprised her by suggesting.

"Are you sure? We still have time to visit the Seattle Center if you like."

"Another time," he said. "Is that all right with you?"

"It's fine; whatever you want." She didn't know why she protested. Getting back to the inn was exactly what she wanted. She yawned once, feeling like she needed a nap. If she fell asleep in the car on the drive back, Roy was sure to guess. She never took naps . . . unless she was sick or pregnant.

They walked back to the parking lot, and she noticed that once more Roy reached for her hand the way he had earlier in the day. She chanced a look in his direction but couldn't read his thoughts. Testing the waters, she offered him a tentative smile.

He smiled back.

Her relief was instantaneous. She could keep her secret a little bit longer.

"What if I buy us a bottle of wine?" Roy suggested. "We can have the cheese, bread, grapes, and wine on the lawn at the inn. That would be a perfect way to end our afternoon, don't you think?"

"It's a lovely idea." Maggie would find a convenient excuse to avoid the wine. She'd always watched her diet whenever she was pregnant, and she wouldn't do anything less this time.

"Shall we drive back instead of the ferry?"

That had been their original plan.

"Sure, and stop at the car museum in Tacoma?" Her husband's look was hopeful.

Maggie smiled and nodded. She'd never paid that much attention to cars, but they were a passion with Roy, who subscribed to a number of car magazines.

Finding their way to the freeway seemed a challenge, but once they were on the main thoroughfare, Maggie relaxed and, despite her best effort, found herself drifting off to sleep.

She shook herself awake and found Roy studying her. "My goodness, what's wrong with you?" he asked. "You've slept more this weekend than you have in the last two years. This last month has been stressful, hasn't it?"

Maggie agreed. "It has."

"Well, you'll get a chance to catch up now. We've weathered this storm, Maggie girl, and our marriage is stronger for it, don't you think?"

What Roy didn't know was that they had even deeper waters to traverse. Nor did he realize that they were about to get caught up in hurricane-force winds.

Chapter 20

~

Ellie hurried to where she'd agreed to meet her father. Her head was spinning as questions hurled themselves at her so quickly it was all she could do to keep focused on where she was walking. Excitement mingled with anxiety about what she would say to this man who was her father and yet a stranger.

In his text message back to her, Tom had suggested the Pot Belly Deli as a good place for Ellie to meet with Scott. It was close and convenient. Looking at the street map provided by Jo Marie, she noticed the deli was next to the hair salon where she'd been the day before. The salon appointment reminded Ellie of everything she had done to impress Tom and the chance she'd taken meeting him. Yet all she'd meant to him was the means to an end. She was just a charity project, a gift for his stepfather.

Seeing that it was the middle of the afternoon, the lunch crowd had already eaten and it was too early for dinner, so there were plenty of empty tables. They would have the privacy they needed. This would be the first time in her life that she'd have the opportunity to talk to the man responsible for her birth, the first time she'd have a chance to hear his side of what had happened in her parents' marriage.

Scott was seated in a booth when she arrived at the deli. He looked up, saw it was her, and offered her what could only be described as a tentative, guilt-ridden smile. As she approached the table, he stood. Ellie glanced around the room to be certain Tom wasn't anywhere close by. She remained angry and upset by his deception, and while she was willing to meet with her father, she wasn't ready to deal with Tom.

As it was, her nerves were stretched to the snapping point seeing Scott Reynolds.

"Thank you for agreeing to meet with me," he said. He looked as nervous as Ellie felt. He folded his hands on the tabletop as if unsure what to do with them. Before she realized what she was doing, Ellie reached for a fork and ran her fingers down the handle. Embarrassed, she set it aside.

Her mouth had gone dry, so she said nothing.

Neither spoke. Scott studied Ellie for a long moment. "You look like your mother," he said, gazing at her so intently that Ellie was forced to look away.

The waitress came, and they both ordered coffee.

As soon as the woman left, Scott returned his attention to her. "How is your mother?"

"She's well."

"I imagine you're angry with me."

Actually, her anger was directed at Tom. She had yet to form an opinion of Scott. Part of her wanted to reach out and hug him and another part wanted to shout at him in fury for the years he'd ignored her.

"Tell me," she said, trying hard to keep her voice level and void of emotion, "in all the years you were out of my life, did you ever wonder about me?" This was the first of many questions that came to mind. The first one that demanded an answer.

"Every single day." His eyes didn't waver from hers. "Not a day went by that I didn't think about you. We might have been apart, but you were right next to my heart, Ellie. Always and forever. I thought about you on your birthday, at Christmas. I wondered how you did in school and if you played the piano the way your mother and grandmother did. I lay awake at night dreaming of the little girl I barely had a chance to know, although I've loved you your entire life."

Ellie wanted to believe him, but she'd seen precious little evidence of it. She hated to be cynical, but she found his declaration of love hard to fathom. "But you never . . . not even once took the time to write or call or contact me."

"No," he said, and hung his head as if the weight of his failure as her father demanded that he look away. "When your mother and I first split, I did everything within my power to get visitation rights."

"I suppose you're going to tell me my mother made that impossible."

"No," Scott corrected. "I think your mother would have been more than willing to allow you to spend time with me on weekends. It was your grandparents. From the first, I rubbed them the wrong way. They had someone else in mind for your mother to marry, some rich guy who was the son of a longtime family friend." His mouth tightened, and anger fired in his eyes.

He stopped talking, and Ellie could see the tension in his squared shoulders.

Then he said, "It does no good to rehash old hurts. The only reason I mention it is so you'll understand that I did my best, but I couldn't afford expensive attorney fees and your grandparents could. They wanted me out of your life and made sure it happened."

"My grandparents are both gone now," Ellie told him, and they had been for a long time. Surely he must have realized that.

"I figured they must be."

"You could have found me. I'm an adult now, and I make my own decisions."

He didn't argue with her. "You're right, of course."

"Then why didn't you?"

He looked down at his hands and she noticed that he'd shredded the paper napkin into a neat stack. "I don't have a good excuse. I guess I was afraid."

"Afraid of what?" She wasn't that intimidating.

It took Scott a long time to answer, and when he did, he couldn't have surprised her more. "I was afraid of you."

"Of me?" She pressed her hand against her chest. "Of me?" she repeated, still unable to take it in. "But why?"

"I was sure you must hate me."

"How could I hate you when I don't know you?" Ellie returned, her voice elevated until she captured the attention of those around her.

Their coffee was delivered, and Ellie reached for two packets of sugar.

Scott reached for two packets of sugar.

Ellie reached for two cream containers.

Scott reached for two cream containers.

Ellie held her spoon with her left hand and stirred counterclockwise.

Scott stirred his coffee counterclockwise, holding the spoon with his left hand.

Ellie watched him mimic her movements. "Do you always drink your coffee with two sugars and two creams?" she asked.

He stared at her just as intently. "Do you always stir your coffee counterclockwise?"

Ellie nodded. "Do you?"

Scott nodded, and then a slow, easy smile started to take shape, transforming his mouth from a worried frown to a smile of delight and pleasure.

"Tell me why you were afraid of me," she said, less demanding now that she was more at ease. Although they were virtual strangers, they were more alike than she would have ever guessed.

It took him a while to formulate his answer. "For all you knew, I'd abandoned you. I couldn't be sure what your grandparents had said about me, if they'd mentioned me at all. Or what your mother had told you about the two of us."

He sipped his coffee, and Ellie noticed that his forehead had creased with a thoughtful frown.

"Whatever you heard about me couldn't have been flattering."

"I heard next to nothing," she told him. As a schoolgirl, she'd asked numerous times about her father, but her questions had either been ignored or gone unanswered.

"In other words, as far as you were concerned, I was a nonentity then." A pained look came over him.

"No," she said. "Twice, once when I was young and again later, I asked Mom to find you because I wanted to write you a letter." She'd asked a lot more often, wanting details about her father, but quickly learned Scott Reynolds was a subject best avoided, especially around her grandparents.

"How old were you?"

"Around five, I think, the first time. I wanted a certain doll for my birthday, and in my mind I thought you would want to buy it for me."

"Did you write me?" he asked. He leaned closer to hear her answer.

"No, it wasn't necessary. Grandpa bought me the doll." Ellie remembered how upset her grandmother had been when Ellie had announced she wanted to write her daddy a letter. She was too young to remember much of the incident other than her seeing the tears in her mother's eyes that night when Virginia tucked Ellie in bed and listened to her prayers. Ellie had reached up and wiped the tear off her mother's cheek. When she'd asked her mother why she was crying, Virginia had hugged her and said that she was sad. Ellie had never understood why her mother would be unhappy until now.

"When I graduated from high school I wanted to write you then, too," she explained.

"And your mother wouldn't let you?" Again the pained look showed in his eyes.

"She claimed she didn't know where or how to reach you."

"I'd left Oregon by that time and moved to Cedar Cove." His hands cradled the coffee mug, and he looked down into the milky liquid. "I remarried when you were around three. I was lonely, and Deana was a widow who had her hands full with two young boys."

"Tom and his brother."

"Yes."

"Did they know about me?"

"No, but every year on your birthday I brought home a cake. They never did figure it out, and that was all right by me. Talking about the daughter I'd never had the opportunity to know would have been too painful."

"But you told Tom." She found it difficult to say his name, seeing how he'd used and manipulated her.

"After Deana passed away so unexpectedly, I realized life holds no guarantees. I told Tom about you and how I'd failed you. My deepest regret was not fighting to have you in my life."

"And so Tom took the matter upon himself . . ."

"I would have stopped him had I known what he intended to do," Scott assured her. "Which, I think, he must have suspected, because he didn't say a word to me until this morning."

"He didn't say a word to me, either," she muttered, with more than a hint of bitterness.

"Please don't be angry with Tom," her father pleaded. "I believe he genuinely cares for you, Ellie."

Ellie shook her head, refusing to believe it.

Her father held up his hand. "I'll leave that for the two of you to settle."

As far as Ellie was concerned, the matter was already resolved in her mind. From this point forward, she never wanted to see or speak to Tom again. What he'd done wouldn't soon be forgotten.

"Tom was afraid I'd never get the courage to reach out to you, and, sad as this is to admit, he's probably right." He swallowed tightly and then boldly met her look. "Can you forgive me for all these years of silence, Ellie?"

Ellie wasn't quite sure how to answer. "I'd like to have my father in my life."

"I'd enjoy getting to know my daughter, too." He smiled then, a genuine smile. "Now tell me everything."

"Everything?"

"What do you do for a living? Do you like to read fiction? Do you play the piano?" The questions rolled off his tongue with such ease Ellie had to believe he'd stored them up for years.

Taking a breath, she answered him, one question after another. "I'm part of a company that helps people organize their homes or businesses and sometimes their lives. And yes, I love fiction. I'm constantly reading. And I do play the piano."

"Me, too." Scott beamed at her answer. "Who was your first love?"

"A boy named Dusty, and he kissed me when we were both four years old. He promised to marry me, but he went the way of all my love interests." She couldn't keep from laughing.

"Did you graduate at the top of your class?"

"I did," she told him.

"I knew it. Your mother was the intelligent one. Did you know she was valedictorian of her high school class? Of course you did. She never liked to brag about her high IQ, but your grandfather found a reason to bring it up in every conversation. He wasn't a bad man, your grandfather, just overly protective."

They spoke for a full hour and went through two more cups of coffee. "Can I see you later?" Scott asked. "Can we meet again? I'd like to take you to dinner."

"Yes, I'd like that," Ellie assured him. It wouldn't be long before she spoke to her mother, and Ellie realized this wasn't something she could keep from Virginia. If Scott had regrets regarding his relationship with her, she wondered how he felt about the woman he'd left behind. "Is there anything you'd like me to tell my mother?"

For the very briefest of moments, Scott's eyes brightened, and then his face went taut as he shook his head. "No . . . nothing. But please let her know I wish her well."

"Mom never remarried, you know."

His head came up, and it was impossible to ignore the surprise in his eyes. "Never?"

"She dated Wally for years."

"Walter Keller," her father said, frowning. "That's the man her parents wanted her to marry. What happened?"

"He died a few years back of a heart attack. It was very sudden and very sad."

"Why didn't your mother marry him? I assumed that once I was out of the picture he'd make his move."

Ellie didn't know the answer. "You'll need to ask her. I think Wally would have liked it if they'd married, but frankly I don't think Mom was interested."

Her father shook his head as if he didn't know what to say.

When it was time to leave Scott asked, "Did you park close by?"

"No, I walked down from where I'm staying."

"Rose Harbor Inn?" Scott said. "Tom mentioned it."

Ellie stiffened just hearing Tom's name. Scott pressed his hand on her forearm and looked her straight in the eye. "Give Tom a chance, Ellie. At least hear him out. His heart was in the right place."

"Maybe I will," she muttered, "but not right away. I need to think this through."

It seemed like Scott wanted to say more but stopped himself.

They set a time and place to meet again later for dinner, and then it was time to go. Scott paid for their coffee and held open the door for her. He was a good-looking man, her father, and because her attention was focused on him, she didn't notice who stood right outside the deli.

"Ellie."

It was Tom. His eyes held hers for the longest moment. "Can we talk?" he asked. "Please let me explain."

Ellie looked toward Scott, unsure what to do. His face was blank, giving her no indication of his expectations.

It would be easy to give in, especially now that she'd spoken to her father. She wasn't sure she could trust Tom again, nor was she completely convinced she should trust Scott.

"No . . ." she whispered. "I don't think that would be a good idea. I've said everything I have to say to you already, Tom. Let's leave it at that."

Chapter 21

I left Mark's house and headed down the hill to the Saturday farm-ers' market, keen on picking up a supply of fresh blueberries and a few baked goods and what I needed for the dinner with my family. I'd meant to get there earlier but had gotten distracted.

Rover enjoyed visiting the market; he got the opportunity to meet up with a number of his dog friends. Several of the vendors were dog owners, and the local animal shelter maintained a booth at the Saturday market. We stopped by each week, and Rover and his friends sniffed butts!

He tugged against the leash in his eagerness to get down the hill, his ears alert. The market is set up in the waterfront park area be-hind the library. I saw that the vendor from Hood Canal was selling fresh clams and oysters this week in addition to Hood Canal shrimp.

Personally, I have a weakness for steamed clams and decided to splurge on myself. I'd steam them for dinner and save the broth for homemade clam chowder later in the week. I hoped he had fresh salmon in addition to the other seafood. I'd make a green salad from the lettuce in my garden and dig up a few new potatoes. My mind was so preoccupied with all that I needed to purchase that I walked right past Grace Harding.

"Jo Marie," she said, stopping me.

"Grace. Hello. My goodness, I don't know where my head is," I said, laughing at myself.

"How are you?" Grace asked, her own arms loaded down with produce and fresh flowers.

"Great." We saw each other in passing once or twice a week, but it'd been a while since we'd spent any real time together. Life gets busy for her and for me. Grace was the head librarian and a wise friend who'd helped me through the shock and grief when my husband's remains had been positively identified. I'd waited more than a year after his death to receive the final word, much the same as Grace had waited to learn the fate of her first husband, Dan Sherman.

Rover barked, demanding Grace's attention. In her spare time, Grace volunteered at the local animal shelter. She was the one responsible for bringing Rover into my life. She didn't have Beau, her golden retriever, with her, and Rover seemed disappointed.

"I mean how are you, really?" she asked again.

Unsure what to tell her, I shrugged. "I'm doing better, I think." I'd had almost two years to get accustomed to widowhood. Time, however, did little to relieve that deep sense of loss and pain. Even now Paul remained in the forefront of my mind and I didn't expect that to change anytime soon. Not a day passed when he wasn't with me in one way or another. I often found myself talking to him almost as if I expected him to answer. I thought to mention the little things—that felt like big things—that I'd noticed I'd lost regarding my husband, but this wasn't the time or the place.

"And how is Rover?" Grace asked, directing the question to my canine friend.

Rover sat on his haunches, and Grace bent down and rubbed his ears. He stretched his chin toward her, and Grace obligingly ran her hand down the underside of his chin.

Looking back at me, she said, "I read an interesting article recently having to do with therapy dogs."

"Seeing Eye Dogs?" I asked.

"Well, I suppose a few of them might be, but this had to do with men returning from Iraq and Afghanistan who'd suffered traumatic physical and emotional wounds. The military had taken to giving them therapy dogs as companions."

Rover had certainly been a companion to me.

"The article said these dogs were extremely helpful to these men and women, offering companionship and comfort. The piece called them 'comfort dogs.' " Her gaze held mine. "I remember you telling me the story of you and Rover and how *he* chose you."

"Rover is my comfort dog," I said. Out of the corner of my eye, I saw Mark was at the market, weaving his way between booths, chatting with Bob Beldon. The two were clearly friends and seemed to be enjoying the conversation.

"I had Buttercup," Grace said, redirecting my attention back to her. Right away I noticed that her eyes had grown thoughtful and sad.

"Buttercup?" I repeated. Beau was the only pet I knew about.

"She died a few years back, and it nearly broke my heart. The interesting part is that I got Buttercup through Charlotte Rhodes, Judge Olivia's mother, shortly after Dan disappeared. Olivia's my best friend. Buttercup was *my* comfort dog." Grace glanced at her wrist. "Oh my goodness, I'm late. My husband and I are babysitting grandchildren this afternoon. I better scoot. Good to see you," she said and gave me a quick hug.

Then before I could say anything more she was off, rushing

toward the library parking lot. I debated whether to seek Mark out or not and felt I wouldn't.

Rover regarded me as if he, too, was wrestling with the decision. Once Grace was gone, I headed toward the fruit vendor and purchased an abundant supply of freshly picked blueberries and had to resist munching on them. They were ripe and oversized, and sweet. The farmer told me she'd picked them that very morning. I'd use them for more than the blueberry muffins. Blueberry pie was one of my brother's favorites, and I'd bake one for him for our Sunday dinner.

I had the blueberries in a bag over my arm when I saw Corrie McAfee. She waved, and, because my hands were full, I nodded back. I pulled on Rover's leash when I saw her weaving through the crowd to get to me.

"Jo Marie," Corrie said, sounding a bit breathless. "You're just the person I was hoping to see."

"Oh?"

"I had a chat this morning with Peggy Beldon."

I knew the two women were best friends and were often together.

"Peggy mentioned you were interested in finding out what you could about Mark Taylor."

My stomach sank. I'd let my curiosity get out of hand. I regretted ever having asked Peggy about Mark. It embarrassed me now, especially since word of my interest had gotten out.

"Not really," I said, with a halfhearted shrug.

"Oh, sorry, I thought Peggy said—"

"I did ask her a few questions, but it's nothing important." I hoped I didn't sound overly defensive for fear she would read more into that than warranted.

"I can tell you one thing I know about him that's a bit out of the ordinary," she volunteered.

"Oh?" I probably should have tried harder, but I couldn't hide my interest. I knew so little about Mark, and while it wasn't important, I remained curious.

"Peggy and I both remember when he moved to town. He bought the house off the Internet. A friend of ours who's in real estate said Mark saw the house online, phoned, and without doing anything more than get an inspection, purchased the house. Furthermore, he paid cash."

"He paid cash?" I didn't know anyone with that kind of money.

"Bob met Mark shortly after he moved to town. He recommended him for odd jobs, and we hired Mark to fix a couple things around the house. I found it a bit unusual that a man who could afford to pay cash for a house would then take on odd jobs."

It'd come to my attention a number of times that while Mark was a good worker with a strong work ethic, he didn't seem overly concerned about money.

"Our porch needed the foundation repaired," Corrie continued, interrupting my musings.

I glanced up and blinked.

"Bob said Mark was our man. He gave us an excellent price, did the work in record time, and as they say, the rest is history."

Mark might work efficiently for others, but that hadn't been my experience with him. Thankfully, I didn't pay him by the hour.

"He's a great guy," Corrie said. "I know he's done quite a bit of work for you."

"He has," I agreed.

Corrie frowned and once more her look grew thoughtful. "Something else . . ."

"Yes?" I probably shouldn't be this openly curious.

Corrie looked uncertain if she should say it or not, but apparently decided she should. "I think he might have served in the military."

That was an interesting observation. "What makes you think that?" I'd never heard Mark make any reference to having been in the service, but that wasn't unusual.

"A while back," Corrie said, "I ordered a bookcase made in Scandinavia, and when it arrived the instructions were in Swedish.

The kit came with pictures, but it was impossible for either Roy or me to follow the illustrations without understanding the written instructions. I was utterly frustrated, and after several tries, Roy was, too. Exasperated, he contacted Mark and asked if he could assemble the project. We were both shocked at how quickly Mark managed to build that bookcase. He had it together in no time. And the thing is, I swear he could read the language."

"It's a leap to assume he'd been military, don't you think?" I said, wondering how Corrie had made the connection.

"Perhaps, but I had that impression a couple other times as well. Roy, too, and my husband has a talent for sensing things about people. He knows a bit of German, and when he asked Mark a question in the language, Mark answered him back in German. It came so easily to him that I have to believe he must be a linguist."

"Mark?" This was an entirely different side of him that I had never seen. It troubled me that I could consider Mark a close friend and know so little about his background.

"I know you said you weren't all that interested in digging up information about Mark," Corrie said, and tapped her index finger against her lips as if mulling over a thought. "But if you change your mind, Roy could help."

I knew Corrie's husband was a retired Seattle policeman turned part-time private eye, but hiring him to investigate Mark was above and beyond anything I would ever consider. Before I could assure her I wasn't interested, Corrie continued.

"Roy knows people who know people who could dig up everything there is to know about Mark Taylor. If you want, I could ask him to find out what he can."

I immediately shook my head. "I appreciate the offer, but no thanks." What I wanted, I realized, was for Mark to trust me enough to voluntarily share his personal history with me. Since moving to Cedar Cove, all the days he'd worked at the inn and we'd shared coffee on the deck or in my kitchen, I was fairly certain he knew practically everything there was to know about me. It stung my pride that I considered him a better friend than he apparently did me.

By now Rover had grown restless and was tugging against the leash, eager to visit his friends. I bid Corrie a good afternoon and then finished my rounds at the market.

By the time we left, my arms were loaded down with clams, salmon, blueberries, fresh ripe tomatoes, French bread, and a bouquet of huge pink dahlias.

Rover wasn't being the least bit cooperative as I headed up the hill. He seemed to feel it was his obligation to mark every blade of grass along the way.

"Come on, Rover," I urged. "This stuff is getting heavy."

"Looks like you could use an extra hand."

I glanced over my shoulder and discovered Mark, walking at a clipped pace directly behind me. Right away I feared he'd overheard me talking to Corrie McAfee . . . about him.

"Hi," I managed.

"Would you like some help with that?"

My cheeks felt hot, and I was convinced they'd filled with color. It would be embarrassing in the extreme if he had overheard us.

"You feeling all right?" he asked, frowning at me.

"Ah . . . why shouldn't I feel okay?" I said, and immediately wanted to bite back the words, knowing they came off a bit gruff and defensive.

Mark did a double take. "I don't know. You tell me."

"Nothing to tell you," I said.

"Do you want help or not?"

My arms ached to the point my upper arm muscles quivered. By this point, Rover was half dragging me up the hill.

"Your choice," Mark said, and hightailed it past me as if I stood still.

"Okay," I called after him. "Please."

He turned back and grinned as if he'd won a verbal battle. "You're in a quirky mood this afternoon."

"Sorry."

He took the heaviest packages, leaving me with the blueberries and the French bread.

We started up the steepest part of the hill. I grew winded faster than Mark, who barely breathed hard. Last winter, after a snowfall, the street had been closed to traffic because it was so steep and dangerously slippery. I had to admit walking up it was good exercise.

"I saw you chatting with Corrie McAfee," Mark mentioned casually. "You both seemed pretty intense."

I swallowed hard. This was what I was afraid would happen. He seemed to be waiting for me to fill him in on my conversation, but, by heaven, if he could keep secrets, then so could I. My mouth was firmly closed. I said nothing, which is what he generally did when I asked him a question he didn't want to answer.

"Everything good with Corrie and Roy?" he asked.

"I assume so." He'd need to torture anything more out of me.

"They're a nice couple."

"I think so, too," I said, eager to agree with him. "Did you know Roy is a retired Seattle detective?" I asked.

"I heard as part of his services he does background checks." Mark looked straight ahead as he spoke.

I swear my vocal cords went numb for two or three seconds. "Oh?"

"You knew that, Jo Marie, admit it."

I pretended indifference and shrugged.

"Are you tempted to hire him?"

"Do I need anyone investigated?" I asked, preferring not to answer his question.

Mark laughed, he actually laughed, and I had the distinct feeling he was toying with me.

It seemed the best approach was a more direct one. "What are you hiding, Mark?"

"Hiding?" he repeated. "Do you honestly think I'm purposely hiding? From what? From whom?"

"I don't know, that's why I'm asking."

"There's nothing to tell."

"You mean there's nothing you *want* to tell."

His eyes grew dark and serious. "You're right. There's nothing I *want* to tell. Leave it at that, Jo Marie."

Chapter 22

~

Maggie had trouble keeping her eyes open as Roy drove south on I-5 toward Tacoma and the car museum. Two or three times she'd drifted off to sleep only to abruptly shake herself awake.

"My goodness, you're a sleepyhead," Roy commented, taking his eyes off the road to glance her way. He seemed to find her inability to stay awake amusing.

"It's the warm car and the chill music," she said, in an effort to distract him from the real reason.

"Maybe I should change to a heavy-metal station," her husband teased.

"Not a bad idea." She managed a smile and hit the scan button on the radio until they landed on a station that played classic rock, which they both enjoyed. The loud beat filled the car, music that they'd listened to while dating.

"You're being a good sport about this car thing," Roy said, and reached across the seat to gently squeeze her hand.

"You're a car freak." She wasn't telling him anything he didn't already know. He'd been wonderfully patient when she'd searched out antique buttons. It felt good to give him this small pleasure. She hoped he would remember this later and think kindly of her.

He hadn't said a word when they'd passed the classic car museum next to the Tacoma Dome just off the interstate on the trip over from Yakima. He couldn't help but notice it. At the time, she remembered, they'd barely been speaking. His eyes had lit up when Jo Marie mentioned it, too. Maggie wasn't that keen on motorized vehicles. As long as they got her to and from where she needed to go and the car was safe for her children, she was content.

Not so with Roy. When shopping for their last family car, Roy had a detailed list of features as long as Jaxon and Collin's letters to Santa. All she requested was that the new car be blue. They ended up with a white vehicle, because that was the only one in a three-state area that offered all the amenities Roy required. Maggie was fine with the color, although she would have preferred blue.

"Do you remember what I said to you shortly after Collin was born?" Roy said, chuckling.

"Like I could forget." Exhausted from the long labor, Maggie had fallen into an elated sleep. After their newborn son had been bathed, weighed, and measured, and the grandparents notified of the latest addition to their family, Roy had settled down in the hospital room with Maggie. While she slept he read his car magazines and talked about one day teaching his sons to drive. It was his way of telling her how pleased he was to have two sons.

"I remember all too well."

"The museum's not far now," Roy said, as they drove through a community known as Fife.

Maggie could see the Tacoma Dome in the distance and would be grateful to get out of the car. Although she'd barely touched her lunch, her stomach had a queasy feeling that left her feeling sick and light-headed. It was all due to nerves, she suspected. Sweat broke out across her brow, and she pressed her hand against her stomach and prayed her discomfort wasn't obvious.

They exited the freeway, and after driving around a bit, found the museum and a parking spot. Maggie climbed out of the car and took in deep breaths of fresh air, hoping that would help hide her discomfort. One glance in their car's sideview mirror showed her face to be ghastly pale. Her cheeks were devoid of color, and she looked dreadful. Her one hope was that Roy would be paying more attention to the exhibits than he was to her.

If he noticed she was unwell, he thankfully didn't comment.

Roy paid the entrance fee to the museum and they went inside. Her husband's eyes widened with appreciation for the variety of vehicles on display.

"I think I'll find a ladies' room," Maggie said, striving to sound as casual as possible.

"Do you want me to wait for you?"

"No, no, I might be a few minutes. I'll find you."

"Okay." He was eager to explore, and for that Maggie was thankful.

She located the restroom area and hurried inside, nearly stumbling in her eagerness to get into the stall. Almost immediately she lost what little lunch she'd eaten. When she'd finished vomiting, she leaned her shoulder against the cubicle wall, letting it support her. She continued to feel light-headed and dreadfully ill.

"Are you okay?" a woman asked from behind her.

Maggie hadn't taken the time to close the stall door. She turned around to find an older, grandmotherly woman behind her. "I'm fine, thank you." Maggie pressed her hand against her forehead.

"You don't look it, dear. Do you need to sit down?"

"I'll be okay," Maggie insisted. She didn't want anyone making a fuss over her for fear it would bring unwanted attention. Grabbing a handful of toilet tissue, she wadded it up and wiped her mouth clean.

"Let me see if I can get you some water," the older woman offered.

"Thank you," Maggie whispered. She needed to rinse out her mouth, and longingly dreamed of a nice soft bed that she could crawl into and curl up in a fetal position.

The woman returned with a paper cup and another woman who worked for the museum.

"Can I get you anything?" the second woman asked.

"Please, I don't want to be a bother."

"It's no bother," the museum employee insisted. "Shall I call someone for you?"

"No, no, my husband is here and I don't want to ruin this for him."

"I understand," the older woman said. "Henry loves these classic cars. My goodness, he dragged me all the way from Olympia just so we could stop by this car museum."

"There's a nice comfortable chair by the entrance, if you feel you need to sit down," the attendant told her, and seeing that there wasn't anything more she could do, she left.

The older woman studied Maggie. "I had the same problem when I was pregnant," she said, lowering her voice. "The first three months were dreadful for me. I couldn't keep a single thing down."

Maggie wasn't about to confirm her condition to this stranger. It would be just her luck to run into the woman later when Roy was close enough to hear and have her spout off something about the pregnancy.

"I think it was something that disagreed with me at lunch," Maggie offered, hoping to turn the woman's suspicions elsewhere.

The woman frowned. "My dear, I've worked as a nurse for a GYN for nearly thirty years. I know the look, and you've got it in spades. If you don't believe me, make an appointment with your doctor or buy one of those pregnancy tests."

Maggie pretended surprise. "Maybe I will," she murmured, not meeting the other woman's gaze. "I . . . I better find my husband," she said, eager to escape.

It took Maggie only a few minutes to locate Roy, who had his eyes on a classic 1936 Mercedes-Benz 540K. He walked all the way around the vehicle with his hands in his pockets as if he was half afraid he would reach out and touch the car like a priceless piece of artwork.

For a few minutes he didn't seem to notice Maggie was beside him. "It's in mint condition," he said, keeping his voice low and reverent, as though speaking in church.

Maggie followed Roy while he admired a number of other vehicles, but she could feel herself growing tired and weak. "Would you mind if I sat down for a bit?" she asked, hoping to downplay her almost desperate need to rest.

She shouldn't have asked, because Roy, who'd bent over to inspect the inside of a 1960 bright yellow Chevy Corvette, straightened and then focused his attention on her.

"Maggie, are you feeling all right?"

"Of course," she said, almost flippantly. "These shoes are a bit tight, and we've done a lot of walking today. I thought I'd take a load off my feet."

"Do you want to go back to the inn?" he asked, as he continued to study her, his eyes filled with concern.

"Not in the least." So she lied. "I'll be by the entrance. I saw a chair there earlier."

Roy hesitated. "I'll hurry through the rest of the museum."

"Please don't. Not on my account. I'm perfectly content to sit for a while. Enjoy yourself and take as much time as you want."

He studied her as if he wasn't sure he should believe her. "This isn't like you."

"What isn't?" she asked, and forced a small laugh.

"Being this patient."

"Roy, that's completely unfair. Even if it was true, don't you think you should take advantage of my generosity and count your blessings?"

"Okay, okay, you're right. Go make yourself comfortable and I'll finish going through the museum."

"Take however long you want."

Again his look told her he was mildly suspicious.

Grateful to leave her husband, Maggie returned to the spot the museum attendant had mentioned earlier. She sank into the padded chair, leaned her head back, and closed her eyes. It felt incredibly good to be off her feet. Almost right away she felt better than she had all day.

She didn't know how long she remained in the chair before Roy came to get her.

"This collection is amazing," he said, and sounded as excited and pleased as their son Jaxon after spending an hour in the park climbing on the playground equipment. "Thanks, honey," Roy said.

"You're most welcome." She was pleased they were able to do something he enjoyed.

"The next time you want to drag me to a chick movie, I promise not to complain."

"That's a fair trade," she said, with a grin, and looped her arm around his.

They started out the exit and were joined by the older woman Maggie had met in the ladies' restroom. With everything in her she silently pleaded with the other woman not to mention their first meeting or her suspicions.

"Hello again," the woman said, and either she hadn't seen or ignored Maggie's plea.

"Hello," Maggie said casually, letting it be known with the lack of warmth in her reply that she wasn't interested in exchanging chitchat.

"Are you feeling better?" the woman asked, hurrying to catch up with Maggie and Roy.

"Much, thank you." She nearly collapsed with relief when the couple headed in the opposite direction once they left the museum.

"You weren't feeling well again?" Roy asked.

"I'm feeling great." Which was a small exaggeration, but Maggie had discovered she was beginning to get better with this subterfuge.

"You don't look it, Maggie. In fact, you look a bit pale."

They reached their car and Maggie made a show of looking in the sideview mirror once again. "I am?"

"Don't you see it?"

"Maybe I have a touch of the flu," she said, hoping Roy would accept the excuse and leave it at that.

"Do you want me to find one of those walk-in medical clinics?"

"Don't be ridiculous," she said, and laughed off his suggestion.

"I hate the thought of you being sick."

"I feel better already."

He frowned in her direction, and it was apparent he didn't believe her. "Shall we return to the inn?" he asked.

"I suppose," she said, as if it was of little difference to her. "Unless there's some place else you'd like to explore."

"The Museum of Glass is just down the road," Roy reminded her.

In other circumstances Maggie would have enjoyed viewing the famous museum and visiting the gift shop, but not now. Her hesitation told Roy all he needed to know.

"You want to go back to the inn."

She hated to put a damper on their weekend, but she really was sick. "Maybe that would be for the best."

"Then you aren't feeling as well as you claim."

"I'm just a bit under the weather," she said, once more brushing off his concern.

He started the car and without much of a problem returned to the freeway. "If I didn't know better I'd think you were pregnant," he said, and the moment the words were out of his mouth, he went completely still.

For one wild second Maggie was afraid he was about to pull off to the side of the road.

Neither said anything for several heart-stopping moments.

"You're taking birth-control pills, right?" Roy asked, his words tight and strange. He hardly sounded like himself.

"Of course I am," she assured him, hoping to sound calm and confident.

"Every single day?" he pressed.

"I might have missed a few times," she confessed. Actually, Maggie had all but abandoned the pill. It hadn't been a conscious decision. At first she'd simply forgotten, and really, what was the point? They'd made love only twice in the last month . . . it'd been his lack of sexual appetite that had alerted Maggie that there was something wrong with their marriage. That *something* turned out to be *someone,* and that someone turned out to be Katherine.

"Maggie." Roy whispered her name almost as if he had trouble speaking. "I notice you didn't immediately assure me you aren't pregnant."

"I didn't?" she asked, stalling.

"Are you or aren't you?" he demanded.

Tension pounded like a gong between them.

"Are you?" he asked again, louder this time.

Hanging her head, Maggie found she couldn't answer him. It might have gone better if she'd told him as soon as her suspicions were confirmed, but she doubted it.

Roy pressed his foot against the gas pedal and the car jerked forward. "I guess that answers that. I'm also guessing you don't have a clue who the father of this baby is."

Chapter 23

"I'm sorry, Ellie. None of this worked out the way I thought it would," Tom said, hurrying after her as she left the deli. Apparently, he refused to accept that she wanted nothing more to do with him. It was hard because she so badly wanted to trust him, but she couldn't allow herself to give in when it was clear he'd used her for his own purposes. She might be able to look past all that if he'd told her beforehand, if he'd confided in her instead of springing it on her without even a hint of a warning.

The conversation with her father had gone better than she'd expected, although there remained a lot of unanswered questions. She hoped they'd be able to talk more over dinner. It was clear there was no love lost between him and her grandparents, but Ellie didn't know what role her mother had played in the breakup of the marriage.

"Ellie," Tom said, keeping his steps in tune with hers. "Say something."

She glanced at him, hardly knowing how to communicate her feelings, which remained mixed. She was terribly confused.

"What did you expect would happen?" Ellie asked, gesturing with her hands. A lot of her anger remained. She wouldn't, couldn't, dismiss his subterfuge lightly. He'd misled her in more ways than the obvious. She'd trusted Tom, and he'd abused that trust.

"I felt terrible after you left the waterfront," Tom said.

"Not any more than I did," she returned stiffly. "How could you use me like this, Tom? How could you?"

"I never meant to hurt you."

"You should have thought of that long before now." She couldn't imagine what he'd been thinking. Nor had he considered how she'd react once she discovered what he'd done. Clearly, he hadn't thought matters through. It seemed to her that after he'd introduced her to Scott he intended to melt into the background. His role was finished, and so he was done with her as well.

"The look in your eyes broke my heart. I can't leave matters as they are, I just can't."

Ellie had nothing to say to that.

"I wanted to tell you before you met Scott," he continued. "I fully intended to explain everything Friday night, and found I couldn't, not so soon. You were so beautiful and you'd taken this big leap toward independence and I didn't have the heart to destroy your faith in me so soon. I was wrong, Ellie. I'm so sorry."

"You should have told me rather than springing it on me unexpectedly like this." Ellie wasn't sure how she would have dealt with the news, but she would have at least had a chance to process it. In some ways it would have been easier to deal with on Friday than it was now. If he'd told her when he'd first come to the inn, it would have been a shock, yes, but she would have known then. But to hit her with it after their dinner date and sailing, after they'd kissed and looked into each other's eyes . . . the wound cut deeper, and made his betrayal feel more intense.

"I couldn't be more sorry, but we met and it felt so good to be with you and to kiss you," he whispered. "I was afraid that if you found out what I'd done you wouldn't want anything more to do with me . . . I wanted that extra time with you. I hoped that after we were together you'd be willing to . . . hell, I don't know what I thought would happen when you met your father. I did this for him, but then later I realized it was for myself. I fell for you, Ellie. I'm not exaggerating or making excuses or anything else. All I want is another chance with you. I'm in love with you. If you believe nothing else, believe that. I love you."

Ellie shook her head as though to shake off his words. She needed more time. Her emotions felt like golf ball–size bits of hail pounding down on her from all sides. She'd met her father. *Her father.* This was the man she'd never had the chance to know. She'd met Scott through Tom, the man she loved, only to discover that Tom had manipulated her, and now he was saying he loved her. It was too much to absorb all at once. She needed to sort everything out in her head before she could deal with Tom.

He started to speak again, but Ellie raised her hand, stopping him. "Give me time."

"How long?"

"I don't know . . ."

"You'll talk to me, though, right? Sometime . . . soon."

She agreed with a simple nod and then held out her hand silently asking him to back away, letting him know she wanted to continue back to the inn on her own. Tom reluctantly slowed his pace and eventually dropped back, letting her go on without him. When she reached the top of the hill she glanced over her shoulder and found Tom standing on the sidewalk with his shoulders slouched, looking as if the world had come crashing down on him.

Ellie continued on toward the inn, her head and her heart in turmoil. Her temple pounded with the beginning of a headache. As soon as she was back in her room, she swallowed two aspirin and lay down to close her eyes. Just as the shock and tension were starting to leave her body and she was beginning to relax, her phone rang. Because she had half expected something like this would happen, Ellie had kept her cell on the bed next to her. A quick glance told her it was her mother.

"Hi, Mom."

"Ellie?" Her mother didn't bother to hide her surprise. "You're actually going to talk to me?"

"Yes . . ."

Right away her mother sensed something had happened. "Honey, what's wrong?"

"Oh Mom . . ."

"Tell me. I can hear it in your voice. It's something bad, isn't it? You know you can tell me anything. Oh sweet heaven, this is exactly what I feared would happen. You know—"

"Mom, stop," Ellie demanded, abruptly cutting her off. She sat up on the mattress, her back against the headboard, and pressed her fingertips against her throbbing temple.

Her mother sucked in her breath, which seemed to vibrate over the phone. "Tell me, just tell me."

Ellie's soft intake echoed that of her mother. "I met my father."

Silence.

Absolute silence.

"Mom, did you hear me?"

"Yes." Virginia's voice was barely above a whisper. "How did that happen?"

Ellie hardly knew where to start, so she gave the short version. "Tom is my father's stepson." Right away, she could sense her mother's indignation, which matched her own.

"They tricked you."

"Yes, Tom tricked me." It'd been a shock, to say the least, but now Ellie had had time to absorb part of it. Yes, she was badly shaken, but she could deal with that; it was everything that had happened since that upset her most. Despite what Tom claimed, it was obvious her so-called father hadn't tried nearly hard enough to connect with her as a child, or even later as an adult.

"Come home," Virginia insisted. "Pack your suitcase and leave for home right away. I can't believe this has happened . . . of all the low, underhanded schemes."

"Mom, there's more . . ."

"More?" Once again, it seemed her mother was shocked into silence.

"I talked to him."

"You actually talked to your father?"

"Yes, and I'm meeting him later for dinner."

"Eleanor . . . no. Absolutely not. I won't allow it." Her mother's voice trembled, but it wasn't with anger. It was a tone Ellie didn't recognize, a plea more than a demand. Was it fear she heard? Regret? It sounded almost identical to what she'd heard in her father's voice when speaking about her mother.

"Why should I scurry back to Oregon?" Ellie asked.

"Ellie, you can't seriously consider staying the rest of the weekend. Not after this. Tom didn't tell you he was Scott's stepson. He misled you, and it only makes sense that Scott was part of this underhanded scheme, too. The only sensible response is to walk out now, before either man hurts you further."

"Mom, I've already agreed to meet my father for dinner."

"But—"

"I have questions only my father can answer."

A noise that sounded suspiciously like a sob echoed through the phone. "Oh Ellie, I'm afraid you're setting yourself up for more heartache."

"You could very well be right."

The same noise repeated itself, and now Ellie was convinced her mother was weeping.

"I loved him, you know," Virginia whispered, "loved him more than life itself. We were both so young and proud. How did he look, Ellie? Is he well?"

The questions took Ellie by surprise. She'd expected a diatribe or some form of denunciation instead of an inquiry. "He looked . . . fine." Ellie found it interesting that her father had asked about her mother first thing, too.

"I didn't recognize him," Ellie added, reminding her mother that no pictures of Scott remained in the house. Well, none that she knew of. The only one she could ever remember seeing of her father had been in her early childhood. His image had long ago disappeared from her memory.

"When are you meeting him?"

"Mom," Ellie said, doing her best to be patient. "What does it matter where or when?"

"It matters to me." The words pitched back and forth on an emotional wobble.

Ellie could hear the tears in her mother's voice, and it shocked her. "Mom, why are you crying?"

"I'm not crying . . . I'm shook up is all . . . your father and I . . . that was a lot of years ago."

Ellie wasn't sure what to make of her mother's reaction. Her father's name hadn't been mentioned in years. The last thing she expected was for her mother to get emotional.

"When you meet him, will you . . . can you tell him something for me?" her mother asked.

"Of course."

"No," her mother said, abruptly changing her mind. "Don't say anything about me, okay?"

"You're sure?"

"I'm sure, say absolutely nothing about me. Wait . . . tell him . . . no, don't say anything."

"Mom . . ."

"Call me after your dinner," her mother instructed, and it sounded more like a plea than a request.

Ellie found she couldn't speak.

"Ellie?" Her mother whispered her name. "Are you still there?"

"Yes," she whispered back. When Ellie was in grade school, she fell and broke her arm. While waiting in the nurse's office for her mother to arrive to take her to the hospital, she gently rocked back and forth, holding her throbbing arm close to her side. The pain had been horrific. All she could think about was that she wanted her mother. Everything would be better once her mother was with her. Ellie felt much the same way now. "I should have listened to you . . . I should never have come to Cedar Cove. This is all one huge mistake. I'm ready to leave."

"No, don't," Virginia whispered.

"Don't . . . but you just told me I should."

"I was wrong. You told your father you would have dinner with him, and for both your sakes, I think it would be a good thing. If you leave now you'll always wonder, always regret the fact that you let this opportunity go. You deserve answers. Don't let my negative experience taint your relationship with your father, Ellie."

This didn't sound like her mother. "Are you sure?"

"Yes. I'll come to you."

"Mom, that's generous, but there aren't that many flights out of Bend, and for you to drive would take a good five to six hours."

The line went suspiciously quiet. "Actually, it won't take that long."

"It won't?"

"I'm here already."

She bolted to her feet. "You're here? In Cedar Cove?" Ellie pressed her hand against her forehead with disbelief.

Virginia made a small, almost indecipherable sound before she said, "If you must know, I spent the night in Tacoma."

"You did what?"

"I never intended for you to know. I was terribly worried that something would happen to you. I know you're probably upset with me, and I can't say that I blame you, but think of it from my point of view. You knew next to nothing about this man you met over the Internet, and I was afraid for you. I didn't dare tell you I intended to be close by, for fear you'd get upset."

Ellie *was* upset, but not for the reasons her mother assumed.

"You followed me?" Ellie couldn't believe what she was hearing.

"Not followed . . . exactly." Her mother seemed eager to defend herself and show that she had only Ellie's best interests at heart. "I wanted to be close by in case something happened, and it has, hasn't it? Please don't be angry with me."

Ellie should be, but at the moment she could only be grateful. "How soon can you get here?" she asked.

"I won't be long," Virginia promised. "Give me an hour."

Ellie used the next sixty minutes to lie down and rest her eyes, not that she was able to relax, let alone fall asleep. By the time her mother arrived, she stood by the window overlooking the inn's driveway, watching and waiting, eager to talk over the events of the day with her mother.

When Virginia arrived, Ellie hurried down the front steps and the two gripped hold of each other and hugged each other close. She touched Ellie's head but didn't mention the new hairstyle.

Her mother looked pointedly toward the inn. "Can we sit down and talk? As you can imagine, I didn't sleep well last night."

"Worrying about me, no doubt," Ellie murmured, well aware that her mother had stayed up past midnight, waiting to hear from her. Right away she felt guilty for the way she'd treated her mother. They were close and had always been that way.

"I had one of my headaches," her mother confessed, "but that's neither here nor there."

Ellie led the way to the inn, up the porch steps to the two chairs set up on the wraparound deck. The water view was amazing, but she didn't comment, and neither did her mother. Ellie didn't say anything until they were both seated. "Okay, Mom, do your worst."

"My worst?" Virginia repeated indignantly.

"You're about to list all the reasons why it was a bad idea for me to come to Cedar Cove to meet Tom." In retrospect, she wondered if it'd been the right thing, seeing all that had happened since.

"I wasn't," her mother argued. "All I wanted to do was protect you. I'm grateful I was close by."

"I am, too," Ellie said, although it was hard to admit.

"Your . . . father," Virginia said after a brief hesitation, "broke my heart. I loved him . . ."

"And he abandoned you," Ellie finished for her, having heard it dozens of times through the years.

"He abandoned *us*," Virginia corrected. "He knew what Tom was up to, didn't he?"

"I don't think so." The shocked look of dismay she read in Scott couldn't be easily fabricated. Her father had looked as bewildered as she'd been when Tom introduced her. "Tom sprang it on him this morning. Our meeting seemed to be as much a shock to Scott as it was to me."

A perplexed look came over Virginia. "You mean to say Tom didn't tell Scott who you were?"

"No. As far as my father knew, I was someone Tom met online and that was it. Both Scott . . . my dad and I were left in the dark."

Something else came to mind. It wasn't until Ellie saw her father that she understood the worried look Tom had had when he'd mentioned his "surprise." If her father wasn't in on this, then she wasn't the only one Tom had misled.

It all started to add up in her mind, and the result didn't make her feel any better. While Tom's intentions had been good, he'd used her gullibility and trust to trick her. Once he'd convinced her to visit Cedar Cove, he had what he wanted. She couldn't deal with her feelings for Tom now, though.

"Don't make the same mistake I did, Ellie. Don't trust Tom. He misled you once, and there's nothing to say he wouldn't again. I'm frightened that if you continue in this relationship you'll end up badly hurt."

"Mom, I'm old enough to make my own decisions. Trust me, will you?"

"I trusted your father."

"Mom . . ."

Virginia straightened, her shoulders tight and square. "It's not fair that he should stroll back into your life at this late date. He doesn't have the right."

Ellie heard the pain in her mother and wished that she was able to ease it, and at the same time realized she had to make up her own mind when it came to her father, and basically he'd already done that for her.

Her mother had a faraway look come over her. "I'm going to tell you something I've never shared with anyone." Her voice dipped to a whisper and trembled slightly. "I wrote your father shortly after he moved out, before the divorce was final. A friend got his address for me, and without my parents knowing what I was doing, I wrote him." Her voice pitched back and forth like a small boat in a storm. She paused briefly to regain control of her emotions before she continued. "I told him I was wrong, and I asked him for your sake and for mine, too, if he would reconsider and give our marriage a second chance. I was willing to do whatever was necessary to be the wife he wanted."

Ellie was shocked. For nearly her entire life all Ellie had heard regarding her father were disparaging words. All along her mother had claimed they were well rid of Scott Reynolds. He'd been a poor provider, shiftless, and on top of everything else, he possessed a weak character. For her mother to have swallowed her pride and reached out to him was huge.

"You never said anything about this before." This revelation took courage, and her mother's honesty surprised her, although it wasn't enough to change Ellie's mind.

"Not even my parents knew," Virginia told her. "My family

would have been dead set against us getting back together, and I knew that, but I loved Scott and I didn't want the divorce."

"What happened?" Ellie asked, needing to know.

Her mother looked out over the cove for several moments before she spoke. "He never answered."

A list of possible reasons immediately came to mind. "Maybe he didn't get the letter; maybe he'd moved and it wasn't forwarded. Do you think Grandma and Grandpa found the letter? And really, Mom, if you wanted to reach Dad, why didn't you just call him?" Then she could be sure that he knew her heart and that Virginia wanted their marriage to work.

"I would have phoned him if I'd had a number," her mother explained. "Things were different back then. There weren't cells or the Internet. My parents were urging me to file for a divorce. We fought and he left and I didn't see him again."

Ellie read the pain in her mother and felt a prick of discomfort herself. When she met Scott she would ask him why he hadn't responded to the letter. She feared it was because he'd fallen out of love with her mother and wanted nothing more to do with either of them. Even if that was the case, she needed to know. Tom seemed to imply that wasn't the way it was. According to him, Scott, too, lived with regrets . . . as well he should.

"Later . . ." Her mother paused and seemed to need a few minutes to compose herself. "I tried again later."

"When?"

"You were five and started asking questions about your dad."

Ellie remembered that vividly. "That was when I wanted that doll for my birthday, wasn't it?"

Her mother nodded. "My parents didn't know, but I couldn't bear to have you asking about your father. It took some doing, but I found him."

"Did he pay child support?"

Her mother lowered her head, refusing to meet Ellie's eyes. "Yes . . . faithfully."

"That isn't what you told me."

"I . . . was hurt and I didn't want you to—"

"In other words, you misled me." Ellie thought about all the things she'd heard about her father not caring about her welfare. Scott had mentioned that he hadn't been given any parental rights and couldn't afford to hire an attorney to fight for them.

"Yes, I lied."

"But why?" That didn't make sense to Ellie.

Again her mother lowered her head as though ashamed. "I have no excuse . . . I told myself it was a protective measure. If you had negative feelings about your father, then he wouldn't have a chance to hurt you the way he did me."

"Oh Mom."

"I know, and I'm sorry, Ellie."

"You said you tried to reach him again later?" She'd gotten side-tracked but wanted to hear what else her mother had to say. "When I was five and wanted a doll for my birthday."

"Yes." She hesitated long enough to swallow and seemed to need to collect her thoughts. "My parents meant well, but my mother spoiled you something terrible. You were her only grandchild and the apple of her eye. But I could see how badly you needed a father's influence. My dad tried, but he was older and often impatient. I was beginning to feel like a burden living with my family. Then you started asking questions about your daddy and I couldn't bear it. I looked for Scott and was willing to do anything to bring him back into our lives, even if it meant standing up to my parents."

"Did you find him?" Ellie asked, and her voice, too, had dropped to a whisper, as if she were afraid speaking out loud would some-how dissuade her mother from explaining the truth.

Virginia wrung her hands and nodded.

"And?" Ellie pressed.

Again it seemed to take several minutes for her mother to gain her composure enough to continue. "I found him . . . he was living in the Tacoma area. I went to see him."

"Did Grandma and Grandpa know what you were doing?"

"No, I didn't dare tell them . . . at least not until afterward, when . . ." She bit off this last part as if she couldn't find it in her to say the words aloud. "Once I told them what happened, my mother was deeply upset. She'd warned me about Scott again and again, but I refused to listen. When Dad heard what I'd done, he was furious with me."

"You found my father?" Ellie didn't want her mother to sidestep what had happened at their meeting. It was important that Ellie know, especially before she met her father for dinner. Already she knew more than she ever had, and she wanted to keep the flow of information coming. "You went to Tacoma to find my father."

"Yes," Virginia answered simply.

"What did he say?" Ellie asked, more gently this time, seeing how fragile her mother looked. Her shoulders had slumped slightly forward, as if weighted down by years of sadness and pain.

"I . . . I didn't speak to him."

Ellie noticed that her mother struggled to keep from weeping. Feeling dreadful for her, Ellie reached across and gripped hold of her mother's hand. "Why not, Mom—you'd come so far?" Seeing that she'd defied her parents and gone to the trouble to locate Scott, something dreadful must have taken place that prevented Virginia from following through.

"I discovered Scott had a new wife and a new family," her mother whispered brokenly. "I saw them all together . . . and they were happy, laughing and joking together. Scott was out in the front yard tossing a baseball back and forth with two young boys. I sat in my car, watching them all."

Ellie could easily picture the scene. Her mother parked against the curb, gathering her nerve to walk up to the front door and knock, only to have Scott come out front to play ball with his step-sons.

One of whom must have been Tom. Ellie swallowed back her hurt and disillusionment.

"I don't know how long I sat in my car, but eventually a woman came outside with a tray filled with glasses of lemonade and cookies."

Ellie knew her mother's heart must have sunk at this perfect picture of the idyllic family.

"Then," her mother continued in the same low tones, "Scott wrapped his arm around this other woman's waist and kissed her. He'd found someone else to love. The boys called him Dad, and that told me everything I needed to know. I was too late. If I'd gone to talk to him I would only have been an embarrassment."

This explained a great deal to Ellie. It was from that point on that her mother's love for her father had turned to something just short of hate. That was the only way Virginia had found to deal with the rejection and the loss. Keeping Ellie away from her father was a form of protection for them both. While that was an excuse, it hadn't been right. Deep down, Virginia recognized that Ellie deserved to know her father.

"I can understand why you left without speaking to him," Ellie assured her mother. Seeing how miserable she was stuck with overbearing parents and a strong-willed child while her ex-husband had found a new family and a new life. To rub salt in her mother's wounds, by all appearances her ex-husband was far happier than Virginia had ever made him.

"I couldn't make myself do it," her mother whispered. "I returned home, sobbing the entire way, and when I got to the house I confessed to my parents what I'd done."

It went without saying how upset her grandparents would have been with their daughter.

"Mom tried to comfort me, but Dad said I deserved what I got by running back to that riffraff."

Ellie remembered something else. "Grandpa bought me the doll."

"He did."

"And I loved it."

Her mother looked stricken. "You didn't, Ellie, you didn't at all."

"What do you mean?" Ellie could remember the delight she felt when she got the special gift she'd longed for the year she turned five. "I was so excited when I opened that present."

"You loved that doll until you learned it wasn't from your daddy. From that point on, you rarely played with it."

Ellie didn't remember it like that.

"In fact, I had to take it away from you because I found you jumping on it and crying. You'd never done anything like that before. I was shocked and put the doll up and out of sight."

That hardly seemed possible. Ellie was always a well-behaved child—at least that was the way she liked to think of herself.

"After a while I gave it back to you. Before I could stop you, you grabbed hold of the doll's arm and tossed it against the wall, claiming you hated that toy."

"I didn't." Ellie's hand came up to her chest in shock that she would treat any of her things in such a manner. Her grandfather would have been outraged.

"You cried and cried and said you didn't want it any longer. I was sure you'd change your mind, but you didn't. In the end, I took it away from you."

The reason was obvious, although Ellie had no memory of any of this.

"A couple years later we gave the doll away to a charity."

All Ellie recalled was how desperately she'd wanted this special doll, but hearing her mother recount the story told her that what Ellie had really wanted was the father she'd never known.

Chapter 24

~

Once home, I unloaded my purchases from the farmers' market and immediately dealt with the clams and fresh salmon, storing them in the refrigerator. I found my conversation with Corrie McAfee enlightening. Little by little, I was learning details about Mark, and key elements were starting to come together in my head. He had money, or did at one time. If so, he lived frugally. What Corrie said about him possibly having served in the military came as a surprise. As we walked back to the inn I asked Mark about that and he'd actually warned me off. Unfortunately the conversation had gotten out of hand, which I regretted.

"Leave it," he'd said to me.

"Leave it," I'd echoed, and then, because he'd irritated me, I'd added, "What exactly does that mean?"

Mark arched his thick brows as if the question caught him off guard. "I beg your pardon?"

"You can't say something like that to me and expect it to go un-challenged."

His forehead creased with a deep frown. "I don't know what you're talking about."

"Yes, you do," I insisted. "You more or less just warned me off."

He shook his head as if I was speaking utter nonsense and then had the audacity to say, "No, I didn't."

If he thought he could downplay the comment, then he was wrong. Maybe I should accept that challenge. "What I should do is call Roy McAfee," I said, staring him down, "and pay him to do a background check on you."

"Go ahead." Mark didn't appear the least bit threatened. He grinned and appeared to be enjoying our outlandish exchange. "There's nothing to find, but if you want to waste your money, then feel free."

I glared at him, half expecting him to laugh. His face, to my dis-appointment, remained completely deadpan. "I hope you know how much you irritate me."

"I irritate you?" he asked, as if astonished. "You're the one who's constantly harping on me."

"I most certainly am not." Oh, the man was impossible. "I am probably one of the most even-tempered, likeable women you'll ever meet." I didn't take this insult lightly. "You know what?" I said. "It might do us both a world of good to stay away from each other for a while." I wasn't sure how serious I was, but I wasn't willing to back down.

He shrugged as if it wouldn't matter to him one way or the other. "That's fine with me. Would you like me to stop work on the ga-zebo? Don't think I haven't got plenty of other projects in the works. If you want me to stay away, then far be it from me to trespass where I'm not welcome."

All of a sudden Rover let loose with a piercing howl that startled both of us. I gasped with surprise, and Mark looked equally taken aback. Rover sat on his haunches and stared up at the pair of us as if to comment that this disagreement had gone on long enough.

"He doesn't like to hear us fighting," I suspected.

"Probably not." Mark looked down and shuffled his feet.

I was willing to admit that I'd let my temper get the better of me. This was rare for me. Generally, I'm not one to fly off the handle or make idle threats. I'd pounced on Mark and felt I owed him an apology. "Rover's right. You're a good friend and whatever is in your past that you're hiding is your business. It's none of my affair."

His brows came together in a thick frown. "Who says I'm hiding anything?"

"Right." It was better not to broach that subject, seeing that we clearly disagreed.

Mark sighed. "I guess I got pretty hot under the collar, too. I take it you still want me to work on the gazebo."

"I do." The one thing I didn't want was for the gazebo project to linger on for months, the way the rose garden had.

He nodded, accepting my peace offering. "If you really want to make it up to me, I'd take a few more of those cookies you baked yesterday morning."

The man was so predictable. "I'll see what I can do."

"Jo Marie?"

"Yeah?" I turned back from the cookie jar to find him staring at me intently. It looked as if he wanted to say something but felt unsure. "What?" I asked.

"I've noticed something about you."

"Oh?"

He hesitated. "You've been acting a bit off lately."

"I have?" I nearly laughed out loud. I was sure this was an exaggeration. Although to be fair, I felt I should give him the opportunity to explain himself. "How do you mean?"

He shrugged as if uncomfortable with the conversation, but now that he'd started, he couldn't very well stop. "First off, you've been prying into my life."

"Yeah, well . . ."

"And you've been moody, too."

"No, I haven't," I argued. Really, this was too much.

"And odd."

"Odd?" This time I couldn't stop myself, and I gave one short laugh.

Mark stuffed his hands into his pockets. "The other day, out of the blue, you started talking about Paul's sweatshirt."

I froze.

"You made some nonsensical comment about it losing its scent."

I didn't move, barely breathed.

"We were talking about something else entirely and then you blurted this out, and for a moment I thought you were about to cry. I don't understand it."

He waited, as if he wanted me to explain. I couldn't. "Is that all?" I asked, making light of it.

"No, there's something else."

There was more?

"You've been in this cleaning frenzy, rearranging cupboards, putting down shelf paper, bringing items out of the attic, and that's only what I've seen. A couple nights I've looked at the inn and your light is on well past midnight. You're having trouble sleeping, too, aren't you?"

That was true, but I wasn't about to admit it.

"As best I can tell, all this odd behavior started about the time you got Paul's last letter."

"Oh." I probably should have put up a defense, explained that he was wrong, completely off base. I wanted to but didn't, mainly because I feared he might be right. This wasn't easy to admit.

All of a sudden his gaze narrowed. "You okay?"

"Of course I am," I insisted, with more bravado than I felt.

He seemed to be waiting for me to hand him the cookies. I did, but still he lingered. "You don't look okay."

"I'm fine," I insisted, and let it be known that I didn't appreciate him pressuring me.

He shrugged as if to say he wasn't willing to argue about it. "If you say so." Before he left, he thoughtfully filled Rover's water dish and then stepped back as my "comfort dog" eagerly lapped it up, splashing water over the sides of his bowl.

After Mark was gone, I couldn't seem to hold still. I moved from room to room with no purpose or destination in mind. I was at a loss; the more I thought about what he'd said, the more upset I got. I wrapped my arms around my middle and fought off the urge to cry.

My husband was dead. I'd watched his casket being lowered into the ground with full military regalia. Paul wasn't coming home. I'd done my best to accept this new reality and I thought I was okay.

Maybe I wasn't doing as well as I'd assumed.

Not knowing quite what to do, I reached for my phone and called my mother. I needed the distraction, and I wanted to put Mark's comments out of my head.

"Hi, honey," my mother greeted, sounding cheerful and happy, in stark contrast to my current state of mind.

"Hi."

A brief hesitation followed before Mom asked, "Is something wrong?"

My mother could read me like a book; she always could. I hardly knew where to start.

"Dinner is still on, isn't it? Your father and I are looking forward to spending time with you."

"Yes, I wouldn't cancel for the world . . . I thought I should tell you Mark Taylor won't be coming." I don't know why I felt it was necessary to give her that information when I had so much else on my mind.

"Oh, that's a disappointment," Mom said with a sigh. "I was looking forward to meeting him."

"I'm fine with it, Mom. I'd like for you to meet Mark, but it's no big deal. He's a handyman and that's all."

"And a friend," Mom added.

"Right," I returned, with no real conviction.

Mom paused. "Sweetie, what's wrong?"

"Nothing," I quickly assured her. I didn't want to get into it with my mother so soon after my confrontation with Mark. Nor did I want to tell her how much I missed Paul.

"I know you're disappointed that Mark won't be joining us for dinner. I was looking forward to meeting him, and your father was, too. Perhaps another time. As for me getting a read on him, I think you'd be a better judge of him than I would ever be," my mother advised.

"I doubt that." I'd already tried, with little success.

"He's obviously important to you—"

"Mark? Important to me?" I said, cutting her off. "You're joking, right? Mark is a handyman and I've hired him because he does good work, but mostly he frustrates me. I don't need that kind of aggravation in my life, and, frankly, I'm through with him. Once this gazebo is finished, that's it." My mind was made up.

"If you say so, dear."

"I say so." And I meant it, too.

I turned around and found a woman standing in the doorway leading into the kitchen. For an instant she startled me, and my hand flew to my chest. I didn't know there was anyone else in the house, especially a stranger. She wasn't a guest, and there wasn't anyone else registered on the books.

"Hold on a minute, Mom," I said. I lowered the phone. "Can I help you?" I asked. Really what I wanted to know was how she got into the house, which to the best of my knowledge had been locked.

"I don't mean to interrupt your conversation," she said. "I'm Virginia Reynolds, Ellie's mother."

"Ellie's mother," I repeated. Oh dear, this wasn't a good sign.

"I was wondering if I could rent a room for the night."

Chapter 25

⁓

After hearing the news that Maggie was pregnant, Roy went cold and silent. She glanced at him as he continued driving back to Cedar Cove and the inn, but he refused to look at her, his gaze steadfastly glued to the road ahead. His hands were so tightly wrapped around the steering wheel that his knuckles had gone stark white.

Maggie wanted to say something, but really, what was there to say? When she'd discovered she was pregnant with each one of the boys, the emotions she felt were so completely different than what she was experiencing now. There'd been joy, excitement and happiness, anticipation and expectation. She felt none of that now. The one dominating emotion was dread.

"How could you have let something like this happen?" Roy demanded.

Anger curdled her stomach. Maggie's instinct was to lash back and remind her husband he wasn't so innocent in this fiasco. She wasn't the only one who'd strayed. He could pretend he was the injured party, but she wasn't about to put up with his verbal abuse.

"I'm going to pretend you didn't ask that, Roy," she said, with all the dignity she could assemble. Her clenched hands rested in her lap as she struggled within herself, fighting down nausea mixed with shock and dismay.

Her husband went silent again.

An eternity passed before he spoke. "What are you going to do about it?"

"It?" she repeated.

"This pregnancy, Maggie. Don't be coy with me."

"A child is not an *it*," she reminded him. That had always been a pet peeve of hers, as Roy well knew. This was a baby, a human being, a life that was growing inside of her.

"To me this child is an *it*," he returned pointedly. "I don't want *it*."

"In other words, you want me to get an abortion." She couldn't believe she would even make such a suggestion. Her heart pounded stronger and louder than a marching band drum corps. It astonished her that no one else seemed to be able to hear it, the sound deafening in its intensity.

"You don't mean that," Roy insisted.

"I don't know what I mean anymore," she said, hardly able to get the words out. "It's what you want. Admit it. An abortion would solve everything, right? We could do away with the baby and everything would go back to normal. That's what you're thinking, admit it, Roy."

"Okay, yes. It would solve everything."

She turned her head and looked out the passenger window. "Have we really been married all these years without you knowing me, Roy?" she asked in a whisper. "Do you really believe I could abort this child and that would actually help our situation?"

He didn't answer, and then finally he whispered, "Okay, you're right. That wouldn't work. If you went through with it, you'd never be able to live with yourself." He sounded more reasonable now, and for that she was thankful.

"Thank you," she whispered.

"That doesn't change how I feel about this baby. I don't want anything to do with this pregnancy or this child. Nothing."

"Or me?"

Again he paused, the silence so loud it felt as if he was shouting, and in some ways that would have been easier to tolerate than this . . . nothingness.

He didn't want anything to do with her? It took a while for the words to sink in, and even then she wasn't entirely sure what he meant. He seemed to be suggesting that he wanted out of the marriage. The mere thought caused her blood to run cold. "But . . . we don't know if this baby is yours or not."

"I'm not taking the chance, because I'm telling you right now, Maggie, I won't raise another man's child."

Maggie was about to argue when Roy cursed and immediately slowed down. Twisting around, Maggie noticed a cop car racing up behind them, lights flashing.

"Were you speeding?" she asked.

He glared at her, and that was answer enough.

Roy pulled over to the side of the road and the state patrol vehicle pulled in behind him. Releasing his seat belt, Roy reached for his wallet and removed his driver's license while Maggie opened the glove compartment and retrieved the registration card and proof of insurance.

When the officer approached, Roy rolled down the window.

"Good afternoon, folks," he greeted.

Roy didn't answer.

"Do you realize how fast you were driving?"

Again Roy was silent and stared straight ahead as he handed the state trooper the necessary paperwork.

"I clocked you at eighty-two miles an hour."

Maggie had no idea Roy was speeding to that extent.

"The speed limit here is sixty."

This wasn't going to be a cheap ticket.

The officer took the paperwork back to his vehicle and returned a few minutes later with the ticket. He recited a list of instructions, but Maggie didn't pay attention, and she doubted that Roy did, either. He seemed frozen in anger.

As soon as the trooper left, Roy rolled up his window and merged with the other traffic.

"I suppose the speeding ticket is my fault as well as everything else," she said.

Roy was silent for the next several miles. The tension was as thick as concrete and just as heavy, weighing on her, dragging her down until she felt as if she were sinking in thick mud.

"What do you intend to do?" he demanded, shocking her by breaking the silence.

"I . . . think that's a question you need to answer, not me." As far as Maggie could see, she didn't really have a choice. She was pregnant, and she would give birth to this child, who was innocent.

His silence told her everything she needed to know. He wanted out of the marriage. Maggie turned her head away and looked out the side window, closing her eyes. They'd come so far this weekend. They'd talked of forgiveness and a fresh start, and now this. A sense of hopelessness threatened to swallow her. That morning, only a few hours ago, she'd been positive that despite everything they would survive as a couple. It didn't look that way now . . . it felt as if all was lost.

"I think we can both agree that it's over. I'm done, Maggie. Done. I can't deal with this."

"You're asking for a divorce?" she whispered, hardly able to believe her husband, praying he wasn't serious and yet knowing he was.

"The marriage is over," he confirmed. "I won't be put in this position, understand?"

Maggie squeezed her eyes closed as the pain rocked over her in harsh waves before she slowly nodded.

"I won't raise another man's child."

"You've made that clear," she whispered, her voice trembling.

"Don't think a few tears are going to make me change my mind. I couldn't be any more serious."

Maggie didn't doubt him. "I believe you."

"I won't pay child support, either. Got that?"

"Got it, but you need not have worried. I wouldn't ever ask that of you." Maggie's hand trembled as she brushed the hair from her face.

"I'm glad we cleared that up."

Thankfully, he'd slowed down to the speed limit.

"Anything else you want to say?" Roy asked her.

"No," Maggie whispered.

"Good." His voice was as cold as arctic ice.

In retrospect, there was. "Actually, there is . . . something I want to say, that is." Knowing any show of emotion would only anger him, she swallowed down her tears. "This very well could be your child, Roy."

He seemed to weigh her words. "It doesn't matter."

Maggie nearly gasped but managed to stop herself. "It doesn't matter?"

"As far as I'm concerned, we're finished."

The only thing left for Maggie to do was to accept his decision. "Baby or no baby, it was already doomed," she told him.

He didn't agree or disagree.

"The night I disappeared," she whispered, "you told me you were worried sick . . . you said you called every hospital in town, contacted the police."

"I didn't know what to think . . . when you didn't come home, I was afraid something had happened to you."

"I nearly had an accident . . ." Even now she remembered slamming on the brakes, narrowly escaping being hit by a large truck, skidding to a stop and shaking so badly she knew she was in no condition to drive. "I could have been killed," she whispered. "It might have been better if I had been."

The only outward evidence Roy showed of having heard her was slowing down to a near crawl. The driver behind them blasted his horn and Roy immediately picked up speed again.

"Don't say things like that," he demanded.

"It would be easier than living through this hell."

"Maggie."

"Don't worry, Roy, I'm not going to do anything stupid." And she wouldn't. One impulsive act and she was about to lose her marriage. She wouldn't fight Roy. He'd made his position clear and so had she. While he might declare his undying love, commitment, and devotion to her, he was willing to walk rather than travel this journey with her.

When he pulled into the parking lot at the inn, Maggie was surprised. Lost in her own world and her thoughts of the future, she hadn't paid attention to the landscape. She didn't have a clue they were back at the inn until he turned off the engine.

Roy continued sitting in the car, but Maggie couldn't get out of it fast enough. Her husband remained inside as she hurried toward the front steps. The best thing for her to do now, she decided, was to pack up her things and leave. Driving back to Yakima with Roy would be intolerable. As far as she could tell, everything that had to be said had already been spoken.

Her steps were slow and her vision blurred by tears as she climbed the porch steps. She paused and leaned against the porch column when unbearable grief struck her. Pressing a hand over her heart, she inhaled a deep breath and drew on her inner strength as she righted herself and continued into the house.

As soon as she let herself in the front door, Jo Marie appeared. "I see you're back. How was your—" she asked cheerfully, and then stopped abruptly. "Maggie, is everything all right? You're so pale."

She managed a weak smile and shook her head.

"Are you ill? Do you need the name of a doctor? There's a good medical clinic here . . ."

"No. It's fine," she assured the other woman.

"Where's Roy?"

Maggie didn't answer. She didn't know how to answer. He might still be sitting in the car. For all she knew he could have driven off and left her for good.

She climbed the stairs one at a time; putting one foot in front of another was all she could manage. By the time she reached the top of the first flight, she was breathless. Grief weighed her down, but pride carried her toward their room.

Jo Marie stood at the bottom of the stairs, watching her, concern written on her face.

Maggie went into the room and closed the door. Her suitcase was in the closet. She took it out and packed her things, which took only a few minutes. What she needed, she decided, was to escape, to get away. But not like she had before.

It felt as if the walls were closing in around her, as if the room was growing smaller with every breath she inhaled, until she could bear it no longer.

Not knowing what to do or where she would go, Maggie stood, her legs wobbly. It came to her that she would need her purse. Funny the things that came into her mind. She opened it and removed the room key and placed it on the mattress. The key would no longer be necessary. Nor was her wedding band, which she removed and placed on the nightstand on top of the novel her husband had been reading.

Then there was the letter, the love letter Roy had written her while in college, the one that claimed he would always love her. No need for her to keep that any longer, either.

Removing the letter from the envelope, Maggie set it on the pillow and then went into the small bathroom and washed her face.

When she came out of the room, Jo Marie remained at the foot of the stairs.

"Maggie," she said, her voice heavy with concern. "Is there anything I can do?"

She shook her head. "I'm pregnant," she whispered.

Jo Marie hugged her. "I'm thinking this isn't a happy discovery."

"Not for my husband."

Jo Marie held her look. "He drove off."

"I thought he might . . . he'll be back," she assured the innkeeper.

Jo Marie followed her to the door. "Where are you going?" she asked. "What should I tell Roy?"

"Don't tell him anything . . . I won't be back." Once again she managed a smile. "Thank you for everything . . . the inn is lovely, and so are you." And that was all she had to say.

Chapter 26

~

I felt sick at heart. Something was drastically wrong between Maggie and Roy for her to leave the way she had, dragging her suitcase, her shoulders slumped as if every step was a burden too heavy for one soul to carry. When I hurried after her to ask if she needed a ride, she shook her head. I persisted and asked if she knew where she was headed. She didn't have an answer for me; she said she wasn't sure where she would go. I tried to talk some sense into her, but it did no good. I followed her halfway up the driveway and realized I wasn't going to be able to change her mind.

The worst part of it was that by the time she left, Roy had, too. He hadn't returned, and the only phone number I had was Maggie's cell, so I had no way of reaching him to explain what had happened to his wife.

Maggie was pregnant. Apparently, this was unwelcome news to

have caused such a drastic reaction. I wanted to help, but I wasn't sure I could or if I should even try. This was the area of being an innkeeper that was most unfamiliar to me. I didn't want to intrude or overstep my bounds, but at the same time I wanted to be helpful.

If what was happening to Maggie and Roy wasn't enough of a concern, there was Ellie and her mother. Virginia had rented a room, and shortly thereafter Ellie and her mother had sat outside, talking intently. Their body language told me they wanted nothing more than to be left alone. I didn't know who or what they were discussing but guessed this had something to do with Tom. My presence wasn't appreciated, and so Rover and I left them to their own devices.

My first thought was to retreat to the covered area on the side yard, where I often sat in the cool of the evenings. The three-sided structure was part of an outbuilding from a homestead that dated back long before the inn was built. The Frelingers, the previous owners, had made it into a cozy retreat. Many a night I'd sat out there and started a fire in the fireplace. This spot held a special significance to me, as it was in that very place where I first felt Paul's presence with me. It was cooler there, shaded from the sun by the shake roof, and would have been ideal if not for one thing.

Mark was back. He was in the yard where I wanted the gazebo built and was busy doing something there. I was fairly certain he didn't see me, which was just as well. If I ventured out it was sure to invite conversation, and frankly, I wasn't in the mood for company; to be exact, I wasn't eager for Mark's company. Our talk from earlier that afternoon weighed on my mind. As much as I didn't want to admit it, he was right. I had been in a cleaning frenzy lately, rearranging cupboards, organizing my spices, sorting through my bedroom drawers. He was right about something else, too. This restlessness had to be connected to the desolation of accepting my husband's death. I realized that I'd grown uncomfortable dealing with my grief and so I'd ignored it by pretending all was well. I'd gotten so good at it that it'd become second nature now. The cleaning had become a distraction, as had my curiosity regarding Mark's mysterious background. I'd been determined to dig up whatever I could find on him because if I concentrated on him then I wouldn't have to think about what was really on my mind. And that was the death of my husband.

Mark stayed only a few minutes. He seemed to find what he wanted and left. He didn't give any indication that he had seen me, though I suspected that at some point he must have. Apparently, he realized I needed time to myself as well.

After a few minutes I retreated to my own room. Rover followed me inside my private quarters and settled down on the rug in front of the fireplace, which was one of his favorite spots. Early on, I'd decided to knit afghans for each one of the guest rooms, but it was much too hot to knit. I had other projects on needles, but knitting didn't appeal to me at the moment. I felt at loose ends, ill at ease in my own home. The restlessness was back, and I found myself pacing the confines of my bedroom, rubbing my palms together, anxious and rattled.

Being agitated by Mark and then deeply concerned about my guests didn't help matters. Desperate to find a way to distract myself, I reached for the novel I'd started earlier in the week and put my feet up, forcing my body to relax. It didn't work. I did my best to get involved in the story, but after a few pages I gave up. My mind wandered like a nomad, traveling from one area of interest to another. I should unload the dishwasher, and then I remembered that I'd done that earlier. Wasn't there wash that needed to be loaded into the machine? That, too, had been accomplished. I supposed I could bake something. I found comfort in baking, but why would I take on that task in the hottest part of the afternoon? My mind might as well have been playing hopscotch.

I must have slammed the book shut because Rover leaped to his feet, looking dazed and startled.

"Sorry, boy," I said. "I don't know what's wrong with me." It would be all too easy to blame Mark, and I considered it. Deep down, I recognized it was more than Mark or even my guests' troubles. What Mark claimed was eating at me like ants on honey.

Rover walked over to my side of the bed and remained there. He focused his gaze on me as if he was trying to tell me something important.

"What is it, Rover?" I asked, slightly impatient. He'd been outside earlier, so I knew that wasn't it.

Obviously I didn't expect him to answer, but the two of us had developed strong communication skills. As crazy as it seemed, I could usually figure out what he wanted to tell me.

After a couple minutes Rover turned his focus to my nightstand. That was odd; it wasn't like I kept doggie treats in my bedroom. I couldn't imagine what Rover would want from there.

I walked over to his side and sat on the edge of the bed; the mattress sank with my weight. Running my hand down his sleek back, I exhaled a deep breath and opened the drawer . . . and froze.

Inside was Paul's last letter to me. The one he'd written in case of his death. A love letter that had come to me from the grave. I'd refused to read it when it first arrived because I hadn't gotten final verification that my husband was dead. For more than a year I held on to the hope, the belief that when his helicopter went down in Afghanistan that somehow Paul had found a way to survive. It took a year for the remains to be located, and then, as fate would have it, not all the bodies were recovered. For a while I clung to the possibility, an irrational hope, that allowed me to believe my husband was alive.

That died a swift death when Paul's remains were found and positively identified. Then and only then did I force myself to read the letter. Blind with grief, I can barely remember what he wrote. It was what I had expected him to say, I remembered that. Be happy for what we had, get on with your life, et cetera.

I read the letter only the one time and then immediately placed it in the drawer on my nightstand. For months I'd chosen to ignore it, to pretend it wasn't there simply because reading his last words to me would bring me more pain than comfort.

I glanced at Rover and saw that he'd lain back down again. Paul's letter was in my hand, and I looked down on the plain white envelope. My stomach muscles convulsed as I removed the hand-written sheets. I noticed that my hand shook, too. Emotion gripped my throat, and for a moment it was all I could do to continue breathing.

My dearest Jo Marie, I read.

Paul had never called me his dearest before, and I paused to take in the significance of this, if there was any.

> *If you're reading this letter, it means the worst has happened and I've been killed in action. Before we met and married, I wasn't overly concerned with the future. I knew the risks when I agreed to become a soldier and there was only my father and a few good friends to grieve or care if I lived or died. There was a certain freedom in that for me, a lack of fear; planning for the future was of little importance. I concentrated on my duty and decided to accept whatever happened without giving it a great deal of forethought.*
>
> *Then I met and fell in love with you. I never expected to meet a woman I could love the way I do you. A whole new world opened up to me with you. A world filled with possibilities and promises. For the first time in a long while I thought about having a home, a real home, and, God willing, raising two or three children. Loving you gave me permission to dream, to look beyond the day, to hope that life held more for me than war and being a soldier.*
>
> *You were a gift to me, Jo Marie. An unexpected, joyful gift I treasure more than my feeble heart or mere words could ever express. You brought me laughter and joy, and for that I will be eternally grateful.*

Soon after we married, Paul and I had talked about starting a family. We'd hoped I'd get pregnant right away, but it wasn't meant to be. With his death, that dream had died along with so many others.

I swallowed tightly and forced myself to continue reading.

Like I said, if you're reading this, those dreams have turned to ash for us both. When we exchanged our vows I promised to love you, and by all that I hold sacred, I do love you, Jo Marie, with all my strength and all my will. I promised to look after you and support you and care for you to the very best of my ability.

I've watched men die. I comforted a friend in his last moments of life, and while I've had experience with death on the battlefield, I know nothing of what is beyond. But I will tell you this . . . if at all possible, I will be with you.

In every way I can I will support and love you as you live out the rest of your life. And if God allows I will reach out to you. I may be gone from you, but my love never will be. Look for me, Jo Marie. I will come to you, protect you. If at all possible, I will find a way to you from beyond the grave.

Knowing you, loving you, I want to ask you to do something important for me. Please listen. Please understand. Don't spend the rest of your life grieving for what might have been for us. I ask only one thing of you—keep your heart open. Live for us both. Make a difference. Fall in love with life . . . fall in love. You have so much to offer, so much to give others. It would be a waste to dwell in the past when the future is holding its arms open with endless possibilities.

It's difficult to know how to end this letter, to say what is in my heart. I'm not good with words. Nor do I know how to say this other than by reminding you once more of how grateful I am to have been loved by you and to have loved you, even if for only this little while.

Remember what I said.

Paul

I wiped the tears from my eyes and held my breath until I could control my emotions. Rover came to me and rested his chin on my thigh as though to soothe me. From the first, I believed Paul had sent me Rover. My rescue dog, but who had rescued whom? Rover was my constant companion, and as Grace had so recently suggested, he was my comfort dog.

"I'm glad I read Paul's letter again," I whispered, and reached for a tissue to wipe my nose. In essence, Paul was telling me to get on with my life and that he would always be with me. He was adamant that he didn't want me to spend the rest of my days grieving for him, but I would. His loss had completely impacted my life. I couldn't help but mourn for what might have been. He asked me to make a difference, and I hoped I was doing it through the inn.

The inn . . .

I'd always hoped this inn would be a place of healing. I'd seen it with a few of my guests. I saw it in those who had checked in with heavy hearts, burdened by the problems of life. Yet by the time they left, their spirits had lifted and they'd found solace in much the same way I had. I believed the inn was making a difference and had become the healing place I'd always hoped it would be . . . until this weekend. As far as I could tell, everything had fallen apart for Maggie and Roy.

Unexpectedly, Rover jerked around and stood in front of my door. I got up and opened it for him. He immediately shot out, pausing to stop and look over his shoulder as if to say I should follow him. As ridiculous as it is to admit, I'd become accustomed to following his orders.

It didn't take me long to discover what the problem was. Ellie had returned and sat in the living room with her mother. Their heads were close together, and Virginia had her hand on Ellie's shoulder in a comforting gesture. I didn't want to intrude or listen in on a private conversation and was about to turn away when Virginia glanced up. She seemed grateful to see me.

"Would it be possible to get a pot of tea?" she asked.

"Of course."

Rover left my side and settled down by Ellie's feet as if to console and reassure her. His chin rested atop her feet as if to hold her in place. If she noticed, Ellie gave no indication. Her voice was low and troubled, and while I wasn't intentionally eavesdropping, I couldn't help but overhear.

"Scott made excuses for him, but I refused to listen or believe anything he has to say any longer. I've learned my lesson."

"What did Tom tell you?"

"What could he say?" Ellie asked, sounding terribly sad. "He never intended to hurt me. He thought he was doing something good for his stepfather, but not once did he take into consideration what he was doing to me."

Virginia leaned her head closer to her daughter and hugged her briefly. "Oh Ellie, I'm so sorry."

"Are you, Mom?" Ellie asked. "Are you really? Isn't this what you've been telling me all along? My problem is I was convinced you were wrong and that I'd show you what it was to find a good man who would love me." She hiccupped a sob as if to say she was the one who'd been the fool.

"I am sorry . . . sorry for tainting your view of men, and giving you a reason to want to prove me wrong."

Ellie's hiccupping sob turned into a sad sort of laugh. "I want to go home . . . this whole trip was a disaster from beginning to end."

"Oh Ellie."

"There's no reason to stay . . ."

"What about your dinner with your father?" Virginia asked.

They were interrupted by the front door being flung open. Normally, Rover would have been on his feet and barking, but he refused to leave Ellie's side.

Roy came into the house as if he intended to tear off the door by its hinges. He looked around and saw Ellie and her mother in the living room and me in the kitchen, paused momentarily, and then raced up the stairs.

Virginia looked at me, her eyes wide. "What's his problem?"

I shrugged, not knowing what to say.

Not two minutes after Roy stormed up the stairs, he returned and confronted me in the kitchen. "Where's Maggie?" he demanded gruffly.

"I don't know."

"Her suitcase is gone."

"Yes, I know. She left shortly after you dropped her off."

Roy frowned. "She didn't tell you where she was going?"

I'd tried to find out but had gotten nothing out of her. "I don't think she knew herself."

"Of all the stupid . . . the woman is irrational and . . ."

"Pregnant," I finished for him.

His eyes narrowed with accusation. "She told you?"

"Just that." I could only assume there was more, and apparently lots more.

Roy clenched and unclenched his fists as if using restraint not to slam one against the wall. "She can't have gotten far."

"No, I don't imagine that she has."

"I'll find her." His face hardened with determination. "And when I do, we'll be checking out."

In his current frame of mind, I wouldn't consider that a loss, but I felt obliged to tell him my policy regarding early departures. "You're paid through Sunday, and I can't give you a refund."

"I don't care," he snapped. "Keep the money."

I didn't notice any love or real concern in him over his wife's disappearance, only anger and something else I didn't immediately recognize, but then it came to me. Roy was dealing with grief and loss.

"Do you know which way she went?" he asked, as he pulled his car keys from his pocket.

I shook my head. "I didn't see her once she left the driveway."

He nodded and headed out of the inn.

It seemed Virginia, Ellie, and I all breathed a collective sigh of relief as Roy left the house.

The teakettle whistled, and I returned my attention to putting together a tray for the mother and daughter. The doorbell chimed, and Rover was instantly alert and rushed to the door.

I opened it to find an attractive middle-aged man with a full head of salt-and-pepper hair. He looked up at me, and for a moment it seemed he didn't know what to say.

"I'm here to see Ellie Reynolds," he said. "I'm her father."

Chapter 27

The instant Scott Reynolds entered the living room, Ellie's mother leaped to her feet. She moved behind the sofa as though to put a barrier between her and the man she'd once loved. Ellie turned to look at her mother and then her father.

She waited for him to speak. With everything that had happened since she'd last seen him, including her talk with Tom and her mother's arrival, Ellie had nearly forgotten that she'd agreed to meet Scott for dinner.

To Ellie's surprise, it was her mother who spoke first. "Scott."

He seemed equally dumbfounded. "Ginny."

Ginny? Ellie had never heard her mother referred to as anything but Virginia. Her grandmother had insisted on it.

The two stared at each other like schoolyard children waiting for the other to make the first move in a game of tag.

Her father's face softened perceptively. "The years have been kind to you," he said, after clearing his throat.

"You look . . . well," Ellie's mother said, almost as if she were in a trance.

Scott ran his hand along the side of his head. "The hair's a lot thinner . . . You look exactly as I remember you."

It seemed both had forgotten Ellie was in the room. She had to resist waving her arms above her head in order to remind them that they weren't alone.

After an awkward pause, Virginia spoke. "I understand you met with our daughter this afternoon."

Her father's gaze shifted toward Ellie. As a young girl and even later as a preteen, she'd built up this fantasy of what her father would be like. She had him pictured in her mind, not so much what he looked like, but how he would be and how much he would love her. He would sit and listen to her play the piano and praise her efforts. He would take her to father-daughter dances and their steps would match perfectly as they whirled around the polished dance floor. When a date came to pick her up, he would drill the young man and be protective. Unfortunately, none of her fantasies had come to pass. Her father had remained nothing more than an absent figure in her life. Until now.

"Ellie's a terrific girl. We met earlier this afternoon, and she's matured into a lovely, capable woman," he said.

She had? Ellie basked in those few words, praise she'd longed to hear from her father, words, however few, that validated her in his eyes.

"Tom thinks the world of her. She's all he talks about . . . It reminds me of when we first met and how crazy we once were about each other."

Ellie was about to tell her father exactly what she thought of Tom, but she wasn't given the chance.

"Tom is your stepson?" her mother asked, although Ellie had explained that fact quite clearly.

Scott nodded. "His intentions were good, although he went about our meeting all wrong. Still, he's a fine young man."

"He isn't all that wonderful in my eyes." Ellie could keep silent no longer.

Both her mother and father looked at her as if they'd forgotten she was in the room, which apparently they had. "Tom misled me. He lied and he used my attraction to him for his own selfish reasons."

"He did it for me," Scott explained, and to his credit, he sounded apologetic. "Tom knew how deeply I regretted not knowing my daughter or being the father she deserved."

"He had no right to lie . . . to mislead me." Ellie wanted to make that one point crystal clear. "None whatsoever."

Her father nodded and took one step closer. "Like I said, his intentions were good, but his methods left a lot to be desired."

"No kidding." Ellie didn't understand what was happening. All her parents seemed capable of doing was staring at each other. This made no sense to her. This was the golden opportunity to let her mother tell Scott exactly what she thought of him. Virginia had certainly shared those feelings with Ellie often enough. Wasn't this the chance Virginia had impatiently waited for all these years? At last her mother could tell this man who had broken her heart exactly how his abandonment had tainted her life. Perhaps she needed a bit of prompting.

"Scott," Ellie said, hoping to break the spell. "You have some explaining to do."

"You're right, I do," he agreed, and advanced another step toward them.

When they'd met earlier that afternoon Ellie hadn't had the chance to ask him more than a couple questions, but that wasn't his fault. She had been overwhelmed by the fact she was talking to her father.

His gaze centered on Ellie. "Seeing you brought back a flash flood of memories of your mother and me."

"I have questions that need to be answered," Ellie said, and as far as she was concerned, there was no time like the present to get the answer to the most pressing one. "I need to know why you walked out on Mom and me. Why did you leave us the way you did?"

His face tightened, and he cast an accusing glare toward Ellie's mother. "I didn't walk out on either one of you."

"Yes, you did. Mom said . . ." Ellie paused and looked at her mother, but her mother refused to meet her gaze. Virginia seemed to find something interesting at her feet that demanded her attention. "Mom?"

"I was given an ultimatum," her father explained. "Your mother wanted me to take money from her family, which I refused to do. When I wouldn't play ball with your grandfather, he had me fired and made sure my life was miserable."

"Dad only wanted to help," Virginia insisted, defending her father.

"No, he didn't," Scott argued just as heatedly. "He wanted to control us, mostly me. He'd had you wrapped around his finger, and when he found he couldn't control me he retaliated. When I couldn't take it any longer, I decided we had to move. I hoped you loved me enough to break away from your family."

"And starve?"

"Ginny, for the love of heaven, we wouldn't have starved. We had little more than each other, and for me that was enough, but apparently it wasn't enough for you."

"You can't live on love," Virginia said.

That sounded like something her grandparents would say, Ellie mused.

"We lived on love the first two years, and, yes, there were hard times. We rarely had more than a couple dimes in our pockets, but we survived and were better for it."

"We did make it," her mother agreed, "but it was hard, Scott. You worked two jobs and I rarely saw you. Ellie has no memories of you. All Dad wanted you to do was accept a loan."

"A loan with so many strings attached that they felt like a noose around my neck."

Ellie's mother shook her head as if to dismiss the accusation. "It was your pride."

Scott looked at her as if weary of the argument that was more than twenty years old. "What does it matter now? It's all water under the bridge."

"Yes," Virginia agreed. "Water that's long since washed out to sea."

Ellie waited for her mother to bring up the letter she'd written shortly after her husband had moved out. Virginia didn't, and in that instant Ellie knew why. It hurt her mother's pride to disclose the fact that she'd reached out to her husband only to be rejected.

The silence grew thick, like fog rolling in off Puget Sound, circling the room.

"I have another question," Ellie inserted, and it seemed both her parents were relieved to move forward.

"Yes?" her father said, looking to her expectantly.

"In fact, I had an entire list of questions I wanted to ask." Ellie felt there was no time like now with both her parents in the room.

Scott grinned. He actually grinned. "You sounded so like your mother just now."

"Ask your questions, Ellie," Virginia insisted. "Perhaps we should all sit down. I asked Jo Marie to brew a pot of tea, which she did. I'll pour."

Scott took the big overstuffed chair while Ellie and her mother settled on the sofa. The tray with the teacups was on the coffee table. Her mother went into the kitchen and returned with a third cup, a mug this time. She poured the tea and handed the first cup to Ellie, the mug to Scott, and left the last cup for herself. They settled back and waited.

Ellie clenched her hand around the teacup. "First and foremost, I want to know why you never answered my mother's letter."

"Ellie," her mother warned beneath her breath. Leaning forward, she set the teacup back on the saucer and then straightened and crossed her arms over her middle.

Scott frowned. "What letter?"

The question was met with silence. Apparently, her mother wasn't willing to discuss the matter. Ellie felt no such restraint. "The one Mom mailed you shortly after you abandoned us."

"You mean after I moved out?"

"However you want to phrase it!"

Virginia placed her hand on Ellie's knee as if to say "Enough."

Scott's brow condensed into thick lines. "You wrote me a letter, Ginny? When?"

Her mother's arms were wrapped so tightly around her middle Ellie wondered how she was able to breathe normally. "About a month after you left."

Ellie had to strain to hear her mother. "A month, Mom?"

Virginia nodded.

"What did you say?" Scott asked gently.

"What does it matter? It's just more water under the bridge, isn't it?"

"No," he argued, "it isn't. This matters."

Virginia pinched her lips together as if to let them both know she had no intention of revealing a single word of that letter.

"Mom only told me about it earlier today," Ellie explained. "She wrote to tell you that she regretted everything and wanted you to come and get us."

"Traitor," Virginia whispered, for Ellie's ears alone.

"Ginny, you wrote me?" He looked stunned. No one was that good an actor. Shock was written on every facial feature, but especially his eyes, which grew wide and intense.

"It wasn't like I had your phone number."

"You didn't want the divorce?"

"No. I was distraught, and afterward I told my parents what I did. They assured me the divorce was for the best and that if you'd had a change of heart you would have responded. It was then that they convinced me to file."

Ellie's father set his mug down on the tray, and when he spoke every word was strong and distinct. "I never got a letter, Ginny. Once I was out of the rental house I never heard from you again."

"But I . . . mailed it myself. I took it down to the neighbor's house and put it in their mailbox instead of our own."

"Mrs. Mullin?"

"Yes. How did you know?"

"My goodness, Ginny, your mother and Mrs. Mullin were thick as thieves. My guess is, she took her own mail out, found your letter, and then gave it to your mother, because, God as my witness, I never got it."

"Would it have made a difference?" Virginia asked, her voice strong and defiant.

Scott didn't hesitate. "It would have made all the difference in the world. I was miserable without you and Ellie. When you returned my letter . . ."

Her mother half rose from the sofa cushion. "What letter?"

"The letter you wrote 'Return to Sender' across and never opened."

"But I didn't do any such thing," she protested. "I never saw a letter." It sounded as if her mother was close to tears. "Every day I prayed I'd hear from you. The minute I got home from work the first thing I did was check the mail, hoping with all my heart that you would agree to give us another chance."

No one needed to explain to Ellie what had happened. Her grandparents had interceded and neither her mother nor her father had gotten the opportunity to communicate with the other.

Both her parents looked at each other as if there was far more they needed to say, but Ellie had other questions she wanted to ask. "Not once in the entire time I was growing up did you ask to see me," she blurted out. "I want to know why."

"I don't have a good excuse," Scott said, his eyes revealing his pain, "and I'll regret that for the rest of my life. When the divorce was final I heard from your mother's attorney. He said if I made any effort to be part of your life your grandfather would drag me through every court in the land. I didn't have the money to fight them, and so I didn't try."

"Why not later, when I was an adult?" she asked again, needing more than what he'd told her earlier. "Do you have an excuse for that?"

"No." His answer was straight and to the point. "No excuse whatsoever. You'd lived nearly your entire life without me. I figured by this time you wouldn't want to hear from me and that you probably hated me. Frankly, I couldn't blame you. In a nutshell, I guess I was afraid."

She pressed her hand to her chest. If only he knew how she'd hungered for a father.

Scott looked away and refused to meet her gaze, and yet every facial feature revealed his regret. "I didn't want to disrupt your life. I could only imagine what your mother and grandparents had said to taint me in your eyes. Ellie, I thought after their indoctrination you wouldn't want anything to do with me."

"I didn't hate you," she whispered. She wanted to hate her father but found she couldn't make herself do it.

"I came to take you to dinner," her father continued. "But I'm here for another reason, too. I came because of Tom. He's afraid he's lost you and it's devastated him. He realizes he should have told you who he was right away, but he kept putting it off and then it was too late and the chance to warn you was gone."

"He destroyed my trust." Ellie folded her arms in much the same way her mother had earlier. "I can't see a relationship working for me and Tom. I wish I could, because I have genuine feelings for him, but I doubt I can get past what he did."

"I want you to reconsider, Ellie," her father urged.

"I don't know that I can." She didn't want to discuss Tom. What was important was going home to Bend, to all that was familiar and comfortable. Then and only then could she analyze the events of this weekend and decide how best to deal with Tom's deception.

It was almost as if Scott hadn't heard her. His gaze remained focused on Virginia, and he couldn't seem to stop looking at her.

"I didn't know Ginny was here."

"I only just arrived," Ellie's mother explained.

"I'm grateful you came . . . so grateful."

"How so?" Virginia asked, blushing as she spoke.

"For the first time in over twenty years I have the chance to tell you how sorry I am that our marriage didn't work out."

Her mother's returning smile was tentative and awkward, as if she wasn't sure how to respond. Ellie read the same regret in her mother and realized that through all these years Virginia had remained in love with Scott Reynolds.

"You did a wonderful job raising our daughter," Scott said, his voice low and intense. "Thank you for that."

For several moments her mother struggled to speak. "That's very kind of you, Scott."

Her father turned his attention back to Ellie. "I wish you wouldn't be so quick to judge. I know my stepson, and he's a good man. He did this for me. He wanted to give me the chance to know you and so he arranged it as a surprise for us both, thinking that was the only way to bring us together.

"He would never have intentionally hurt you. If anything, I believe he fell deeply in love with you. He's beating himself up over what's happened, and I feel I'm the one to blame."

"Go to him, Ellie," her mother urged.

Ellie couldn't believe what she was hearing. "Mom?" After all the warnings her mother had issued about trusting men, this was completely out of character.

"Don't make the same mistake I did and let pride get in the way."

"Or the mistake I made in leaving you behind when I should

have been fighting with every ounce of strength I possessed to be part of your life," her father added.

"Go, Ellie, go to Tom."

Her heart was shouting one thing and her stubbornness was saying something else entirely.

"Don't live with regret the way I have," her father urged.

"And I have," her mother added.

Undecided still, Ellie stood and after a moment asked, "Where is he?"

Scott told her and then handed her his car keys. "You'll need these."

"She's more accustomed to driving my car," Virginia insisted, and hurried from the room, returning in a matter of seconds with her purse. She dug out her keys and handed them to Ellie.

"Will you two be all right while I'm away?" Ellie asked her parents, half joking.

"We'll be fine," her mother insisted.

"Yes, we will," Scott agreed. "It seems we have a lot to discuss."

Chapter 28

~

By the time Maggie had walked down the hill dragging her suitcase into Cedar Cove she'd managed to get her emotions under control and dry her eyes. She had purpose now. First things first. She'd need to find a way back to Yakima, to home, without her husband.

She paused and slowly exhaled. From now on she had to stop thinking of Roy as her husband. He wanted a divorce and she would give him one without putting up a fight. Pain gripped her, and she nearly stumbled forward. Her marriage was over. It'd been over when Roy had started the emotional affair with Katherine, only she'd been too stubborn and too much in love to realize it. It was easy to lay blame at his feet, but they were both at fault. They had failed each other. Her life revolved around their children and she'd ignored her husband's needs. She'd been blind and foolish, but then Roy had, too. Her one hope was that they could get through the next year without coming to hate each other. Divorces could be messy; she would do her best to make sure bitterness wasn't part of the dissolution of their marriage.

Once she was on Harbor Street, the main road through town, Maggie found a coffee shop called the Java Joint. Stepping up to the counter, she checked her purse, unsure of how much cash she had on her.

"Can I help you?" asked a young man with a name badge that identified him as Connor.

"I'd love a cup of herbal tea," Maggie said, realizing she would need to alter her diet and avoid caffeine now that she was aware of this pregnancy.

"We've got several herbal teas to choose from," Connor informed her cheerfully. "Go ahead and look over the list and make a selection." He pointed to an upright menu that listed the names of several teas.

Maggie chose chamomile, hoping the tea would help calm her nerves.

"You just get to town?" Connor asked, eyeing her suitcase. "The shuttle bus stops close by, and people often come in for a cup of joe."

Maggie wasn't sure how to answer without inviting other questions. "Sort of." She wasn't interested in starting up a conversation with the teenager.

"Cedar Cove is a great town." He rang up her order and then announced, "That'll be a dollar fifty."

Maggie slid a couple dollars across the counter.

Connor handed her back the change, and she noticed the tip jar was front and center and dropped a quarter inside.

"Thanks," he said. "I'm saving up for college but decided all the tips I collect on weekends will go toward a ticket to a Seahawk football game. A guy's got to have some fun, right?" As he spoke, he reached for a large insulated cup and filled it with steaming hot water and handed it to her, along with the tea bag.

The Java Joint had two other customers, and Maggie settled down in the back, away from the window. The other couple left, leaving her the sole occupant. She opened the tea bag and dipped it into the nearly boiling hot water, letting it steep. She liked her tea weak. Her thoughts wandered back to Roy and she was nearly overwhelmed with sadness. She was lost in her musings when Connor approached.

"You can put your used tea bag in this," he said, and handed her a plastic spoon and a couple napkins.

"Oh, sure, thanks," she mumbled. Taking out the tea bag, she wrapped the string around the spoon and squeezed out as much of the liquid as she could. She tasted the tea and nearly burned her lips.

"Do you want ice chips?" Connor called from behind the counter. "That water can get really hot."

The youth was apparently looking for something to keep himself occupied.

"No, thanks."

"I make a mean latte if you're looking for something to tide you over until dinnertime. The special of the day is salted-caramel mocha. It's one of our best sellers."

"Thanks, but no thanks." Maggie wished she'd sat with her back to him, but to change places now would seem rude. Because she sat facing him and it was just the two of them, it seemed to encourage conversation. Maggie didn't feel up to chatting.

After a few minutes, she tried her tea again.

"I've got to go to the back room for a few minutes," Connor announced. "If anyone comes in, tell them to ring the bell on the counter."

"Will do." Peace at last, but then Maggie realized there was no peace for her. Not now, and probably not for a very long time.

She checked her cell phone and saw, thankfully, that it was fully charged. Logging on to the Internet, she scanned rental car agencies. Getting a car was sure to be cheaper than flying back to Yakima. Once home, she'd need to look into a number of matters. Her cousin

Larry Morris was an attorney, and he'd help her through the divorce proceedings. It would be necessary for her to find employment outside the home, although finding a position now would be difficult, seeing that she'd need time off when she delivered this baby.

The baby.

Aborting the pregnancy sounded like a quick, easy solution, and for some it might be, but not for her. In reality, it would solve nearly everything. It might even help save her marriage for the time being, but it wouldn't help for long. An abortion would be only a Band-Aid to what was really wrong with her and Roy's marriage. For a moment, just a moment, she reconsidered. Maybe she could do it . . . maybe it would help. The thought didn't last long, though. She knew it would be pointless, and she'd be riddled with guilt afterward. Maggie knew herself well enough to realize doing away with the pregnancy wasn't the answer for her. Thankfully, Roy recognized the truth of that as much as she did.

What distressed her with a divorce was the thought of her two sons growing up with a part-time father. The fact was, Maggie didn't want this divorce. If she could turn back the clock a month she would never have left the house the night of their fight, but then hindsight didn't do her a bit of good now.

A baby.

Maggie wished with everything in her that she wasn't pregnant. Roy didn't want this child. And the truth was, she wasn't the least bit excited to be pregnant. Her upper body rocked with indecision, swaying with doubt, with fear. Yes, delivering this baby would be problematic. Frankly, she didn't know how she'd manage raising three children on her own, working forty hours a week, and keeping up with the house, and still have any semblance of a life. Maggie stiffened with determination. Other single mothers had managed all that and more and, with grit and determination, she would, too. She had the advantage of a college degree. She was employable.

Still, her heart ached and she was forced to swallow down a

bubble of near hysteria as worries and reservations pounded against her like rocks bouncing against an embankment in a landslide.

Needing a distraction, she returned her focus to the Internet and read through the rental-car specials. She booked the cheapest one she could find, which unfortunately meant she had to travel into Seattle, near Sea-Tac Airport. Earlier, Connor had mentioned a shuttle bus that went to the airport, where she could collect the vehicle. If she could get the information for that, it would be perfect. No doubt Connor would be able to direct her.

The cell phone was still in her hand when a text message came through from Roy. Where are you? I don't appreciate you disappearing like this. I want to leave as soon as possible.

Maggie texted back a rely: Then go.

As far as she was concerned, everything had already been said. This wasn't a game, nor was it a trick, and after all these years together, Roy should know that.

When she'd broken up with him while they were in college it wasn't a trick or a scheme to get him to change his ways. She'd never been one to throw out idle threats; she meant what she said.

With the phone in her hand, Maggie hungered for solace, for a connection with her family—she needed to talk to her sister . . . not about her current situation. She couldn't, wouldn't mention anything about that . . . not yet. First and foremost, she needed to get home, back to her children. Then and only then could she orient herself enough to explain to her family and friends that while it was unfortunate, her marriage was over.

Without putting much thought into the decision, she phoned her sister, Julia.

"Maggie," Julia answered, sounding upbeat and happy. "How's your getaway weekend going with Roy?"

"Great," she said, forcing enthusiasm into her voice. "We spent the day in Seattle and went to Pike Place Market, and took a tour of Underground Seattle."

"Seattle has an underground? I didn't know that."

"It was fascinating. A great history lesson. I recommend you take the tour the next time you and Sam get to Seattle."

Julia laughed skeptically. "The only thing Sam wants to see in Seattle is football. It's a four- or five-hour drive from Spokane but you'd think it was across the street the way he acts, and in the middle of winter, no less."

"Everything good with you?" Maggie asked.

"It's great." Her sister hesitated. "You okay? You don't sound quite right. You haven't for the last month. Something's on your mind, isn't it? You think I can't tell? Come on, Maggie, I'm your sister. What's up?"

"I'm fine. What could be wrong?" she said, downplaying the mess she'd made of her life. "You have to remember, I'm on a romantic getaway with my husband. We have three glorious days without kids."

"B-u-t . . . ?" Her sister dragged out the word so that it became a question.

It was irrational to think Maggie might be able to fool her sister into thinking everything was all well and good. "Guess what?" she teased.

"I'm not guessing," Julia said, her voice somber and serious now.

"I'm pregnant." She tried to sound happy but failed.

"Maggie, that's wonderful . . . isn't it?"

"Yes."

Julia hesitated. "I'm not hearing the joy. I know you and Roy had considered a third child. The last time we talked about it, you said Roy was hoping for a girl next time."

"He'd like that."

"I take it the pregnancy wasn't planned."

"You could say that." If only her sister knew the truth. Eventually, Maggie would tell her, but not now.

"I agree three is a handful," Julia said, "and I should know, but you'll adjust. It was the biggest transition for me after having Trevor and Travis. Then Ted arrived and it was pandemonium for the first six months. When I found out I was pregnant with Tracy, I didn't know how we would manage, but it was fine. Going from three to four is not nearly as difficult."

Maggie needed to hear her sister's chatter. It helped calm her nerves, helped her deal with the present and not think ahead to how she would handle the future.

"Where's Roy?" Julia asked, out of the blue.

"Resting." Which, unfortunately, was a necessary white lie. "We're staying at a bed-and-breakfast here in Cedar Cove. It's the perfect location. Roy's mom has a romantic heart, and she's the one who paid for this anniversary gift. If you and Sam need to get away, I can't think of any place better."

"You went away for the weekend and discovered you were pregnant. We have our family; I'm not taking the risk," her sister teased. "Is Roy happy?"

The question caught Maggie off guard. "Happy?"

"About the pregnancy."

Maggie wasn't sure she could get away with another lie. "Truth is, it's a bit of a shock to us both."

"It takes a while to set our minds to the idea sometimes. A new baby is a major adjustment in a family. Have you told Mom and Dad?"

"Not yet . . . you're the only one I've told."

"If you need anything, you'll let me know, right?"

Maggie's mind wandered to the garage, where they'd stored the boys' baby furniture, and immediately bounced to another concern. She might not be able to keep the house. "No worries there. I saved the crib and everything from the boys."

"I wasn't talking about baby furniture, Maggie. I mean emotional support and encouragement. I've been there. I'm your big sister and I'm here to lend a hand if you need me."

"Thanks, Julia."

Her sister had no idea of how badly Maggie was going to need her in the upcoming months.

They chatted about the kids, a safe subject, for a few minutes before Maggie was ready to end the call.

"I better go," Maggie said, when she noticed Connor had returned to the counter. A man came into the Java Joint.

"You're sure everything is all right with you?" Julia asked again.

"Of course. All is well," she answered.

"Like I said, you don't sound like yourself," Julia murmured. "Something is up. You're probably not ready to share it, but know that I'm here when you are, okay?"

Maggie could hear the frown in her sister's voice. "I'm fine, really," she insisted. "I'll call you next week and we can talk more then."

"It's a date."

Once she ended the call, Maggie returned her phone to her purse. The man at the counter had collected his drink and left. Connor was busy filling the sugar and artificial sweetener containers. He glanced up when Maggie approached the counter.

"You need a refill? They're complimentary."

"No, thanks. I'm full up." She placed her hand on her stomach as if she'd recently finished a three-course meal. "I was wondering if you could tell me about the shuttle bus that leaves from Cedar Cove to the airport, the one you mentioned earlier."

"Oh sure. It's the Sea-Tac Transporter. I have a schedule. A lot of folks stop off here and collect coffee before heading out, especially the morning and mid-morning buses." He opened a drawer and took out a plastic-coated sheet and handed it to her.

"Do I need to make a reservation?" she asked, noticing that they were recommended.

"It wouldn't hurt, but it shouldn't be a problem getting a seat."

Maggie wrote down the phone number, stepped away from the counter, and made the call. Just as Connor had predicted, she was able to book a seat. The woman on the other end of the line told her the pickup point, which didn't seem to be far from where she was.

"The bus should arrive within the next fifteen minutes," the woman told her.

"I'll make my way there right now," Maggie assured the reservation clerk. "I'm a short distance away."

"The driver doesn't wait."

"I'll be there," Maggie promised.

She returned to the table for her suitcase and thanked Connor on her way out the door. Just as she was leaving, another customer entered the store. The other woman held open the door for Maggie to go out first, and she would have except for one thing.

Roy.

Her husband drove past the Java Joint at just that moment. Maggie shrank back into the coffee place, nearly tripping backward in her rush not to be seen. "You come inside first," Maggie insisted, as she all but plastered herself against the wall. The woman gave her an odd look but then complied. It took a few moments for Maggie's breathing to return to normal before she ventured outside a second time.

Her one objective was to get to the bus stop and board without Roy seeing her. He could look all he wanted, but Maggie was determined not to be found.

Chapter 29

~

I heard voices in the other room and poked my head around the corner of the kitchen to find the man who'd told me he was Ellie's father talking with Virginia Reynolds. They were alone, and the two appeared deep in conversation. They didn't notice me, which was just as well. I wondered what had happened to Ellie, who was nowhere in sight.

The front door was left partially open, which told me that perhaps Ellie had left. When I checked outside I saw that Virginia's vehicle was missing, which was a good indication that Ellie had taken the car. The Porters' car was gone as well. The last time I saw Roy he'd been in a bear of a mood. I hoped that improved once he found Maggie. I remained worried about the couple, who were clearly having marriage problems. I thought matters had improved, but I'd guessed wrong. Just that morning before they'd left for Seattle I had had a strong feeling that whatever had troubled them had been resolved. Clearly, something had happened since that time that had deeply upset them both. I suspected it must be the discovery that Maggie was pregnant. Really none of this was my business, but I couldn't help being concerned. I'd never considered myself nosy and briefly wondered if I was seeking yet another distraction.

Looping the handle of a white wicker basket over my forearm, I collected my garden scissors and headed toward the side yard, where I had two large hydrangea plants. Mark was busy sorting through the lumber he'd unpacked earlier. He had the plans for the gazebo spread out on the tailgate of his pickup. I watched him refer to those drawings a number of times.

One thing I admired about Mark: When it came to his work he was a perfectionist. It might take him longer to complete a project than I wanted, but by the time he was finished, whatever he was working on was beautifully done.

I was about to ask him a question regarding the gazebo when Roy Porter unexpectedly returned, spitting up gravel as the car's tires spun. He came to an abrupt stop and turned off the engine. He didn't seem to be in a hurry to get out and sat for several moments before exiting the vehicle. Whatever was eating at him didn't appear to be resolved, because he slammed the door closed with enough force to rattle the car's windows.

Mark straightened and set down on the grass the two-by-four he carried. "You got a problem?" he called out to Roy.

The other man paused and sent Mark a hard look. If Mark thought he was helping, he was wrong. The anger in Roy's eyes was hot enough to fry bacon.

"Everyone's got problems," Roy replied.

Mark chuckled. "And most of them involve women."

I didn't take kindly to that comment, but went about my business and pretended not to hear.

"You're telling me!" Roy said. He walked over to where Mark

stood and jabbed his hands into his pockets. "What are you building?"

"Jo Marie wants a gazebo for weddings and the like." Mark walked over to his truck and picked up the plans to show Roy. "I understand you're in construction."

Roy reached for the plans and appeared to be studying them before returning them to Mark. "You're right about women being the root of most problems."

"Don't I know it," Mark muttered. "They can make a man's life a living hell."

Like he would know! Mark lived alone, and if he was ever married there was no evidence of it. I couldn't help but wonder if he was speaking from experience, although it seemed unlikely.

"Are you using treated lumber for this?" Roy asked, abruptly changing the subject.

"Yes, it was more money than what I'd budgeted, but I figure it will save Jo Marie problems in the long run."

Roy walked over to Mark's truck. Apparently, I was far enough on the side of the house that neither man could see me, which was just as well. They wouldn't be comfortable knowing I was listening in on their conversation.

"I've decided to divorce Maggie," Roy announced.

Oh dear, no wonder she'd been upset.

"Sorry to hear that," Mark returned casually, leaning against the tailgate. Both men stood there with their arms crossed. Neither seemed eager to talk, and I wondered if Roy would return to the house. I was somewhat surprised when he didn't.

"It's for the best," Roy told him.

"So that's why Maggie left?"

Roy shrugged. "You know how women get. She went all emotional and irrational on me and walked away. She took her suitcase with her and didn't say a word about where she was headed. Seems she wants to find her own way back to Yakima, which is fine by me. I looked for her and couldn't find her. I did what I could, right?"

"Right," Mark concurred.

"Actually, it's probably better this way so I don't have to deal with her hysterics."

"Yeah, it's probably for the best." Mark was more than agreeable.

I was about to intercede and tell them both they were dead wrong but stopped myself. Mark quickly changed the subject and asked Roy a couple construction questions. The conversation went on for about five minutes. I'd long since finished cutting the flowers I needed for the bouquet and was ready to head back into the house when Mark spoke again.

"I'm sorry to hear that Maggie is a bad mother. You have two boys, that's what you said, right?"

"Right. Jaxon and Collin."

"They'll be better off without her," Mark finished.

Roy straightened away from the truck. "Maggie's a great mother. It's the other stuff I can't deal with."

"Oh sorry, I must have misunderstood. I assumed you'd want custody of your sons."

"No," Roy said reluctantly, as if taking this into consideration for the first time. "It would be better if the boys stayed with their mother for the time being. They're still young enough to need her. If I had them, it would mean they'd be stuck in day care all day, and we agreed before we had kids that Maggie would be a stay-at-home mother."

"So Maggie doesn't work outside the home?"

"No, we're fortunate that way. She has her teaching certificate but put her career on hiatus in order to be with the boys."

Mark nodded as though weighing this information against other concerns. "From what I've heard some women can be good mothers and lousy wives. A man has needs, you know, and their wives get so caught up in the mommy scene that they forget they're married."

I rolled my eyes. It was all I could do not to march out and demand to know how he was such a know-it-all when it came to marital problems. My handyman sounded like a professional counselor. From the way he was talking, he could hold seminars on the subject.

"Maggie's been a good wife," Roy said, with some reluctance.

"Well, no worries, there are plenty of fish in the sea. You'll find another woman in no time, and next time you'll know what to look for."

"Next time?"

"You aren't going to let this experience sour you, are you?" Mark asked. "That would be a shame. Besides, your sons will be just as happy with a stepmother."

Roy shook his head. "I'm not ready to think about remarrying."

"Of course not," Mark agreed, "it's early days yet, but it gets lonely, and after a while you'll be looking for companionship. It's not right that you be alone, especially if you want the boys to stay with your ex-wife."

"Maggie's not my ex-wife."

"Not yet she isn't," Mark agreed. "But she will be soon enough, right?"

"Right," Roy said, conviction marking his words. "This isn't what I wanted, but I don't have any choice."

"This isn't what you wanted?" Mark repeated. "I thought you told me you're the one's decided to file."

For just an instant Roy looked confused. "Yeah, I guess I did."

Mark removed his hat and scratched the side of his head as if what Roy said made no sense.

"Maggie's not the woman I thought I knew," Roy explained. "She stepped way over the line, and now . . . now there are consequences. A man can overlook certain things, but not others, if you know what I mean."

"Sure I do." Mark was certainly agreeable. "A guy works his fingers to the bone in order to support his family only to have his gut twisted by a no-good, cheating wife. We're oblivious, gullible, and easily fooled because our focus is on taking care of those we love. It's all work for us. Work, work, work."

Roy walked away from the truck. "It wasn't like that with Maggie."

"Oh sorry, I assumed, you know, that she was running around on you behind your back."

"Not really," Roy murmured, and then seemed to gather his resolve, "but some things can be forgiven and others can't. To be fair to Maggie, it wasn't all one-sided . . ."

"You're right again," Mark said. "There are certain aspects to marriage vows that a man can't easily overlook or forgive, even if he's looked at another woman a time or two himself."

"Don't misunderstand me," Roy said, his hands deep inside his pockets. "I've made my share of mistakes."

"Of course you have, we all have, but nothing as bad as what Maggie did."

"Right," Roy returned, but without the same conviction he'd had earlier.

"The thing I've noticed with women," Mark continued, speaking again as if he were an expert on the subject, "is that it isn't in females to forgive. They might claim they have, but with every disagreement, every slight we've ever committed gets thrown back in our faces. A woman can drag up sins that are twenty years old. Forgiveness isn't part of their emotional makeup."

Roy looked away and then commented, "Maggie's never been like that."

"You're joking?"

"No," Roy murmured. He started to pace, although I realized he probably wasn't aware of what he was doing.

"No problem, man," Mark said. "Your mind is made up. You know what to do, so good for you. From what I read, statistics say it's women who most often file for divorce, not the husbands. You're making a stand and you aren't going to allow Maggie to push you around."

"That's not her way," Roy murmured.

"Oh, she's one of those subtle types, is she? You know, the passive-aggressive kind. She cooks you dinner, but it's cold; does your wash and puts your underwear in with the colored clothes so they come out red."

Roy looked up at Mark as though he'd spoken a foreign language.

"Let another man deal with her and all her baggage," Mark suggested.

"Another man?" Roy repeated, as if this was something else he hadn't considered.

"Well, sure. Like I said, there are a lot of fish in the sea. You'll eventually remarry, and in every likelihood, so will Maggie."

I watched as Roy abruptly stopped pacing as if the truth of what Mark said jolted him.

"If you're going to let her keep custody of your sons, it will take some getting used to when there's another man in the house. Not all stepdads make decent fathers."

Roy started across the lawn, heading back to his vehicle.

"Where are you going?" Mark asked.

Roy shook his head as though he didn't want to answer. He opened the car door and looked back over his shoulder. "I'm going to find Maggie," he said. "I'm not fooled. I know what you're doing. You're making me look at the idea of getting a divorce in ways I didn't want to see. You're right, though. Maggie and I need to work this out. I don't want to lose my wife, and I don't want my sons being raised by another man."

Mark joined him and gently slapped Roy across the back. "Some things are easier to forgive than others, just like you said, but it takes a big man to forgive a bigger offense. Find your wife, Roy, and do what you can to hold your marriage together."

"That's exactly what I plan to do."

Once more Mark patted his back. Roy climbed into the car and drove off, and this time there was no spitting gravel.

I waited until Roy had disappeared from the driveway before I stepped out from the side of the house. Mark's gaze met mine.

"You handled that well," I told him.

He shrugged as if it was no big deal. "Sometimes all anyone needs is a little guidance."

"Anyone do that for you?" I asked.

He sighed and slowly shook his head. "Are we back to that again?" he asked, as if growing impatient with me.

"Actually, no."

"No?"

"No," I repeated. "Roy isn't the only one who took your advice. I did, too."

Mark went still, and his gaze rushed back to me. "You read Paul's letter?"

I nodded. "It was a beautiful love letter . . ." I found it impossible to add more. The things my husband had written were strictly for me and me alone. My throat started to close up. I wasn't about to get emotional in front of Mark. "You don't need to worry, I won't be hounding you for any more of your secrets."

"Good to know . . . not that I have any secrets."

"Right," I murmured mockingly.

Mark's gaze went to the flowers in my wicker basket.

"For dinner with my family tomorrow afternoon. I thought I'd put together a bouquet for the centerpiece. The hydrangeas are really lovely this year." I had both pink and purple blooms.

"If you want, I'll fertilize them for you later in the season."

"No need; I can do it." My budget was limited, and I wasn't willing to pay for anything I could do myself.

Mark seemed to read my mind. "I didn't plan on charging you."

"In other words, you're willing to work in the yard out of the goodness of your heart?" For a long time, I wasn't convinced Mark had a heart.

"Not exactly."

"Ah, the truth comes out," I said, having trouble holding back a smile.

"I figure I owe you for all the cookies and meals you feed me."

"Good point, in which case feel free to work in my yard anytime you want." As far as I was concerned, it was a good deal all the way around.

I headed to the house and paused on the top step and turned back to Mark. He stood where he was, watching me. "Thanks again," I said, "for talking sense into Roy." And then I did the oddest thing.

I blew Mark a kiss.

Chapter 30

~

Ellie's heart beat so frantically it felt as if it had grown too big for her chest. Even now, as she parked in front of Tom's house, she wasn't sure coming to him was the right thing to do. Furthermore, she wasn't entirely sure she was ready to forgive him, despite the excuses and justifications Scott had mentioned.

It was the look in her mother's eyes that had convinced her she needed to do this. The message was familiar, and Ellie could read it easily: Don't make the same mistakes I did. Only this time it wasn't a warning not to trust men or to give her heart away. Instead, it was encouragement to be willing to do exactly the opposite, to fall in love, find joy, and be happy. To say Ellie was confused would be grossly understating the facts.

For a long time all she did was sit in the vehicle, nervous and unsure, toying with her options, the most appealing of which was to start the engine and drive off. Even now she wasn't sure what she would say to Tom. Thinking it was a lost cause, she inserted the key and started the car, intent on leaving, but then just as quickly changed her mind and turned it off.

Her hand remained on the keychain when she saw Tom. He must have noticed her car out front because he stepped onto the porch. He stood there with his hands tucked inside his back jeans pockets, elbows jutting out while he waited. His gaze seemed to focus directly on her.

If he hadn't moved outside, Ellie might have given up and driven off. Confronting him wouldn't be easy, but realizing that he'd seen her, she felt compelled to act, to do something. Filled with equal parts of dread and anticipation, she got out of the car and stood next to the driver's side for several tense moments. Neither of them moved.

Tom continued to stand exactly where he was on the porch, all the while watching her. With her mother's car as a barrier between them, Ellie felt more secure. She willed him to make the first move.

He didn't.

The look he wore reminded her that she'd claimed she never wanted to see him again. The first move had to come from her. Ellie could be stubborn, too, but pride hadn't helped her father or mother, and it wouldn't solve matters for her, either.

"My dad . . . Scott came to the inn," she said, slowly moving around the car while keeping her hand on the hood as if she needed it to guide her. "He and my mother are still there . . . they're talking."

"Your mother?"

Ellie nodded. "She came by . . . she was in the area." No need to explain further.

"How's it going with the two of them?"

"Good, I think. They discovered that they'd written love letters to each other after they separated that neither of them ever received."

Tom walked down the three steps leading to the concrete walkway. Ellie stepped away from the curb. They met halfway between the house and the car, and while it was a short distance, Ellie felt like each one of those steps was a mile in length. She walked with the care of a soldier traversing a minefield.

"Did you get a chance to have Dad answer any more of your questions?" Tom asked.

"A few."

"He always loved you, Ellie, always, but he was afraid you'd been brainwashed against him."

Tom said that as if it explained everything, only it didn't. "He could have at least tried."

"You're right, but the fact is, your father has a lot of baggage from his first marriage."

"We all have baggage," Ellie argued.

"But some more than others. The longer one drags it around, the heavier it seems. I'm hoping you're willing to look past that disappointment and appreciate how hard it was for him to meet you, knowing that you might possibly hate him."

Ellie didn't see it like that. It seemed wrong to hear Tom defend her father, but then she realized Scott was a safe subject. Discussing the older man's fears and doubts made it easier to avoid talking about their own troubles. Ellie found it interesting that her father had defended Tom. It hurt that Tom had such a strong relationship with him and she didn't.

"Can we not talk about my father?" she asked.

Tom agreed. "Fine by me."

Silence followed, as though they were each afraid to venture beyond to anything else. Finally, Ellie couldn't bear the tension any longer. "You hurt me," she whispered. "You took my feelings for you and used them for your own selfish purposes."

"I know, and I'm sorry." He didn't deny it, didn't make excuses.

"Sorry," she repeated slowly, thinking it was such a weak, insipid word.

"I take that back." He stood directly in front of her now. They were both on the sidewalk, facing each other. Tom reached out and gripped her shoulders.

"You're taking back your apology?" She tried to break his hold, but he wouldn't let her go.

"I don't regret contacting you, reaching out to you. Okay, you're right, my original purposes were less than stellar. My intent was to introduce you to the father you'd never known in a casual, non-threatening way. I assumed that after the first few days I'd nonchalantly mention I happened to be Scott's stepson and let the conversation go from there."

"Why didn't you?" The words were more accusation than question.

"Because I was afraid that once I told you who I was that you would block my name and I wouldn't be able to talk to you again. It was a risk, but one I was willing to take for my dad's sake, and for yours, too."

Although privately Ellie was pleased, she felt obliged to say, "That's not a good excuse."

"Maybe not," he agreed, with some reluctance, his eyes pleading with hers for understanding. "But, Ellie, I found it increasingly important to keep you in my life."

Ellie had felt the same way, too, although she wasn't overly keen to admit it. Hearing from Tom each day had become progressively more important as their friendship developed. By the time they'd moved on to emails and phone calls, she was half in love with him.

"You have to remember my intentions were good," he said, as if that was enough to wipe out all the hurt this entire mess had caused her.

"No, they weren't. You used me . . ."

"You had a right to know your father," Tom argued. "A right to know that he loved you and regretted the past. It didn't take me long to realize that you'd been fed nothing but lies about the man I'd only known to be decent and good and honorable."

"My mother was looking to protect me."

"By keeping your father out of your life?" he demanded.

"She . . . I think it was a matter of several unfortunate incidents that kept them apart."

"I didn't want that to happen to us, Ellie. You have every right to be upset with me; I understand that. But look at it from my point of view. I wanted to bring a father and daughter together. Yes, I made mistakes, and yes, I was insensitive to you both, but I couldn't think of any other way to go about it."

"I wish you'd been honest with me from the first."

"Would you have let me in your life if I had?" he asked.

That was the real question, and one Ellie wasn't sure she could answer. "I . . . I don't know." She'd like to think she would have welcomed the opportunity to meet her father, but she couldn't be certain, couldn't be sure. Besides, if Scott had wanted to be part of her life, wouldn't he have reached out of his own accord instead of letting his stepson do it for him?

"That's just it," Tom went on to say. "I didn't want to take the chance of losing you, and then I realized by going about it the way I did I'd basically guaranteed that once you discovered the truth I was in a no-win situation. That's why I asked you to trust me, no matter what happened this weekend."

"If Scott hadn't come to the inn, you would have," she whispered. She'd been angry and determined, and even now she wasn't completely sold that she should let Tom back into her life again.

Exhaling slowly, Tom leaned his forehead against hers. "Tell me you're here because you're willing to give me another chance."

"I'm here because my parents urged me to talk to you." As of right this moment, Ellie wasn't sure of anything. Then it hit her. As she said *parents,* she realized that this was the first time in her life that she'd ever referred to her mother and father as parents, *her parents,* because they were together and in agreement with each other.

"I'm glad you're here, no matter what the reason," he whispered, and ran his hands down the length of her arms. "More glad than you know, and I promise if you give me a second chance I won't blow it."

The warmth of his touch chased away the chill that had come over her from that morning on the water and all that had happened afterward.

"The last thing I ever wanted to do was hurt you. If you believe nothing else, believe that."

"My father said basically the same thing," she confessed, with a sigh, and accepted that loving someone left her heart open and vulnerable to hurt and to so much more, including love and joy. "I do want my father in my life, and I believe he wants to get to know me, too."

Tom kissed her forehead and then her nose and the curve of her chin before asking, "What about me . . . in your life?"

His kiss made it difficult to think clearly, especially as he eased his way toward her lips. "That has yet to be determined," she whispered suggestively.

He settled his mouth over hers in a lingering kiss that left her weak in the knees. "Does that help you decide?" he asked.

"I . . . it helps."

"Good," he whispered, and kissed her again, with even more intensity. Ellie clung to him, wrapping her arms around his neck and standing on her tiptoes as she felt her heart opening up to him.

When they ended the kiss they were both breathing hard.

Still, there were things Ellie had to know. "What would you have done if I hadn't driven here to talk to you?" she asked, her voice barely above a whisper.

"I don't know, but I can tell you this—I wouldn't have left matters as they were. You're too important to me to let you walk away without putting up a fight."

"Really?"

"Yes, really."

Ellie sighed and felt herself weakening. She was being drawn into his arms, and it felt as if this was exactly the place she was meant to be. It would be too hard to live without him now.

"Are you willing to give me another chance?" Tom asked, drawing back enough to be able to look her in the eye.

"That depends on if you have any more surprises to throw at me." She held his gaze, willing him to level with her.

"Some women like being surprised."

"I'm not some women, I'm me."

"Okay, no more surprises."

Ellie laughed and, looping her arms around his middle and pressing her face against his chest, said, "Then we're in business."

Tom laughed, too, and hugged her close for a long time. He released her but reached for her hand, intertwining their fingers. "I think both your mother and Scott would like it if we stopped by the B-and-B."

"You mean . . . now?"

"No time like the present," Tom suggested, keeping her close to his side. "And later you can tell me more about the love letters they wrote to each other that you mentioned a bit ago."

"Okay."

Ellie's mood lightened considerably as they drove in separate cars back to Rose Harbor Inn. Standing outside the inn, she filled Tom in on the letters and what each of her parents had learned about the other.

"It seems your grandparents have a lot to answer for," Tom said when she'd finished.

Ellie agreed, but at the same time she understood that they, too, had been motivated by good intentions. "I believe my grandparents assumed Mom would marry again. They had someone else in mind, but it never panned out."

"Why not?"

Ellie had never been sure until now. "She was in love with my father. At one point she swallowed her pride and went to him, but it was too late. He'd already married your mother."

Tom tightly gripped her hand. "I'm sorry about that."

"Don't be. I believe that life flows the way it was meant to be. We're in charge of our own futures, but only to a certain point, and then God takes over, and that's for the best."

"You have a forgiving nature," Tom said, "and I for one am grateful you do."

"If Mom and Dad had reunited when I was a kid, there's every likelihood that we would never have met," she reminded him.

Tom mulled that over for several moments and then agreed. "Your father is a good man, Ellie, and once you get to know him you'll learn that for yourself. He made mistakes in his life; we all do. I have and you have, but we can't allow ourselves to get bogged down by errors in judgment."

Ellie hoped that was the case with her parents.

Tom took her hand as they walked toward the front steps. Rover was at the door to greet them, but he didn't bark or put up a fuss. Instead, he wagged his tail as if to say how pleased he was to see that they were back and that they were together.

Virginia Reynolds glanced up when Ellie and Tom came into the living area. Her gaze went to their linked hands and she smiled.

"Did you two work everything out?" she asked.

"We're getting there," Ellie explained, sitting down on the sofa next to her mother. Tom took the chair beside Scott. They hadn't discussed the future. That had yet to be determined. For now, it was enough that they'd cleared the air and decided to move forward. She didn't know what the future held for the two of them, but she sincerely hoped they would have one together. Time would tell.

"It seems to me," Scott Reynolds said, "there are plenty of reasons for a celebration. I'd like to treat us all to a wonderful dinner at DD's on the Cove."

Virginia looked to Ellie as if seeking her permission. "I think that would be lovely," Ellie said.

"It's time I got to know my daughter."

"Time I got to know my father," she returned.

Virginia shifted and looked a bit uncomfortable. "Perhaps it would be better if I stayed behind."

"Mom, no," Ellie insisted. "I want you to come. It wouldn't be the same without you."

"But . . ."

"Ginny," Scott said evenly. "I invited you as well. I'd like it if you'd join us."

"I'm going," Tom told her. "I don't want to waste a minute of the time I have with Ellie before she heads back to Oregon."

Virginia glanced from one to the other and then agreed. "All right."

Ellie knew her mother well enough to recognize that she wanted to be talked into joining the group. She read subtle hints that told her that while she'd been away her parents had talked and, she hoped, cleared the air. As far as she was concerned, it was twenty-two years later than it should have been. Still, it pleased her immensely that they were able to communicate now.

"S-o . . ." Tom said, dragging out the word and looking to his stepfather. "Are you two . . . talking?"

"We're talking," was all Scott would say.

But Ellie noticed that her mother blushed ever so slightly. "We're talking," she concurred. "There's been a lot of hurts and a lot of misunderstandings. I fear I misjudged Scott terribly."

"Your family . . ." Scott said, and then bit off the rest of what he intended to say. "Like we agreed, what's done is done. This is a brand-new day."

"It's early evening," Virginia corrected.

Scott chuckled. "You always were a stickler for details, Ginny. All right, it's a brand-new early evening. I have both my daughter and the son of my heart by my side, and my ex-wife and I are talking."

"Just talking," Virginia reminded him.

"Just talking," Scott agreed, "but that's a vast improvement."

A vast improvement, indeed. Ellie's gaze met Tom's and he winked, and, smiling, she winked back.

It was a start for them all, and for that Ellie could only be grateful.

Chapter 31

~

Maggie took a seat near the back of the bus and sat with her head pressed against the window. It felt cool against her skin. Exhausted, she closed her eyes and tried not to think of all she would need to do once she reached Yakima.

The thought of facing her family with the news that she and Roy were separating twisted her gut. She didn't know what she would tell her boys when they started asking why their daddy didn't live at home any longer. Sadness nearly overwhelmed her. The weight of loss and grief was almost more than her heart could absorb.

"Are you feeling all right?" the woman sitting across the aisle from Maggie asked.

She offered her fellow passenger a weak smile. "I'm just tired," Maggie said. "I'll be fine."

"Late night?" the woman pressed.

"Something like that." Maggie closed her eyes again, not really in the mood to strike up a conversation with a stranger.

"My goodness, would you look at that," the woman said.

"At what?" she asked, although she wasn't really interested.

"That car," the woman continued. "He's pulled up on my side of the bus and is waving at the driver to pull over."

Maggie sat up straighter and glanced out the window. No, it couldn't be. The vehicle was the same make and model as Roy's car, the very one they'd driven over from Yakima, with the same bumper sticker for Jaxon's T-ball team. Half standing now, Maggie pressed her hand over her mouth. Obviously, it had to be Roy. She nearly gasped as she sat back down. Having him come racing after her like a madman was the last thing she needed. Or expected.

"Some clown is trying to pull you over," another passenger called out to the driver.

"It happens," the driver shouted back. "People miss the bus and then try to catch up with me. It doesn't work that way. Our policy is clear. I leave on time, and if they aren't at the stop, then I head out. It's as simple as that."

Maggie heard the horn honk.

"What's he doing now?"

One thing was sure, Roy had everyone's attention. He continued to press against the horn while the driver did his best to ignore him.

"This fellow's pretty insistent," the woman across from Maggie said, shaking her head.

"He's weaving in and out of traffic now."

"It isn't going to do him any good," the driver called. "I don't stop, especially on the highway. Not for anyone. It's company rules. I've been driving for ten years, and I'm not about to lose my job over some bozo who can't tell time."

"Good for you."

As far as Maggie could see, the passengers agreed with the driver, including her. As for why Roy would want to stop the bus, she could only speculate. She wanted to believe he'd reconsidered filing for divorce, but she doubted that was possible. He'd been adamant about what he wanted, and it wasn't for them to work on their marriage. Surely he didn't believe it would be possible for them to travel back to Yakima together. The three-and-a-half-hour ride over had been difficult enough. Following their last discussion, it would be impossible to be in the same car together. Roy had to recognize that.

The bus exited the freeway, leaving Maggie to wonder if the driver had changed his mind about stopping.

She sat up straighter and turned to her chatty neighbor. "What's the bus driver doing? Why did he pull off the freeway?"

"There's another stop ahead," the other woman explained.

"A stop? You mean the bus stops in other towns?"

"Oh yes, there are six along this route. Cedar Cove is the second one. There are four others."

"Oh." It made perfect sense. This wasn't welcome news, although she should have realized the bus wouldn't go directly to the airport from Cedar Cove. The bare fact was, Maggie hadn't been thinking. She wasn't in an emotional place to let trivial matters such as bus stops enter her already overtaxed mind. Under normal circumstances it wouldn't have mattered, but this was anything but usual.

"The car is following us off the exit," her seatmate informed her, craning her neck to look out the window.

"Good thing, because that blasted horn was beginning to irritate me," someone else said, and took his fingers out of his ears. "What's the matter with people today?"

No one had an answer for him, least of all Maggie.

She glanced around for some sign of where they were but saw nothing she recognized. As far as she could make out, the stopping point was little more than a transit parking lot. There didn't appear to be anything commercial within sight—no convenience store, no service station, no fast-food restaurants. Just a parking lot, and a sparsely used one at that. But then it was Saturday.

Maggie saw a couple people standing next to their suitcases. The bus pulled up close to the two women and gradually eased to a stop. Both women boarded the bus, paid their fee, and then claimed their seats in the middle.

The driver was about to close the door when Roy leaped on board. He stalked past the driver.

"Hey, buddy, you need to buy a ticket," the driver called after him as Roy continued down the aisle, headed directly to where Maggie had slouched in her seat. She kept her head down, her chin tucked against her chest, refusing to make eye contact with him.

"Maggie, you need to come with me," he said, standing directly alongside her seat.

Maggie pretended not to hear.

"Maggie," he said, louder this time. "Come with me."

She crossed her arms over her chest. "Why?"

Roy exhaled loud enough so she'd know how deeply she'd tried his patience. "We need to talk this out."

She did her best to sound calm and reasonable. The two of them had the attention of everyone on the bus. The last thing she wanted was for Roy to make a scene. "I believe everything has already been said. Please, just leave. If you want to talk, we can do it once we're in Yakima."

"This can't wait," Roy insisted.

"It'll have to." She could be just as stubborn as her soon-to-be ex-husband.

The driver stepped behind Roy. "Either you pay your fare or you get off the bus," he said.

"Give me a minute," Roy pleaded.

"Listen, buddy, I've got a schedule to keep. Do I need to call nine-one-one and have you deal with the sheriff?"

"This is my wife," Roy told the driver.

"Not for much longer," Maggie informed the driver.

"Okay, you two, listen up. I'm a bus driver, not a marriage counselor. So I advise you to settle whatever marital problems you're having elsewhere. I got people catching flights."

Maggie could see that delaying everyone else wouldn't be appreciated. From his stance, she could tell that Roy wouldn't easily be moved until he got his way.

In reality, Maggie didn't have much choice other than to gather her purse and vacate the bus. She wasn't happy about it, but her options were limited.

"Thank you," the driver said with apparent relief when she stood and scooted past the woman sitting next to her. Her seatmate gave her an encouraging smile and gently squeezed her hand as she slipped by.

The driver got off the bus to retrieve her suitcase. The passengers on board applauded as Maggie moved past.

The driver gave Maggie a hand as she climbed down the stairs off the bus. "I'm not a marriage counselor or a doctor, but I delivered a baby a few years back while on my route," he said proudly. "I even made the Seattle newspapers and did an interview for the nightly newscast on Channel Five. You look like a nice couple; I hope everything works out."

"Thanks," Roy said, as he moved past the driver and picked up Maggie's bag.

She didn't hold out much hope that their talking would solve anything. They'd come too far, said too much, to the point that raw nerves were exposed.

As soon as she had her suitcase, the bus drove off, leaving Maggie standing with Roy in the middle of a nearly deserted parking lot.

For someone who had come chasing after her, honking his horn and holding up a bus full of people in order to get to her, Roy didn't seem to have anything of importance to say.

The driver's side of his car had been left open, indicating that he'd leaped out in an all-fired rush. That sense of urgency appeared to have deserted him now that she was with him.

Silently, he walked around to the passenger side and held open the door for her. Then he took her suitcase and placed it in the back. While he dealt with that, Maggie got inside the car and closed her door. Then she leaned her head against the window and closed her eyes, much the same way she'd done while sitting on the bus.

Roy slid into the driver's seat and shut the door, but he didn't start the engine.

"How'd you know where to find me?" she asked, still not looking at him. But her eyes were open now, wide open, and she was curious.

"You didn't make it easy."

"I didn't think you'd care."

"I care," he returned. In answer to her question, he added, "Connor told me you'd asked about the bus."

"The young man at the Java Joint?"

"I drove all over town looking for you and got a little desperate when I couldn't find you. So I started asking folks on the street and in the shops, showed them your photo, and the kid said you'd been in there, drinking tea and asking questions about catching the bus."

"Why were you looking for me?" she demanded. She found it hard to understand why he found it so important to talk to her now.

"Why do you think?"

His answer infuriated her. "Please, Roy, I don't want to do this. You made your feelings clear. You're finished with me. You don't want this baby. Nothing has changed in the last few hours. As far as I can see, there isn't anything left to say. All I want now is to get home, wrap my arms around my children, and make plans for my future and theirs." A future that didn't include him, other than as the father of her sons.

Roy didn't seem to have anything to say. When he did speak, she noticed that his hands had a steel grip on the steering wheel, as if he were driving through an intense storm. "It's a difficult thing to find out the woman I've sworn to love could very well be carrying another man's child," he said, the emotion in his voice stark, his expression bleak.

Maggie turned her head away as tears blurred her vision. She had nothing to add, nothing to say.

"And something else entirely, to think of living the rest of my life without you. The thing is, Maggie, I don't think I could manage it. We've been one for so long that tearing us into two halves isn't going to work. I was a fool to have suggested we try."

Swallowing tightly, Maggie held her breath for fear if she did breathe it would come out as a sob.

"You left your wedding ring behind in the room. At first it just made me mad . . . I saw it as a dig, a way of getting back at me. In all the years we've been married, I don't ever remember you taking it off."

She had, but only out of necessity, never in anger or despair. Not until that very day.

"You left the letter, too. The one I wrote you in college."

Like she would forget when she received it.

"I read the letter . . . I remember writing it, how I measured every word. I thanked you for making me a better man. I said that I would always love you." He hesitated, and then in a low voice added, "I meant every single word of that letter."

"At the time," she qualified.

"I mean them now." Again, his words were low and rough. "I mean them now," he repeated. "You're right, nothing has changed in the last few hours except the fact that I realize I don't want to live without you. It isn't easy dealing with this pregnancy. But I'm trying. Give me a chance. I can't promise to be perfect, but at least give me credit for making the effort."

Maggie lifted her head and turned to look at her husband. To her shock, she saw tears rolling down his cheeks.

"I don't know how we'll get through this, Maggie," he whispered brokenly, "but we will. We'll survive this and whatever else life throws at us."

"The baby . . ." Her cheeks were moist as well, and she found it difficult to speak. The lump in her throat felt as large as a tennis ball.

"I promise you I will do everything within me to love this child,"

Roy said. "From this moment forward I will work on accepting this child as my son or daughter."

Maggie cupped her hand over her mouth, unable to hold back the sobs. "But I don't know who the father is."

"It doesn't matter."

"How can you say that . . . how can you learn to love another man's child?" She'd realized almost from the first moment she'd discovered she was pregnant that she was asking Roy to do the impossible. He would always wonder, always suspect, always fear.

"I'll love this child because while we might not know who fathered this baby, there will never be a doubt who the mother is," Roy said, as he gently wiped the moisture from her cheeks. "You're the mother, the woman I love."

A sob escaped her, and she pressed her forehead against her husband's shoulder.

"This is our baby, Maggie, yours and mine. There won't be a paternity test. There's no need for one. We're in this together. I don't expect it will be easy for either one of us, but I can't let you go." His arm came around her as he buried his face in her shoulder. "I want to be a better man, Maggie," he whispered, "a better husband and a better father. I've failed you, but I swear by everything that is holy, I won't again."

She was weeping almost uncontrollably now, and Roy was, too.

"I vowed to love you. I meant it when I wrote that letter, and I meant it the day we were married. I mean it now. Nothing you could ever do will make me love you any less than I do right this minute."

Maggie would have said the same to him, only she found it impossible to speak. Roy brushed the hair from her cheek with tenderness and love while he rubbed his chin over the crown of her head.

"I love you, Roy."

"I know, baby, I know."

"I want to go home."

"Me, too, but can we wait until the morning?"

"Okay," Maggie whispered.

"Promise me one thing," he said, kissing the top of her head.

"Anything."

"Don't ever leave me again."

Maggie grinned. "You got it." She wrapped her arms around his middle and sighed, suddenly tired and depleted. "We're going to be okay, Roy." She felt it in every fiber of her being. Their marriage would survive, and they would grow stronger as a couple and as a family because of this.

"I'm hoping we have a girl this time."

"And if it's a boy?" she quizzed.

"Actually, I'll take whatever God gives us."

While it didn't feel like it at the moment, Maggie was convinced that in time it would be true. "This baby is a gift, Roy, a precious gift."

"You would have had a hard time convincing me of that earlier, but I think you may be right." He kissed her again, before he continued. "He or she has yet to be born and already this unborn child has shown me how to be a better husband."

"And me to be a better wife."

"You ready to go back now?" Roy asked.

Maggie released a shuddering sigh and nodded. She was more than ready.

Chapter 32

First thing Sunday morning I fed my guests breakfast: fresh fruit, toast from bakery bread, crisp bacon, and an egg casserole, all of which were popular breakfast items. I couldn't help but notice that the atmosphere was completely different this morning than it had been previously. Everyone appeared to be in a jovial, happy mood.

Ellie and her mother were in good spirits and promised to get in touch soon to book rooms for a return visit the following month. Before Ellie had time to bring down her suitcase, Tom arrived. The two sat on the deck and talked for some time. I heard Ellie's laugh and watched Virginia smile.

"They get along so well, don't they?" Virginia said, as I carted the dirty dishes into the kitchen.

"They certainly seem to."

"I invited Tom to visit us in Oregon, and he accepted my invitation, and I think Scott will come with him."

This was quite a switch in Virginia's attitude from what Ellie had mentioned earlier. The inn had worked its enchantment once again, healing wounded hearts, lifting spirits, blessing all who stayed. This was the promise I had gotten from Paul that first night, and it had certainly proved itself this weekend.

The story was the same with the Porters. I was never quite sure of what was going on between the couple, although I was able to piece parts of the story together. Maggie herself had mentioned she was pregnant and she'd said it as though in shock, struggling to hold back tears, and then she'd disappeared. At first Roy had seemed more angry than concerned, but his attitude had changed after his chat with Mark, and he'd set off determined to find her.

When Maggie returned with Roy, her suitcase in tow, I noticed a drastic change in them both. In some way I felt I needed to thank Mark for talking sense into Roy Porter. This morning I felt I was looking at two entirely different people. They acted like newlyweds, so deeply in love they couldn't take their eyes off each other.

The first thing Roy did when they sat down at the breakfast table with Ellie and Virginia was announce that Maggie was pregnant.

"It's our third," he said. "We're both hoping for a girl this time."

"Do you have names picked out?" Ellie asked, after congratulating the couple.

"Not yet," Maggie said, resting her hand against her abdomen.

"Margaret for a girl," Roy insisted.

Right away Maggie waved her hand, dismissing his suggestion. "Names are still under consideration."

"We'll be checking out right after breakfast," Roy told me. "Mark asked me to stop by his place on our way out of town."

"He did?" That was odd, but I didn't stop to question Roy, seeing that I had quite a bit of work to do before my family arrived for dinner later in the afternoon. Plus, I had guests checking in, but they wouldn't arrive until later in the day.

The house was empty before noon, and I started stripping down the beds. I had a busy Sunday ahead of me and wanted to get as much of the housekeeping chores finished as possible before starting the dinner preparations.

I figured my family would arrive around three and we'd eat about five. The weather was perfect, sunny and bright. I glanced out the window a couple times and realized I was hoping to see Mark. Not much chance there. My guess was, I wouldn't see hide nor hair of him all day. He'd as much as said so.

Frankly, it was a relief. I'd regretted asking Mom to ferret out information about my elusive neighbor and handyman. Curiosity had taken root in me and I'd allowed it to get out of hand, making uncomfortable demands of someone I considered a friend. I'd since made peace with Mark's need for privacy.

That wasn't the only reason I was eager for a breather from my neighbor. The kiss I'd blown Mark after his chat with Roy Porter had been an impulsive gesture. After a night of mulling it over, I still couldn't imagine what had prompted me to do such a thing. I'd seen Mark's eyes widen with surprise, but his shock was no greater than my own. It embarrassed me now, and I was afraid Mark would take delight in bringing it up in conversation. That would be just like him. Talking about it, analyzing it, was way out of my comfort zone, and if Mark insisted, I'd tell him so. Once that was decided, I immediately felt better.

The phone rang in my office as I cleaned the kitchen, indicating a business call. Any personal call would come via my cell.

"Rose Harbor Inn," I answered, using my best professional voice.

"Oh hi," the woman on the other end of the line said, as if she was surprised to hear a real person. "I'm calling about booking a room," she said, and then quickly added, "Actually, two rooms." She mentioned a date in early September, less than a month away.

I checked my reservation schedule and saw that I had two rooms available.

"It's for my best friend and me," the woman explained. "It's our class reunion. I'm Kellie and my friend's name is Katie." She laughed as she said it.

"You graduated from Cedar Cove High?"

"We did. Time really does fly when you're having fun. My mom and dad live in Arizona now and I'm in San Francisco, and Katie lives in Seattle. We could commute, it's really not that far, but we didn't want to have to worry about getting back to Seattle if the night gets late."

This should be interesting. Best friends coming back to Cedar Cove for a class reunion. "I've got you down for that weekend and have reserved two rooms for Friday through Sunday."

"Perfect. See you," she said, and the line was disconnected.

I stared at the phone for a moment and shook my head. I could hardly wait to meet Kellie and Katie.

As I expected, my family arrived around three. Also as I expected, my mother was full of questions regarding Mark.

"I'd hoped he would have a change of heart and join us for dinner," Mom said, almost as soon as she was in the front door.

"If you're referring to Mark, then the answer is no. He won't be joining us." I hated to disappoint my mother. Really, there wasn't anything more to say.

My father was even more inquisitive about Mark. Clearly, my parents had been discussing my relationship with the handyman, which made for an uncomfortable conversation. Dad stepped into the kitchen and dipped his finger in the salad dressing, licked it, and then gave me a nod of approval. "You like this fellow, don't you?"

"Dad! Mark is a friend, nothing more and nothing less."

"Nothing else?" he pried, his thick brows arched with the question.

"No," I insisted, and busied myself getting the salmon ready for the grill in order to avoid further questions.

Unfortunately, their inquisitiveness started up again once my brother and his family arrived.

"Mom said you'd invited some guy you wanted us to meet," Todd said, looking about the room.

"It's Mark, and before you ask, he's a friend. He's done quite a bit of work around the inn, and he's just a friend," I repeated, emphasizing our relationship didn't go beyond the bond of friendship.

"I remember," Todd said, brightening. "Mark's that handyman who irritates you."

"I feed him cookies and that helps tame the beast in him," I joked, and looked for a way to change the subject.

Todd grinned. "You like him, though, right? I mean, that was what Mom seemed to insinuate."

I didn't know how many times I was going to have to repeat that Mark wasn't a potential love interest. "I like him as a friend."

Todd gave me that know-it-all look that said he read between the lines. Arguing would only convince him he was right, and so, hard as it was, I didn't further the discussion by protesting overly much.

Everyone left around seven, and even if I say so myself, dinner turned out fabulous. Better than I'd expected. I'm sure all the cooking I've been doing since taking over the inn has vastly improved my skills in the kitchen.

My guests were out for the evening, and the inn felt especially quiet after my family left. In the end, I was eternally grateful Mark had stayed away. I would hate to think of the interrogation he would have undergone had he arrived unexpectedly. Thankfully, Mark seemed to have a sixth sense when it came to such matters.

After brewing myself a cup of coffee I ventured outside to the alcove. Rover followed me and we sat in the chairs close to the fireplace. I'd come to love this little haven. Mark had strung lights around the frame, and as dusk settled I turned them on. Sipping my coffee, I had a one-sided conversation with Rover. He'd loved spending time with my brother's two kids. He would have made a great family pet.

I was chatting away when Rover lifted his head and I felt someone's presence behind me. Twisting around, I found Mark.

"Do you always talk to yourself?" he asked, plunking himself down in the chair next to me.

"I was talking to Rover."

"Does he answer back?"

I shrugged. "He does in his own way."

"Bet he doesn't argue much."

"Not like some people I could mention," I said pointedly.

Mark grinned and leaned back in the chair, making himself comfortable.

"Roy Porter mentioned that you'd asked him to stop by." He hadn't mentioned why, and I couldn't help being curious.

"I finished that cradle I've been working on for the last few months."

"It's beautiful."

"I figured he and Maggie might put it to good use."

I could hardly believe it. "Mark, that cradle was a work of art and you gave it away?"

He shrugged as if it was something small and quickly changed the subject. "How'd the dinner go with your family?"

"Great."

"No questions about where I was or why I hadn't bothered to show?"

He had to ask! I could fib, but I don't think it would have done much good. Mark would see right through me. "A few," I said, hoping he'd leave it at that.

Thankfully, he did, and we sat in relative peace for several moments, each taking in the beauty of the evening.

"Question," Mark said, breaking the silence.

"Sure." I wasn't the least bit sure, because I had a feeling I knew what was coming.

"You blew me a kiss."

I knew it, I just knew he would bring that up. "I was hoping you'd overlook that."

He'd gone still and serious. "Did you mean it?"

"The kiss?" If I played dumb long enough, maybe he'd change the subject.

He didn't answer right away. "I'm afraid we're wading into dangerous territory, Jo Marie, and it worries me."

Dangerous territory?

"How so?" I asked, rather than head straight into flat-out denial.

He clamped his hands together and went silent. It felt as if everything around us did the same. Even the breeze wafting the leaves ceased. The birds no longer chirped and the street traffic faded away.

"Mark?"

"My given name is actually Jeremy."

"Jeremy?" I repeated, confused now. "Then exactly where did Mark come from?"

"It was my father's name. He was a good man who worked hard his entire life, who loved my mother and his children. He believed in God and family and the American way."

"And Jeremy?" I asked, and as soon as I said the words I was sorry.

"Jeremy is dead." His voice was stark and hard.

Now I really was confused. "Listen, it's not important that I know. You don't need to tell me a thing."

"I think it is important."

"Because I've been pressuring you? I'm sorry about that. Whatever reason you have for keeping it a secret is fine by me. It's not my affair."

"It's funny."

"What is?" Personally, I wasn't finding anything amusing about any bit of this. I don't know when I'd seen Mark more serious. He looked nervous and unsure. Everything about him said as much, the way he sat, leaning forward and gently rocking, the way he tapped his foot as if looking to run away from a past he didn't want to confront.

"What's funny," he clarified, "is that a couple days ago you couldn't have gotten me to tell you this if you'd had me water-boarded."

"What changed your mind?"

His eyes skirted to mine. "That kiss you blew me."

"The kiss?" I couldn't imagine what that had to do with any of what he insisted on telling me.

All at once Mark was on his feet, his hands inside his pockets. "You have to know the way I feel about you, Jo Marie."

My mind and my heart started racing. I stared up at him, my mouth dry.

"I make every excuse imaginable to spend time with you."

He did? I found myself incapable of speech.

"Don't pretend you didn't know."

"I didn't." It shocked me that I could be that oblivious, but then little things started adding up. His anger when he saw me climbing a ladder last spring, and how he'd kept Peter McConnell out of the inn and insisted he stay overnight at his house.

My eyes and body language must have betrayed me, because Mark said, "I see you're filling in the blanks."

"I . . . I didn't know—"

"Before you say anything," Mark said, cutting me off, "let me tell you this thing I feel, this attraction, isn't going anywhere. I'm nipping it in the bud right now."

My thoughts were spinning, and I placed both hands on top of my head, looking to make sense of what seemed impossible.

"The only reason I'm telling you this now," Mark continued, "is that I can see you're starting to return those feelings, and it's got to stop."

Return his feelings? That was how he'd read the meaning behind that silly throwaway kiss?

"For the sake of argument, can you explain why you feel there could never be anything . . . romantic between us?" This was all pretty new to me, and I needed clarity.

Mark started pacing the tight area inside of the alcove. "There are things about me you don't know, things I don't want to talk about."

"It's okay, Mark. I'm sorry I pressed you for information you aren't willing to share. It doesn't matter to me what your past is."

"It matters to me," he said, nearly shouting, and then he repeated himself, lowering his voice. "It matters to me."

I didn't know what to say or how to respond.

He crouched next to me and reached for my hand, gripping it with both of his own. His eyes held mine. "You were married to Paul Rose, and he was a hero. He gave his life in defense of our country. He's everything I'm not. I'm the antithesis of a hero, make no mistake in that. I'm blemished. Flawed. Broken. I'm crawling out of a black hole. By all that's fair and just, I should be the one who died, not Paul."

Again, I was at a loss for words.

He straightened and started to leave, but I leaped up, reached out, and grabbed hold of his elbow. We were only a few inches apart. From the time I took over the inn I'd seen a good deal of Mark Taylor, often two and three times a day, but he was right. I didn't know him at all.

"This doesn't change anything," I whispered.

His eyes were filled with sadness. "You're wrong."

"Not on my end."

His gaze didn't waver, and I could see him struggle with indecision within himself. "Like I said, we're headed into dangerous territory."

"Maybe so," I agreed, and then I said it again. "Maybe so."

"I think it might be best if I moved on," Mark told me, his voice low and serious.

"You mean leave the area?" I couldn't believe he'd even suggest

such a thing. Then I remembered that he'd mentioned earlier that in
the past he'd drifted from town to town. At the same time he'd also
mentioned that he was content in Cedar Cove.

"It's time."

"What about the gazebo?" I asked desperately, trying to think of
something, anything, to get him to reconsider. "You don't seem the
type to leave a project unfinished."

He hesitated. "All right, I'll finish that, but then I'm leaving."

From the look in his eyes I could see nothing I said would be able
to change his mind. I suspected it earlier, but now I knew the truth.
Mark was running from his past.

It seemed the healing powers of the inn weren't strong enough to
heal the man who had become my closest friend.

ABOUT THE AUTHOR

DEBBIE MACOMBER, the author of *Blossom Street Brides, Starry Night, Rose Harbor in Bloom, Starting Now, Angels at the Table,* and *The Inn at Rose Harbor,* is a leading voice in women's fiction. Nine of her novels have hit #1 on the *New York Times* bestseller list, with three debuting at #1 on the *New York Times, USA Today,* and *Publishers Weekly* lists. In 2009 and 2010, her *Mrs. Miracle* and *Call Me Mrs. Miracle* were Hallmark Channel's top-watched movies for the year. In 2013, Hallmark Channel produced the original series *Debbie Macomber's Cedar Cove.* She has more than 170 million copies of her books in print worldwide.

ABOUT THE TYPE

This book was set in Sabon, a typeface designed by the well-known German typographer Jan Tschichold (1902–74). Sabon's design is based upon the original letter forms of sixteenth-century French type designer Claude Garamond and was created specifically to be used for three sources: foundry type for hand composition, Linotype, and Monotype. Tschichold named his typeface for the famous Frankfurt typefounder Jacques Sabon (c. 1520–80).